THE DRIVING SEAT

A NOTE ON THE AUTHOR

After graduating with a first in English, Abigail Abbas began her career in financial PR. She left the City to raise her children and worked as an illustrator, later embarking on an MA in Illustration at Camberwell College of Art. *The Driving Seat* is her first novel.

THE DRIVING SEAT

Abigail Abbas

Polygon

First published in 2026 by
Polygon, an imprint of Birlinn Ltd

Birlinn Ltd
West Newington House
10 Newington Road
Edinburgh
EH9 1QS

www.polygonbooks.co.uk

1

ISBN 978 1 84697 692 6
eBook ISBN 978 1 78885 745 1

British Library Cataloguing-in-Publication Data
A catalogue record for this book is available on request
from the British Library.

Typeset by Initial Typesetting Services, Edinburgh

FSC www.fsc.org MIX Paper | Supporting responsible forestry FSC® C018072

Printed and bound in Great Britain by Clays Ltd, Elcograf S.p.A

For Ali and Lily

Chapter 1

The woman hollered across the bays, 'Are you going to pay for those?'

She meant the blueberries. Everyone turned to look at me, the blueberry thief.

'Shh,' I whispered, exhaling all breath. I pointed at the pram.

The woman looked at the baby.

I pulled the packet out of the carrier bag and scanned it performatively. I put it back into the bag.

'Sorry,' I said. 'I'm just a bit tired.'

She eyeballed me. She had heard it all before. There were no flies. No wool for the pulling.

Someone else's checkout was pinging, glowing red. They were waving a bottle of wine about like a Neolithic club. They could not buy their wine until the checkout supervisor let them. Vanquished, she moved on. That got me off the hook.

I stowed the carrier bag in the net beneath the pram and steered it out through the fruit and vegetable maze, down the little slope and out through the automatic doors. I was a creature of such heft and breadth with my pram and my carrier bags. In a moment I was on the High Road in the blistering daylight – out into the carnival of buses and vans and cars and all the people in whose way I was getting. A clunking, inconvenient juggernaut. What a nuisance I had become!

My eye hurt. I was squinting against the light as if I had just been released from a pit. There was something wrong with the white – it was red. I needed to get it looked at. But I was terrified of doctors and hospitals ever since I'd had the baby. It was a hot, new fear I had. It must have had something to do with the amount of time I'd spent in them – in hospitals – believing that there was something wrong with the baby when the doctors kept telling me there wasn't. If someone asked me to describe hell to them, I would say it's hospitals.

Back at home, the baby asleep in the pram in the hallway, I unearthed the shopping from its polyester cradle and went into the kitchen, which was a slim galley, and stored the contentious berries in the vegetable drawer in the fridge. They were a blue-black reminder of my very near misdemeanour.

I will give you a glimpse of my life as it was then, and I will try to keep it brief.

If I was just pottering around the flat, I would sometimes open the fridge and imagine that an officious health missionary from one of those television programmes about eating was standing next to me, or perhaps even someone from social services, and as they appraised its contents, they would clock the blueberries and would understand that all was well in this household. It was clean, salubrious; it was *good*. I was scrupulously domesticated and I, Emma Propeller, was not someone to put on a list, or on watch, because I had blueberries in my fridge. They could move on to the next person, and perhaps that person had half an onion face down on the fridge shelf that had been in there for a couple of weeks or an opened tin of baked beans with a spoon marooned in it.

That's what I pretended, and I think it helped me to keep things to a passable level of hygiene. Whatever it took. It's like that thing people say, 'dance like no one's watching', but it was the actual opposite for me: 'mother like everyone is watching, all the time'.

Dinner that night was a messy affair, one of the messiest I had encountered. The baby had squash all over it. It was riddled with squash. I decided to bathe the baby. It wouldn't very well sleep with squash all over it, and I loved the baby and regarded washing off the squash as an act of love that I could get on with without having to think too much about how I felt while I was doing it.

I had bought a little plastic tub, a miniature bath, that I could place anywhere I wanted in our flat: in the kitchen, in the living room, in the nursery. There was no bath so I couldn't draw a bath for the baby. We had a shower room, and that should have been as good a place as any to wash the baby, but I did not like to bathe the baby in there because there was an atmosphere in that room that I did not like and to which I did not wish to subject it. I can't say what it was apart from ascribing it to *dark forces*, a sense I had of not being entirely alone, and I felt this acutely when I was sitting on the loo; I would be in and out of there so fast that sometimes I would leave with a trickle down my leg. I've always been attuned to that sort of thing, to the supernatural. I put it down to my mum. She was into that too. Beliefs permeate, like osmosis.

My husband told me to use the kitchen sink as a baby bath, but I once watched a video on YouTube that itemised all the bacteria that live in sinks. There are so many, and they are horrifying in their unique infanticidal roles that I couldn't bring myself to do it. I bought the miniature bath instead and made a pact with myself to use it, installing it in the living room while *Pointless* was on. I had to fill it in bowl-loads from the kitchen tap, while the baby sat in the bouncer gawping at Alexander Armstrong. I had to prove to my husband that it was not a frivolity, which is what he said it was. I'm not sure why he even cared – he was hardly ever home; he made sure of it. I knew that he hated it there.

I checked the time on my phone, taking care not to drop it in the bath. Dropping my phone in the baby bath would be the start of the end of everything. I couldn't imagine ever recovering from an event such as a phone in the bath or down the loo. I doubted I would adapt to life without it. I would have to tell myself *this too shall pass*. That is what I had been telling myself ever since I had had the baby because that is just something that people say. It's a word pill, like *let me kiss it better*, or *you'll just feel a little scratch*, or *I do*. You say it in the same way you might take a paracetamol.

When I first heard *this too shall pass*, I found it frustratingly unhelpful, but when the difficult things did pass, I could see that it is true – things pass. Although I have to say that I never want the good things to pass. They can stay. They don't though. And no one ever says, while you're having a great time, *this too shall pass* because it would be a real downer and I have tried and tried not to be that person.

I had been gazing for several minutes at the phone yet had failed to register the time. I had wandered off again into a daydream. I checked it again and made sure to take notice. It was saying half past six. James's flight had landed according to the airport app. He would be at passport control now. He had hand luggage only. He was a frequent flyer. I wasn't. (I used to be.) I was not thinking about that. I had put those thoughts to the back of my mind and would not allow them to creep out of that hazardous brain cave.

So, no bags. There would be no need for him to hang around at baggage reclaim with the pedestrians, as he called them. He'd miss bedtime.

Getting in an Uber. 40 mins.

There was no kiss. It was a conspicuously kiss-free message.

I put the baby to bed and, with haste, poured myself a glass of wine, knowing that I would need to get it into myself with a practised swiftness and in enough time for the smell to disappear from my breath. My husband didn't like me to drink. He didn't drink. He wasn't allowed to, not since he got caught with three of grams of cocaine in his wallet and a bottle of Jack Daniels clamped between his thighs, driving the wrong way down Curtain Road, EC2. We didn't talk about that because he was easily triggered.

I stowed my secret wine in the bottom of my closet under a heap of old trainers and drank it while watching things on the television that he thought were stupid like *Gogglebox* and *Love Island*. When I was on my own, there was no requirement to consider his happiness. And if the baby woke in the middle of the night, I would bring the baby into bed with me. I would have only one glass because I did not want to crush the baby I loved so dearly in my sleep.

A face-down onion would be the least of my worries were I to drunkenly crush the baby I loved.

At that time, I tended to sleep in the nursery with the baby. It was easier that way because sleep was important to my husband, much more so than it was to me, he said, and if he did not get enough sleep, he would not be able to do his job and his job was the most important thing in our lives. He worked in the music business and had to work long hours and travel far and wide.

I had a job too but that's a long story. That wasn't working out for me. I had every intention of being a financially independent woman. But I wasn't the great success I hoped I'd be, let's just say that.

Forty minutes came and went. An hour passed, then two. I texted him: *Where are you?*

There was no reply. I called him instead. The first time, the phone rang and I left him a message asking him if everything was all right. I left it a little while and then I phoned again. But the second time, the phone went straight to voicemail and I assumed that perhaps he was in a tunnel or on the phone himself. Or he was in an area with no signal and had not been able to reach me. I phoned a few more times for good measure, but it still went to voicemail, so I stopped doing that. I was repeating the same action and expecting a different outcome.

It was now 9 p.m. and there still was no sign of him. I had no idea what to do. Yes, there were times where he'd go out at night and not come home until four or five in the morning, when he'd said he would be back at eleven, or when he said he'd call if he was away on business but forgot to, and I was used to that level of unreliability, but this was different because there had been an incongruous sense of certainty about his text.

I became keenly aware that I was going to have to act in what appeared to be an actual crisis. My brain was awash with complicated, panicky feelings. I was beginning to feel too much.

I phoned my sister.

'What do you mean he's gone missing? Chance would be a

fine thing.' Hannah chortled. I could hear her sucking on her vape.

'He sent me a text when he was getting in the Uber and that was around half six. But he hasn't come back yet.'

'I wouldn't worry about it,' she said. 'He's a grown man. You know what he's like. He probably got a text from a mate in town and he's gone to meet him for a drink. He just couldn't be bothered to tell you. Or he's too much of a coward. He's done that before, right?'

'Yes,' I said.

'Well, there you go. Don't worry. Get an early night. Have some you time. Have some of your special chocolate. He's probably just gone out on a bender. I wouldn't put it past him. What a shit. You must be shattered from looking after the baby on your own all this time.'

'Okay,' I said. 'I am. I really am.'

I was feeling sorry for myself. I was feeling sad and holy. And then I had some of my special chocolate and I fell fast asleep. I always found that sleep came easily when I ate my special chocolate.

Chapter 2

I had eaten too much special chocolate.

I was feeling at a remove from myself. It was not the best frame of mind to begin the mission of finding my errant husband. He had still not returned.

I flung some blueberries into my mouth hoping that they would neutralise the effects of the special chocolate and went to see Hannah, which is what she told me to do if James did not materialise, and because it was a Saturday, she would not be at work but at home, around the corner from me in Hammersmith.

I took the baby with me. I would never have left the baby behind!

•

'You'll see that this is absolutely the best thing for you,' my sister said.

She was standing next to the window in her living room, looking at Hammersmith Bridge, which was empty – a ghost bridge – because cars weren't allowed on it anymore. She slammed the sash. She tied the belt of her kimono too tightly and it made her wince. Her hair was tied up in a towel, having just been washed.

'What is?'

'Him leaving you.'

'Is that what's happened?' I asked.

'I think it is obvious that that is what has happened,' she said, returning to the sofa and picking up her hand mirror and pair of tweezers. She proceeded to pluck the hairs on her chin. 'So while I was waiting for you, I called the top divorce lawyers in the country. It's Saturday, so I could only leave messages. I've done the one whose name sounds like a shark and the one who did Prince Charles. If you want to get a good divorce you have to call around the best lawyers first and engage them so that James can't and he's left with the worst. I saw it on *Succession*. And some of the firms won't even charge you until they secure a settlement from the other party. I've put the ones that do that on the top of the list.'

She wrenched a hair from its follicle, brought it into her line of sight and scrutinised it as if within that delicate fawn strand lay the answer to the mysteries of the universe.

'But he sent me a text telling me he was on his way home,' I reminded her. 'Also, we don't have any money. What's the point in getting a top divorce lawyer if there's no money?'

She lowered her mirror and tweezers and said, 'The mother's got money though.'

'Do you think I should call the police?' I asked.

'Do you think that's necessary?' she asked back.

The baby had fallen asleep on my lap. I looked down at the baby's skin. The baby had beautiful, impossibly perfect skin. I stroked the baby's nose. The baby stirred. My hand froze.

'I think it might be necessary,' I said.

'Okay, then call them.'

'What number do I call? Is it 999? Is this an emergency?'

'I would have thought it was the opposite.'

Hannah was typing things into Google on her phone. She read from the screen. 'Right. Here we are. Report a missing person. It says: *Are they in immediate danger?*'

'I have no idea,' I told her. 'How would I know if he is in immediate danger if I don't know where he is?'

She shrugged and continued: '*You do not have to wait 24 hours to report someone missing. It is not wasting police time to report someone missing. We are here to protect you and your loved ones.*'

'What a beautifully phrased statement,' I remarked. 'So much humanity in that. It's not what I would have expected.'

Hannah continued: 'Call 999 if a person is missing and you believe it is an emergency or call 101 if a person is missing and you think it's not an emergency.'

'So 101?'

'Bit silly,' Hannah said. 'How do you know if it's an emergency when you don't know where the person is? I would have thought that if a person is missing, they either want to be missing, in which case they will be impossible to find and not in any particular danger, or some agent – some*one* – has made them missing, and are doing terrible things to them, in which case it probably would be an emergency.'

I pictured James bound and gagged in a dank cave under a railway bridge in Vauxhall, having his fingers julienned. While I believed that many people would not mind too much if he was dead, I couldn't imagine that they would expend the effort of taking his death into their own hands.

'Who would want to make him missing?' I pondered. 'He's a grown man. Isn't it quite difficult to make a grown man missing?'

'Look,' she said, pointing to a band of text. 'It says call 101.'

'Can you?' I asked her.

'No, you have to do this yourself.'

'I don't think I can,' I said. 'I've got this terrible feeling that I'll incriminate myself and the police will think I've got something to do with his disappearance and then they'll arrest me and the baby will be left without a mother and a father.'

Hannah was growing impatient with me. She was breathing out loudly, which was her 'tell'. And then she slammed the mirror and the tweezers down onto the coffee table with so much force that I thought she'd shatter the mirror, wantonly sentencing herself to many years of bad luck.

She said, 'Fine, give me the phone.'

She called and spoke to the police. But as she was speaking, I sensed that she was selling him as a miscreant and painting me as a lunatic because she kept saying, 'She's just had a baby,' which I have come to recognise as code for 'she's gone mental'.

And then she said, 'Okay, officer, will do. Thanks so much for your help. I will.'

She hung up.

'What will you do?'

'I'll tell you to try not to worry.'

I nodded. 'What did they say?'

'They've taken the details.'

'Anything else?' I asked. 'Did they think he might have been murdered?'

'Jesus.'

'Well, isn't it a possibility?'

'They didn't seem to think so. People go missing and then they reappear. I got the feeling that they believed, because I felt that he wasn't in any immediate danger, because he has done this sort of thing before, that he will probably turn up, but they have his details anyway. They said we should ask around his friends and family. Places he tends to go. That sort of thing. Be our own detectives.'

'Be our own detectives?'

'Yes,' Hannah said. 'What a bore.'

'So that's it?'

'That's it.'

She got up from the sofa and disappeared into her bedroom, further confirmation that the conversation had come to an end.

'Fancy some lunch?' she called from the other room. 'Angie's has just come on Deliveroo.'

I didn't know how she thought I was supposed to eat at a time of such uncertainty. But I had noticed that my stomach was beginning to rumble. I went onto the app and scrolled through all the food they had and when I saw Eggs Royale (which I was tempted by – although I had reservations about how well a hollandaise would travel) I suddenly remembered something.

'Oh God!' I exclaimed. 'What time is it?'

Hannah reappeared. She had removed the towel from her head. There was a little spume of unassimilated mousse on her crown.

'Half eleven,' she said, picking up her phone from the coffee table and showing it to me. I had my own phone of course, but it had become wedged between the sofa cushions. Hannah had a designer sofa, and it was beautiful.

My sofa wasn't beautiful. James had bought it, and it was aggressively ugly. I had wanted a navy-blue velvet one from John Lewis that my friend had bought as a wedding present to herself, which I had admired, but he said no and ordered one instead from an outlet on the North Circular and a few weeks later came a black leather article that made me want to cry. I fantasised about taking a chainsaw to it and throwing its dismembered parts into the Thames or burning it, or even keeping it and making James sit on it, while I, with some money that had miraculously made itself available to me, bought the navy-blue velvet one, which I would forbid him from ever sitting on.

I dug about in the sofa, retrieved my phone and then I ran around the living room like a crazy thing, amassing my belongings. What is it they say? In that space between stimulus and response there is freedom. Not for me. Once I am stimulated, that is it, I am a slave.

'Chill. You need to chill.'

'James's mother!' I shouted. 'She's meant to be coming round. I'd completely forgotten. I can't believe I've forgotten.'

'You've got to start saying no to things,' Hannah said. 'You've got to start putting your foot down. Stop being a pushover.'

'Sorry,' I said. 'I'm so sorry.'

And with that, I stuffed the baby in the carrier, and it screamed, because it had been in the most restful sleep, listening to the calming, familiar chatter between my sister and me and I legged it out of Hannah's flat, all the way across Hammersmith Broadway.

Chapter 3

Hilary was standing by the front door when I arrived back at the flat. Her eyebrows were arched steeply with dissatisfaction. She had always hated me! I know I'm not the easiest person to get on with. I'm not a horrid person but I am gauche. I am an awkward person and I always have been. But I am not a *horrid* one. I suppose that if you were to see me for the first time, you might avoid me.

My mother used to think it had something to do with 'energy'. She used to talk a lot about energy – positive and negative – and she put my particular kind of energy down to my brush with death as a child. I won't go into detail, but I'd like to think that was the cause, because then this energy would not be something that I was born with but rather a consequence of something *happening to me*. I will always be grateful to my mother for assigning blame for my deficiencies in character to that.

I often wondered that if Hilary had known a bit more about me, about that part of my childhood, she might have hated me less, but there was never a good time to tell her and she wouldn't have wanted to hear it anyway. Hating me was her prerogative and it was something she was good at. I would never be good enough for her son. I suppose that is the universal experience of daughters-in-law.

So, there she was, right in front of me, standing on the steps of the mansion block, like an evil beacon. In appearance, there was something violently geometrical about Hilary. She had a chiselled jaw and a sharp brown bob. She was tall and used to loom over her husband who was now dead and who can blame him? I had a nickname for her: Old Hairy. I'm not sure where it came from, but it suited her so well.

She would ask me a question, and because I was terrified of her, I would stammer and trip over my words and she would say things like 'spit it out'. I longed for my mother when she did that because I knew that she thought that I was stupid, and I wanted someone to hold me or stroke me on the head. I was also so angry with her because she had done such a bad job of raising her son and sanctioning his release into the world. More than that, though, she had no idea of the extent of the dreadful job she had done. She just could not see it.

Hilary was very happy standing on the top step looking down at me, I could tell. How I wish it had been a colder winter, the steps slippery with ice, and that moment might have brought an end to her tyranny, but that was not how she was to meet her maker. Alas, that November was unseasonably warm.

'Gorgeous day,' she said to me, but I wasn't buying it.

The day was too bright. The light hurt my eye.

And then she looked down at her watch so I took the opportunity to scowl at her lividly.

'Well, aren't you going to let me in?'

She sounded just like Katharine Hepburn: like an American impersonating an Englishwoman impersonating an American.

I was looking forward to sharing the news with her, truth be told. I wasn't sure whether to tell her there on the steps or to protract the moment and wait until she was in the flat, sniffing around my things, wiping surfaces with her index finger.

'James hasn't come back yet,' I told her, hoping it would make her leave and never return.

'What do you mean?'

'He was meant to come back last night, but he hasn't. He texted me when he was getting in the Uber from the airport, but then he didn't turn up.'

'Well, have you tried calling him?'

'Yes, I've called and texted, but there's no sign of him. His phone is turned off.'

'Turned off?' she said.

'Try calling him,' I urged.

She snatched her phone out of her bag with her nasty raven-claw hand and pressed a couple of buttons in that strange way she had, as if the phone was going to bite or poison her. She put the phone to her ear so that it flattened the nest of her starched brown hair and she glared at me, burning holes through my skin.

'James, honey, call me when you get this message. I'm outside your apartment building and I was expecting you to be here. I just can't wait to see you. Love you, Mommy.'

Nothing sounded as sinister as Hilary saying Mommy.

And then she looked at me as if she would definitely have more luck with that. As if I had been doing the calling and texting thing all wrong my entire life.

Inside the flat, she stood in the hallway and declared that she was going to use the loo. I panicked. I couldn't remember if I'd flushed it. Sometimes I don't if it's a wee. I would always flush a number two. But if I had done a wee I would be thinking carefully about flushing in case I disturbed the baby because the baby screamed if woken by a flush.

'Let me just check,' I said.

And I ran to the loo and my arms went all over it, so rapidly, that I took on the form of an octopus. I neatened the towel. I flushed. I put the loo roll the right way on the holder. I cleaned the basin with my hand, scratching away the limescale with my fingernails. I scrubbed the loo pan for any tiny trace of poo because I did not want to give Hilary content, anything of value to share among her coven: not that she would have been able to see anything anyway – she was always complaining about her macular degeneration. (Although I struggled to believe that there was anything wrong with her eyesight because I used to catch her running a silent inventory of the wrinkles on my face and my new grey hairs. Believe me, she saw everything. *Everything.*) I needed to get a hold of myself. I felt woozy, unsteady, as if I were submerging. I had to tell myself to calm down.

'Go ahead,' I said to Old Hairy as I re-emerged from the room. A clammy sweat coated me. I was flushed.

'Would you like some coffee?' I shouted down the hall, and just before I heard the door lock, she said, 'Americano.'

She was in there for the longest time. I couldn't hear a tinkle or the rush of water from the tap. I wanted to ask her if she was okay but I'm pretty sure she would have muttered something beneath her breath about me being a 'stupid girl', which is something she liked to do.

I asked the baby, 'Do you think Gan Gan's alright?'

The baby blew a raspberry.

I went up to the bathroom door and put my ear against it.

I couldn't hear a thing. I knocked and there was no answer. I knocked louder and I shouted and shouted but there was no response.

'HILARYYYY!' I shouted. 'ARE YOU OKAY?'

Bang-bang-bang went my fist on the door. I pulled at the handle and I shook the door about for a bit. She was definitely dead. I was in no doubt. Hilary was dead. The dark forces had taken her. Perhaps they weren't so dark after all. I phoned Hannah.

'Hannah,' I said.

'I'm on my way to a thing,' she said. The world sounded very busy wherever Hannah was.

'Oh, sorry,' I said.

'Are you okay?' she asked.

'I think Hilary's dead. I think she's dead in the loo.'

'Who's Hilary?'

'My mother-in-law.'

'Good riddance,' she said and she chortled again, but it was much more forceful than the chortle she had produced when I told her James had gone missing.

'What do I do?'

I was in such a state by this time. I could not reconcile what was going on inside my head. I'd gone bananas. All these things were happening at once and I was not the person to have them happen to. And there was the baby to think about! I had completely lost my grip on the feeds and the naps. The baby must have been wondering what on earth was going on.

'Call an ambulance. I've got to go. I'm running late. Just call an ambulance. Let me know how you get on.'

Chapter 4

'Mrs Propeller?'

The caller was muffling a snigger. It was a familiar response.

'Yes,' I said. 'Speaking.'

If I said 'speaking' like that – a bit haughtily – it added a formality that I believed helped to counteract the absurdity of my surname. (It wasn't actually my surname, it was James's and it wasn't even his. He changed it by deed poll on a dare and refused to change it back, so we were all stuck with it.)

'My name is Dr Naidoo. I'm a trauma consultant at the Queen Charlotte Hospital.'

Trauma consultant? I was confused. I had thought my mother-in-law was being dealt with by a vascular surgeon for the massive tear in her aorta.

'I'm calling about your husband.'

'Yes?' I said shrilly.

'He was admitted a few hours ago. I'm afraid he's not particularly cogent. We found your number in the emergency contacts in his phone.'

I had done that. I'd put myself in as James's emergency contact in his phone because he had refused, thinking that emergencies were for 'ninnies'. I had been the prescient one and had taken that precaution because I knew something terrible would happen to him sooner or later. I had been right!

'I'd like you to come in, Mrs Propeller. I think it best if we talk in person.'

When she said that, I thought she was implying that he was about to die.

•

He wasn't about to die.

'By the sounds of it,' the doctor said, 'your husband befriended the Uber driver who supplied him with some illegally made fentanyl – we are running a toxicology report – but it looks as if that is what we're dealing with, and it appears that your husband has got himself in a fair amount of trouble while under the influence.'

That explained the presence of the man sitting in the cubicle with Dr Naidoo and me. He later introduced himself as a plain-clothes policeman, or the 'arresting officer'.

'When your husband regains consciousness, we hope to get a clearer picture of what happened,' she said.

'Where did you find him?' I asked, as if I had mislaid a water bottle or a lipstick.

At this point, the man in the chair piped up. 'Wandsworth,' he said.

'Wandsworth?' I said, stunned. 'He has never stepped foot in southwest London in his life. It's one of his boundaries.'

'Boundaries?' the man asked.

'Never mind,' I said. 'It's just odd that he should go there. He doesn't ever go to Wandsworth, so I wonder what he was doing there, officer. Is it officer?'

'You can call me Steven. I am the arresting officer.'

'Oh dear,' I said. 'That doesn't sound good.'

'It's not usually.'

Steven was a very good-looking man. I had thought, and I don't want to offend anyone here, that policemen tended not to be so good-looking only because on the television they usually aren't. But in real life this guy was really something to look at. I wondered if he'd consider having an affair with me, and then I pictured us in bed together under the sheets without any clothes on and the thought of it horrified me. I never wanted anyone to see me without clothes on ever again.

I was a wreck that day. I was at my dowdiest. Dowdiness is an insidious thing. Before I had the baby, I had promised myself I wouldn't be one of those mothers who let herself go, but that's really what I did. Why? I suppose I didn't see the point. Who was I grooming myself for? The baby. No. My friends? I hardly saw them anymore. James? To James, I was now aunt-like. I was his aunt, and in turn he was my nephew: close enough but distant too.

'Fentanyl,' I said. 'What is that?'

'It's an opioid,' he replied. 'It's about fifty times stronger than heroin.'

'Gosh,' I said. I liked the sound of fentanyl.

I looked over at James lying on the hospital bed. He was unconscious. There was no risk of him waking up any time soon. I noticed that more grey hairs had sprouted up in the tufts of his sideburns and I smirked because I knew that he had probably thought (before this near-fatal overdose) about whether he could get away with dyeing them. I knew that was exactly the type of thing he'd be thinking about because that was the kind of man he was, and I took a guess about what percentage of his brain expended time thinking about dyeing them.

Thirty-four per cent.

'Mrs Propeller?'

Steven had to stir me from my reverie.

'There must be some mistake, Steven,' I said earnestly. 'He's never done anything like this in his life.'

'Ah, well,' he said. 'That's not technically true, is it?' Steven was talking to me as if I were a fibber. 'Our records show that he has a drink-driving conviction.'

'Oh yes!' I exclaimed. 'I'd completely forgotten.'

Steven did not appreciate the felicity of my response.

'Yes, officer,' I said solemnly. 'You are right.'

'Is there anything else we should know about your husband, Mrs Propeller?'

'No,' I said.

I had no idea what my husband was up to and how he was spending his time, whether his life was growing and expanding. He didn't tell me anything and I didn't ask. He used to tell me things and I used to listen. But the things he used to tell me turned out to be lies so I listened less and less.

'You'll have to ask him, Steven,' I admitted. 'But for what it's worth, he's never used that drug – what is it?'

'Fentanyl.'

'Yes, fentanyl,' I repeated. 'He's never used it to my knowledge.'

Just coke and pills and weed and ketamine and MDMA.

'That's helpful to know.'

'I'd better get home,' I said. 'My sister's looking after the baby and she's not so comfortable with doing bedtime.'

'No problem,' he said.

'What are you charging him with?'

'Breach of the peace,' Steven said. 'He wasn't caught in

possession of any narcotics. He's a lucky man. And we can't technically charge him, but we can arrest him. We have to see that the threat he poses has passed.'

'What exactly did he do?' I asked.

'I think I'll leave it to him to tell you that,' he replied.

Chapter 5

I got off the number 94 a few stops earlier and walked through Bedford Park. If I had to describe that neighbourhood in one word, I would call it *bucolic*, because of all the trees and hedges and the Queen Anne-style houses with their symmetry and big windows. Whenever I went there, I felt as if I was somewhere else, no longer in the city. I was transported. It's called a *garden suburb*, but I don't much like that name. There are so many trees in Bedford Park, more than its fair share.

It was a magical evening, walking home in the gloaming, in that celestial, cossetting twilight. There was a sense around me of everything turning inward; I love the gentle darkness autumn brings. It is a relief to me when summer is over. All that sweating and skin and flesh. There is no hiding in the summer.

A mystical fogginess hung in the air that made the light emanating from the windows of the Norman Shaw houses glow like amber eyes. They watched me as I passed (one scowled and I felt affronted, but, on closer inspection, I saw that it was just the way the Roman blinds hung in the windows, slanted). I had read a poem once about a yellow fog and wondered if it was the same yellow fog that I was seeing. But it wasn't a jaundiced or sulphuric yellow – it was warm and mellow. I wanted so much to be in one of those beautiful houses, and as I approached a fairly large one on Addison Grove, I slowed my pace to see if I could get a good look inside, if the lights were on and if the curtains had not yet been drawn. I was careful not to linger too long; I did not want to be mistaken for a Peeping Tom.

Up ahead I heard the clatter of the Tube on the railway bridge overlooking Acton Green. That was the downside to where I lived. Noise came from every vehicle you could think of – trains, planes, buses. It was cacophonous. The planes were especially loud, because they flew so low, being so close to Heathrow.

We lived in a mansion flat overlooking Acton Green on The Avenue, so I heard the rattle of the Underground all day and most of the night when the Piccadilly line stormed past and I'd wake up with a jolt and the baby would shriek. The baby had the sweetest shriek. Out in the suburbs, the Underground is not underground. The trains hammer the rails out there, rattling like a sack of scrap metal. It takes some getting used to. I wore bright yellow ear plugs to bed every night and they blocked out most of the noise. They're the type you use to protect your eardrums from heavy artillery and industrial machinery. You can get them from Boots.

Once, when the baby was sitting on the floor with the shape sorter in the living room, I'd absentmindedly left a packet of earplugs nearby, and the baby managed to open it and put one into its mouth. From the kitchen, I heard choking, so I ran into the living room and the baby's face was bright red, turning purple, the colour of a burst blueberry cooked inside a muffin. I grabbed the baby and ran out of the flat, screaming *my baby is choking, my baby is choking*, banging on my neighbours' doors. No one was at home. They were all at work. I was the only one there in the day. I was always the only one there. I can't say what came over me, or how this thought had entered my head, but I turned the baby upside down and I slapped the baby on the back and out came the offending yellow sponge.

The only sound that gets through those earplugs is the baby crying. That has always amazed me.

The noise aside, I loved where we lived. I loved the florist by the Tube station, the deli under the bridge where I bought my coffee beans and where they ground my coffee for me when my grinder broke and I thought the world had ended. There were no delis with coffee grinders where I came from, just fields, a road without a pavement and a scantily stocked Spar at the end of it. (You could get a Starbucks from the Sainsbury's on the bypass but it would take you the best part of a morning.)

More than anything, though, I loved the fact that Hannah lived so close by in Hammersmith. She was always just around the corner, always there when I needed her. I had never wanted to leave.

But I was delaying going back. Hannah would be waiting for me at home with the baby, and she would want to know everything. I had no idea how to tell her. I thought about starting with Steven, the handsome arresting officer, and how she might enjoy that. And then she'd know to ask no more. I supposed it was a good thing that Mum wasn't around to see how it had all unfolded.

In my bag, my phone lit up. I must have left it on silent when I was on the ward with James. Whoever called left a voicemail. I picked it up. It was from the hospital, but it was regarding Hilary, not James. They said that she was refusing to stay in Queen Charlotte's a moment longer and was insisting on a transfer to a private clinic and could I arrange it with her private health insurance.

I often wondered if Mum had had private health insurance, whether she'd still be alive.

Chapter 6

'Fuck me, you look awful.'

The look on the nurse's face. It bore a hole through me. I could feel the grip of it in my gut.

'I know. I'm sorry,' I said. 'I haven't had a chance to wash. It's been quite mental.'

'Oh,' he said, 'I can imagine. Mental for you. Not for me. Not me, in this hospital bed, barely able to walk, let alone wipe my arse. You know they're calling in a shrink, don't you? Have you got anything to do with that?'

James was up. His leg in plaster. He had murderous bags under his eyes.

'Dr Naidoo said–'

'Dr Naidoo? She's a quack. Your job was to say that everything was fine. That's all you had to do. Say my drink was spiked.'

'But it wasn't.'

'So? They don't know that. That's the problem with you, Em. You've never been able to think on your feet.'

The nurse left the room. She kept her eyes locked on the floor as she closed the door behind her.

'I was worried about you.'

'You'll be more worried when we have no money because no one will employ me again after all this.'

'But what about your job at the label?'

He looked down and fiddled with his cannula.

'Gone.'

'Gone?'

'Yes, gone. They cut me. I got the text almost as soon as I landed. In mid-air.'

'But you've been there forever. I don't understand.'

He did that thing with his eyes where he looked me up and down, ensuring as he did to convey his disgust. He shrugged.

'Why?' I asked.

'Stop questioning me. It's done. Over.'

'Is that why you took the drugs with the man in the Uber?'

'Where's the baby?' he asked.

'With Hannah. I don't know what I would have done without her. She's helped me so much.'

'With Hannah?' he exclaimed. 'What did we agree about letting Hannah look after the baby?'

'But what else was I meant to do?'

'Hannah is a mad alcoholic.'

'She's not mad. She's just having difficult time.'

'Then her life is one long difficult time,' he said.

'She's my sister,' I protested.

'I don't like her being around the baby. I don't want her to have any influence.'

'Influence? The baby is six months old.'

He was just lying there, immobile, on the bed. I wanted to injure him more. I wanted to kick him in the chest with my foot. I would have preferred to kick him in the back, because backs are preferable to kick. There is too much yield in the chest. But I had no access to his back.

'This is the last thing I need,' he said, putting his head into his hands.

I wished he had been on life support so I could have turned it off.

'Why didn't you call my mother?'

'Your mother is currently on her way to the London Clinic in an ambulance.'

'Oh, right, yeah,' he said. 'I'd forgotten about that. I thought I'd imagined it.'

'Do you want to know how she is?' I asked. 'You haven't even asked what happened. Her artery ruptured. You do know she nearly died.'

'Oh, she'll be fine. She's made of steel. You know that. She's the strongest woman I know.'

What he meant was that I was the weakest.

'Her surgeon is saying she will need to be looked after while she recovers,' I said. 'He said for about six weeks. Six weeks. He says that someone will need to look after her for six weeks.'

Dr Naidoo appeared. She was wearing a lovely dress. It was the type that buttoned up the middle like a long shirt. I assumed that she was allowed to wear proper clothes because she was a consultant and didn't have to wear scrubs. She wore Celine loafers on her feet while the junior doctors wore Crocs. I wanted to tell her how much I liked her shoes, but she saw me looking at them anyway and I imagined that was approbation enough for her.

She stood opposite me, this paragon of woman, with her accomplishments and her tasteful wardrobe. She had a lovely posture. My back was hunched. I straightened it. It hurt. I braced myself – I was soon to be on the receiving end of her difficult words.

'How's the patient today?'

'He's okay,' James said, and he shot her a grin. 'He's all the better for seeing you.'

He was flirting with her. *Oh no*, I thought to myself. For the record, I wasn't jealous about the flirting (we were past the point of jealousy), but I was humiliated. That was the worst thing about the philandering – the visibility of it.

I felt a shift in Dr Naidoo's energy. I wanted to leave the room so that I no longer had to bear witness to James's offensive.

'The results of the psychiatric review have come back,' she said. 'And while it has been agreed that you are now ready to move on to the rehabilitation facility and begin your recovery there, it has flagged something else up.'

'Flagged what up?' he asked.

I wanted to listen to what was coming. I had a feeling I was going to enjoy it.

'Have you heard of a condition called narcissistic personality disorder?'

James's eyes bulged. He looked over at me as if I was the architect of the diagnosis. I shrugged.

'It would explain the suicidality,' Dr Naidoo said.

'But I wasn't suicidal,' James said. 'I was spiked.'

'So you say,' Dr Naidoo replied.

'Is there any treatment for that?' I asked.

'What the evaluation is recommending is talk therapy,' Dr Naidoo explained.

James rolled his eyes demonstratively and said, 'Utter lefty bullshit.'

And then Dr Naidoo said to me, 'The impact of this personality trait on the family dynamic can be severe so we would recommend that your husband undergo some CBT or similar.'

'CBT?' I asked.

'Cognitive behavioural therapy.'

'This is completely ridiculous,' James said. 'I've been under a lot of stress. That's all. My life is extremely stressful. So what if I choose to unwind now and then? Is there a male doctor I could speak to? Who's your boss?'

'I am the boss,' Dr Naidoo said. 'But if you would like a second opinion, do pursue one. It's fairly standard practice to seek out second opinions.'

'Well, I'll do that,' James said.

'For what it's worth, you should know that your wife has been quite extraordinary through all of this,' Dr Naidoo said, addressing James. 'She's had quite a lot to contend with.'

Chapter 7

Time passed. I hadn't wanted it to, because while both James and Hilary were convalescing in their respective institutions, I hadn't had to spare much thought to looking after them both. I must have been in denial. I had made no preparations, mentally or on a practical level. It was just the baby and me, pottering around the flat, walks in the park. At the back of my mind, I knew it wouldn't last. Things were about to change.

I visited both now and then, Hilary in her clinic (actually only once. I couldn't bear more than that) and James in rehab, where I was included in a few family therapy sessions. I brought the baby, and the baby brought joy to the group, but I sensed that James envied the attention that the baby was getting. No doubt he believed that he was the worthier recipient. That must have been a feature of the narcissism that Dr Naidoo had been talking about. It struck me that, despite his constant complaints, he was enjoying rehab, because he could talk about himself all day long and I wasn't sure whether this was curing his narcissism or enabling it. I could see from the therapists at the centre that James's enjoyment was not mutual. I knew their pain and I avoided eye contact with them, in the same way I do when I see a new mother out and about with a newborn. It's for the best.

Hilary was released a week earlier than expected because she had made an astonishing recovery, according to the vascular surgeon, who made it clear to me that, despite this, her predicament was 'precarious' because her blood vessels were 'like rotten tripe'. I collected her from the hospital in a taxi and we spent the journey in complete silence. I thought about throwing myself out of the cab on the Westway so that I would not have to deal with what was to come, but I couldn't reconcile the act with the tacit commitment I had made to the baby.

By the time we arrived back at the flat, it was only half past two. I now had Hilary, all day and all night. It was such a long time until bedtime. I had no idea what I was going to do with all the hours. I had the baby, and that would keep me busy or at least provide me with an excuse to get away from Hilary. I needed to know how long she was going to stay if I were to survive another minute. It was something to iron out immediately, so as I was putting her into the bed in my bedroom (she was to have our bedroom, James the nursery when he was back, and I was going to bunk up in the living room and sleep on the sofa bed, with the baby's cot next to me) I said, 'I can't remember the consultant saying how long you would have to recover for.'

I had learnt from James's deft manipulation of all situations to ask questions by making vague statements rather than direct enquiry.

'Trying to get rid of me already,' she said meanly. She was so mean. I thought: *get out of my bed, harpy*. I would have to incinerate those sheets as soon as she was gone.

Then it occurred to me that James must have learned that questioning technique from someone and it was clearly from Hilary because I was preaching to the converted, if that's the right metaphor.

'No, I–'

And then she started talking over me with a list of demands. I zoned out because it was extensive and the sound of her voice made me want to pull all my skin off.

I wondered in that instant if her housekeeper, Mercedes, should look after her instead – she would do a much better job I reasoned – so I considered calling her up and seeing if she'd relieve me of my anguish, but before I could pick up the phone, Hilary said, with an eyebrow raised, 'I've allowed Mercedes to have a sabbatical while I'm away.'

She was always two steps ahead. Hilary wasn't convalescing, I began to realise. She had engineered an opportunity to infiltrate.

'You'll have to wash my hair now,' she said, pointing to the things in her bag and then pointing at the places she wanted them to be put.

'What?'

'I can't very well entertain with my hair like this,' she said, indicating the matted mess on her head.

'Entertain? But you're meant to be resting. Entertain who?'

'Yes,' she said nastily. 'Ent-turt-tayn. The twins are coming to visit me.'

'Twins?'

'Yes . . . the twins,' she said, unravelling her jewellery roll and skewering a stack of rings onto her gnarled fingers. 'Biddy and Morwenna. My dearest friends. You're going to help me host them. I can't possibly do it myself.'

'But I've got a meeting to prepare for,' I said. 'I have a meeting tomorrow.'

Hilary snarled. She was looking at me as if I was an outrageous fantasist. 'A *meeting*? Who on earth are *you* meeting?'

'My business partner,' I said. 'I have a meeting with my business partner.'

'Business partner?'

The doorbell rang.

'They're early!' she exclaimed. 'Quick, pass me my headscarf.'

She pointed at a garment whose pointed end poked spikily out of her suitcase.

I threw it at her. Frustratingly, it floated. Frustratingly, it landed gracefully.

'Don't just stand there!' she shouted. 'You can't let aristocrats hang around in doorways! Let them in.'

•

The women introduced themselves as Morwenna and Biddy. They were the kind of old I remember old women being when I was young. They had that old lady greyness that you don't see much these days. They smelled the way I'd imagined the Queen Mother would have smelt, of stale cigarettes and Yardley perfume, day-old Tanqueray. I supposed they were roughly the same age as Old Hairy, yet they looked as if they had walked out of the 1970s before facelifts and lasering had been invented. Hilary, I suspected, kept her bob at a certain length and angle to hide the tell-tale scars around her ears.

'Biddy?' I said, nervously, to both. 'Is that short for anything?'

'Elizabeth,' Biddy said shortly.

She wasn't going to give me a thing.

'Are you identical?' I asked.

They looked at each other and then around me searchingly for the person whose care I must have been under. And then, seeing that I was unsupervised, they examined my appearance, protracting the act. They registered the ptosis on my eye that dragged my eyelid down when I was tired and which I had to prop up most of the time with the help of the corresponding eyebrow. They were looking at the skin around my jowls, at the exact point where the creases were at their most entrenched. They lingered awhile on my slippers. They were wearing matching patent black Ferragamos and had not even considered removing them on entering the flat. Hilary never removed her shoes either. I wondered if it had something to do with class. My mother always told me to take my shoes off because of all the shit outside.

Morwenna or Biddy (I couldn't tell which) had a dog, and its head poked out of her handbag. It had a name that didn't fit it like Bannockburn or Banquo, heavy on the Bs. I can't remember. It was all too much.

•

I decided to hide in the nursery under the pretence of needing to feed and change the baby. The baby was coming in handy. I did not want to go back out there. No way. Not into the snark and the inquisitions and the 'spit it outs' and the 'where is your nanny?' and 'what do you mean you don't have a nanny, who looks after the baby?' and all the flinching when I said that there wasn't one.

They were talking furiously in the room next door. My room! I thought of all the bottoms on my bed and the dog in the handbag – no longer in the handbag but on a rampage, shedding its furs all over my duvet cover.

Theirs was the strangest language – some discussion about

a marquess and a marchioness. I thought they were talking about people from Mars or that massive boat that sank, but it soon became clear that they were talking about people they knew and not just in a loose way but in an extremely closely related way.

From what I could gather, Morwenna and Biddy's brother, David, the marquess, had an estate in Perthshire close to a town called Dunkeld and he had recently been involved in a car accident that had left him comatose in a hospital in Dundee. Hilary kept asking questions, which I felt were impertinent to the point of prurient, but the twins seemed not to mind. In fact, they appeared to relish the unseemly direction the conversation was taking.

'Do you think *she* had anything to do with it?' Hilary asked. 'What's her name? David's wife. The marchioness.'

'They'd been having problems for a long time. And then, suddenly, this happens,' Biddy said.

'Surely it's not in her interest for David to die,' Hilary said. 'I hate to sound so cynical, but isn't it the case that were he to die, she'd lose her claim to the estate. There are no children? No issue?'

'Correct,' Biddy said.

'So, it would all go to . . .' Hilary said, deftly nudging the narrative along.

'Us. No entail. Co-heiresses.'

'And what would happen to the marchioness?'

'Dowager.'

There was a silence. Someone cleared her throat heavily, which I took to indicate displeasure.

'A house on the estate I'd imagine,' said Morwenna. 'Where Mummy lived.'

I was so engrossed in this conversation that I hadn't realised I was holding the bottle the wrong way and had been feeding the baby air. I sat the baby up on my lap and rubbed its back. It belched. The noise it made exceeded its size.

'Everything okay in there?' Biddy asked.

'Yes, fine!' I shrilled, but I knew it wasn't a sincere question and, if anything, it was a way to tell me to shut the belching baby up.

'She's visiting him almost every day. It's a long slog to the hospital. A two-hour round trip.'

'Doesn't help that she's refusing to drive herself,' Morwenna added.

'Why won't she drive herself? How utterly bizarre. Entitlement, is it? Does she expect a chauffeur?' Hilary asked.

I put Hilary's apparent fascination with this discussion down to there being no aristocratic system where she came from on the Upper East Side. I can't remember ever hearing her so engaged with anything. I can't say I wasn't interested too. I wanted to know more about the marchioness who wouldn't drive. I inched closer to the door.

'She's convinced she's going to die in a car accident. Convinced of it. She will no longer drive. Point-blank refuses to. It's all very odd if you ask me, but this what we're dealing with.'

'Where was he going?' Hilary asked. 'The day he had the accident.'

'St Andrews.'

'Whatever for?'

'Guest lecturing.'

'For what?' Biddy asked.

'Not now, Biddy. It's not important. The point is that she's now convinced that if she drives, she will die.'

'Lunacy,' Hilary hissed.

The twins grunted in unison.

'We saw in the back of *The Lady of the House* that she is advertising for a driver. A female driver. That's her stipulation. No idea why she can't have a male one. Who ever heard of a female chauffeur?'

•

They didn't like the dinner I had made for them. I had tried hard on that one. Of all the things I cooked, that had the most potential to be edible.

Hilary made it clear: 'It's dreadfully bland.'

She was digging through the rubble of my tuna pasta bake. The twins raked theirs across the plates, forming little heaps while masticating arduously.

'Is this canned?' Morwenna glowered.

I gawped at her. I didn't know that tuna came in any other vessel.

'And is it skipjack or albacore?' Biddy asked.

'I can make you something else if you like,' I said. 'I'll just put the baby down.'

'No!' Hilary exclaimed, seizing the tray with her gigantic knuckles. 'Nothing else.'

Then it dawned on me that I could shorten my suffering by starving the woman to death.

Chapter 8

I had a meeting. Ever since I had had the baby, I would tell anyone who would listen that I had a meeting. I rarely had meetings anymore. Ahead of this meeting, life stirred inside me, fire coursed through my limbs. I put on shoes that weren't trainers and a coat that wasn't a parka. I added some earrings and I left Hilary in the flat, ruminating on the piece of toast I had given her earlier that morning. She had not slept well, and it was the first thing she told me when I opened the door to her room.

'This mattress is dreadful,' she complained. 'And the noise! The noise from outside. It's a war zone. I've ordered a new mattress from Harrods and it will be here this afternoon. But the noise. I really don't know what I'm going to do about that.'

You could go home, I thought. And I definitely was not going to tell her about the bright yellow earplugs. I wondered if it meant that I'd get to keep the new mattress after she'd left, but before I could even reach the end of that train of thought she said, 'It'll go in the guest suite when I get home. The one in there is a little tired too.'

I put her cup of coffee down on the bedside table, having had my fill of Hilary. She didn't even think to ask me how the baby slept, how we both slept for that matter, shacked up in the living room together. (Up at two, one feed, straight back to sleep, awake at seven. It was a good night, and I was so grateful to the baby for that.)

When I arrived at the café for my meeting, after a twenty-minute ride on the number 94 to Notting Hill Gate, I noticed that Vanessa was sitting in a seat with her back to me. It struck me as odd because whenever we met before I'd had the baby she'd always get there early and choose the better seat, the one that looked out at the restaurant.

I knew something wasn't right. It was to ensure that I couldn't see her face, I was certain of it, because if I had seen it, I might have been able to read it, and there was something on there that she wanted me not to see but her problem was that her face was so hopelessly expressive.

'You've brought the baby with you,' she said.

She looked at the baby as if the baby was Yoko. The baby was in the BabyBjörn, facing outwards, drooling onto my lap. I couldn't see the baby's face, and I worried that the baby would start crying because of the lack of humanity that Vanessa was displaying on hers.

'It's been a bit crazy lately,' I said. 'I've had no one to watch the baby.'

I was about to tell her about Hilary's ruptured aneurysm and how it had come to pass that she was living with us and James's disappearance and subsequent reappearance, but I could see that she wasn't interested because she reached for the bag that had been sitting next to her on the banquette and pulled out a thick wad of papers. She did that thing people do when they're being serious about something. She pushed her glasses up the bridge of her nose with both hands and looked down as if she was reading an X-ray or a pathology report, but I knew that those glasses were not prescription lenses and she wore them to make herself look intelligent because she told me so when she had had too much to drink on a business trip we'd gone to in Frankfurt. That's where we bought the stuff we sold on the internet. The doggy stuff. Some cat stuff too.

'What are they?' I asked, referring to the papers. 'I thought you wanted to touch base about the business.'

'I do,' she said.

'Because I've been sending you business plans and mood boards and proposals but I've heard nothing back,' I continued. 'I almost feel like I'm being ghosted.'

I laughed, hoping that Vanessa would laugh too and correct my misapprehension but a correction never came. I could see that she didn't know how to say what she needed to tell me, so she looked down at the papers, turned them around and pushed them towards me like a croupier with bad hand.

'This is the paperwork for the termination of your directorship from Companies House.'

'Termination?'

'Yes,' she said.

'But I don't want to terminate my directorship,' I said.

She took the glasses off her face and one by one folded the arms and placed the glasses on the table. She was lining them up with the end of the table, obsessively and compulsively, making everything perpendicular. What she needed was a protractor. Why didn't she just carry a protractor around with her? She carried fake glasses around with her, so she might as well have carried around other mad things. I could see that she was procrastinating. This right-angle bullshit was a stalling tactic. She was doing everything to avoid looking me in the eye. Beneath the table I made my hands into fists.

'I just don't think you fit in the company anymore,' she said. 'I think we've outgrown you.'

'Who's we?' I asked.

'Me and Camilla.'

'Camilla? She's my maternity cover. I thought you said she's only meant to be temporary. I thought that was the deal.'

'I've promoted her. She's bringing so much to the brand. Social media. New contacts. All this Instagram money. I'm going to make her a director. She's great. She's young and energetic. She's hungry. And she doesn't have a–'

'A what?'

Vanessa looked at the baby and then at me.

'You can't pretend it's not made a difference. You said nothing would change, but that's not the case, is it?'

'I'm still technically on maternity leave.'

'Maternity leave?' She said. 'When I had Lorenzo I was back in the office after a fortnight.'

'It was different for you,' I said. 'Your husband paid for your nanny. I can't afford a nanny and continue working. You know that James won't contribute to childcare.'

'That's not my problem,' she said. 'You chose to have the baby, knowing what the situation was.'

It occurred to me that all this negative talk about the baby would hurt the baby's feelings somewhere deep down, so I covered the baby's ears with my hands. I couldn't risk the repercussions of such triggering talk eighteen years down the line.

'Really?' Vanessa said.

I removed my hands.

She caressed the papers, stood them up and shuffled them a bit.

'This might be the best thing for you,' Vanessa said. 'Time for you to start something new. Or, you know, you could stay at home with the baby.'

Expression-wise, Vanessa produced one of her finest. It was a mixture of repulsion, upper-lip curling and dead horror behind the eyes, and her head was pushed backwards, which made her neck wrinkle up. I wanted to take a picture of her neck and show it to her. The baby began to whine. I started bouncing in my seat.

'Don't I get a say in this?' I asked. Blood was rushing through me at the rate of knots; my whole body was aflame. I was getting hot and I could feel that, round about where my heart was, there was a throbbing, a heavy slapping. A rage was threatening. 'I started this company with you. I put five years of my life into it. I know we haven't made the kind of money we'd hoped to make, but I know it's just a matter of time. I'm a shareholder. I should get a say.'

'But I'm the majority shareholder,' she said. 'The final decision comes down to me.'

Just then, a waitress appeared at the table and stood over us. She asked me if I'd like anything. Vanessa had a latte. I didn't want to order the same drink as she had ordered in case she saw it as some kind of approbation, so I said no.

I had said it too angrily. I tried to temper it with a 'thank you'.

'Okay,' the waitress said, and I smiled at her and she sort of smiled back at me but it wasn't genuine. It was in that appalled way.

'Actually,' I said to the walking-away waitress. 'Could I have a double espresso?'

Vanessa looked at me. She only ever knew me as a latte drinker.

'I'm not sleeping very well,' I said, even though I had slept brilliantly the night before. I thought she might take pity on me and forget the whole thing.

'We want you to terminate your directorship,' she continued unfazed. 'And I'd like you to surrender half your shares.'

She pushed another wad of papers towards me that read *Transfer of Company Shares.*

'But I really don't understand,' I said.

I was confused. I was weary, so weary. And I was angry. Angry and weary. It was a hard blend to metabolise.

'If you don't,' she said.

'If I don't?' I repeated.

'I know things,' she said. 'I know a lot of things.'

She was talking about things I had told her about James from a long time ago. That's what she was talking about.

I hung my head. Tears sprung in my eyes, poured from my eye sockets. My eyes were reddening. Good! Let her see the pain she has wrought on me, I thought. Although I wished I had brought my sunglasses for when I left the café. Being a mother with a baby in the pouch and sobbing is a tragic look, one that I've achieved more often than I'd like to admit. I snatched the papers, stood up and walked out.

Chapter 9

James was due to be collected from the rehabilitation centre the following week.

I still had the documents that Vanessa had forced upon me at the café in the baby bag, which I had dashed lavishly with my tears, holding them beneath my face, so that they would fall onto the paper. That's what I did while I was sitting at the bus stop, waiting for the number 94 after leaving our meeting. The wetness had dried but had left the papers crumpled in places. Very well, I thought. Let her see the product of my grief. I could not bring myself to sign them.

After that meeting with Vanessa, I had delayed returning home and spent the rest of the day mooning around Turnham Green Terrace with the baby. I sank three lattes and became jittery, borderline wretched. Whatever was necessary to avoid returning to nasty Old Hairy I did, but eventually I saw that I had no choice because the baby's nappy was bulging and I had neglected to bring any spare. The night was drawing in. The temperature had dropped. It had started to feel much more like November. The baby's cheeks were getting cold. I couldn't in good conscience subject the baby to frostbite simply because I was terrified of my mother-in-law.

During those weeks at home after Hilary's discharge, I toiled in my new role as carer, trying not to apply much thought to the emotional fabric of my days but rather contemplating the practical ways I might end my suffering. I was homing in on the idea of poison as a good method. I wondered about the availability of arsenic, whether I could buy it on Amazon or, failing that, the dark web, but I didn't know a thing about accessing it. I had read a book when I was a kid called *Flowers in the Attic* about some siblings who had been locked away in their loft and had resorted to incest and, very, very slowly, were being poisoned by arsenic. Someone was putting arsenic into their doughnuts. It was slow and it was painful. Perhaps arsenic was no longer as fashionable a poison as it was in the early 1980s and now you were looking at the more sophisticated poisons, like Novichok.

This was my life. No job, no plan, apart from poisoning Hilary.

James wasn't alone when I arrived at the centre. I was expecting him to be standing at the entrance with his suitcase in hand looking chastened and pious. But he wasn't doing that. He was inside in the waiting room, sitting in one of the enormous armchairs, absorbed in conversation with a woman I didn't know and hadn't once met during our group therapy visits. She had a bag with her too. It stood at her feet. I assumed that they were both being discharged at the same time and this had given them something in common, a reason to talk to each other.

I must have been standing there for several minutes when at last James caught sight of me. It was the strangest thing because, having seen me, he continued to talk to this person as if he had not. And at that moment I knew that he was pretending not to know me because acknowledging me would have endangered whatever he was trying to achieve.

Clearly, I had been standing in the middle of the room for such a long time that the woman he was talking to turned to me and, registering the baby in the pouch, said, 'Are you okay there?'

Then James turned to face me. I can't remember ever being regarded with such disappointment. It wasn't even disappointment. It was dismay. His mouth bent into a rictus.

'I've actually come to pick up my husband.'

I looked at James. He stood up. The woman watched him rise.

'You're late,' he said.

'I'm actually early,' I said, picking my phone out of my pocket and glaring at the screen. 'They said noon. It's eleven-thirty.'

I looked at the woman. Then James looked at her.

'This is Anya,' he said shortly. He was embarrassed by me. I would have been embarrassed by me too. I wasn't looking my best. The skin around my eyes was raw from crying. In truth, I wasn't dealing well with this Vanessa business despite what I had been telling myself.

'Hi,' I said.

She lifted a hand in half-hearted salute.

'The cab's waiting outside,' I said. 'We'd better go.'

I turned to leave but noticed that James wasn't coming with me. 'Are you coming?' I said. 'I think the meter's running.'

'I have to tell you something,' he said.

He sat down again and placed his hand on the woman's hand. I wasn't sure what I was watching. I felt the world start to turn the wrong way.

'I have fallen in love.'

'Sorry?'

'I have fallen in love. I'm in love.'

He turned to Anya and she squeezed his hand and said, 'That's it. Well done.'

He nodded. He hung his head in saintly self-regard.

'I've found Anya. She understands me. At last, someone understands me. We want to be together.'

•

'Where is he?' Hilary screeched. 'Where's my boy? Where's my beautiful boy?'

The front door slammed shut behind me. There was a draught in the flat. Hilary had opened the bedroom window. I could smell cigarette smoke and knew that it was coming from the twins chugging on their Dunhills. I could hear them all in my bedroom. I had told them not to smoke when they lit up after dinner the day Hilary came back from the hospital. I had warned them about the dangers of smoking around the baby. I had pleaded.

'I hope you've brought some food with you, Emma,' she said. 'There's absolutely nothing of merit to eat here. No doubt my boy needs a proper meal. I can't imagine they've been feeding him properly over there. Although I suppose he's used to it.'

I entered the room. They all stared expectantly at me. Morwenna was at the window, blowing smoke into the cold air, while Biddy perched at the end of the bed. Hilary was lying in state with a stack of pillows behind her.

'Well, where is he?' Hilary asked.

'Where *has* he been?' asked Morwenna. 'Hilary, you still haven't told us.'

'Rehabilitation,' Hilary answered. She glared at me. She was bringing serious game to her eye work. She had a secret. I knew her secret.

'Oh dear,' Morwenna replied. 'Poor chap. Skiing accident?'

And just as Hilary was about to open her mouth, presumably to confirm this misapprehension, I said, 'No, not for a skiing accident. Not that. He was in rehab because he's an addict and because he was arrested for breach of the peace for shitting in public on the Wellington Arch when he was high on fentanyl that he scored off an Uber driver on the way back from Heathrow. He was a bit glum, you see, having been fired from his job for screwing his boss's daughter. That's where he's been, and the reason I know this is because that is what he told me, about an hour ago, right after announcing that he was leaving me for some woman he's met in rehab. He is leaving me, but they are planning to live together in our flat with me and the baby and you, Hilary, because neither of them can afford to live anywhere else. They're on their way here now in fact. As you can imagine, I didn't fancy joining them on the ride.'

Hilary swooned. Morwenna's fag flew out of her hand. Biddy retrieved it. But it had already singed my seagrass rug.

Chapter 10

When I look back at that time, I can see that I was suffering from a kind of cognitive obliteration.

I was in the darkness of the nursery with only the night light on. I watched it cast its spell upon the ceiling while it played *Eine kleine Nachtmusik* to me. I found myself rocking in the feeding chair while the baby slept in its cot. At first, my rocking was gentle, like the motion of a pedalo on water, but then it became frantic.

Through the small gap in the door I saw Morwenna handing around a plate to Hilary and Biddy in the living room. Biddy had her feet up on the coffee table, on my second-hand Assouline books, the ones I had spent years collecting, trawling eBay for and she was crushing them, crushing, crushing. She was sinking a glass of Glenfiddich, decanted from a bottle that she had brought with her. Hilary was sobbing, occasionally yowling. Morwenna must have found the Carr's crackers and the packet of Philadelphia in the back of the fridge that had seen better days. I noticed that Hilary kept shooing the plate away. She must have lost her appetite. I didn't much feel like eating either.

James and Anya weren't back yet. James was reliably delayed.

I was not going to leave the nursery. I had decided to barricade myself in there. I did not want to go into the living room with Hilary and the twins. I knew that she was constructing a narrative that would seek to blame me for everything.

I stopped rocking and steadied my feet on the carpet to cease the chair's motion. I looked across at the baby who was wriggling, making little grunting, fitful noises in its sleep. Behind me was the window, leading out to the fire escape stairs. I pulled at the sash. It was stubborn. I couldn't remember ever opening it. Paint had warped it shut. After a tussle, I managed to lift it. The cold night air swept in. I wanted to be on the other side of that window. Out.

I needed to gather my things. None of my things was in the nursery. The baby's things, I reasoned, were of the greatest importance, like the car seat. I'd need that. That was in the hall where I'd left it after returning from rehab. I had no idea where my phone was. I couldn't think. I couldn't remember.

At a speed so fast and with energy so frenzied that the women next door would have struggled to compute what I was doing, I leapt into the living room and from there dashed to the hall to retrieve the car seat. I grabbed the baby bag that I had abandoned next to it and slung it over my shoulders in the manner of a commando.

Behind me, I heard the tell-tale click of the front-door latch, the creaking hinge.

It was him.

I ran back into the nursery and did not come out again.

Chapter 11

The cottage was perched on the tip of the highest hill in the area, and, as areas went, it was already very hilly given that it was in the Highlands – Perth and Kinross to be exact. The beauty of the cottage was wrapped up in the view it had. It looked onto the Tay Valley, which had a river flowing through it, and it bulged with salmon, but you couldn't see the salmon from where I was standing. From that height, the valley was as picturesque as a postcard or a poster urging calm. On either side of the valley sheep grazed. It was hard to believe that what I was seeing was not just a figment of my imagination.

How does that saying go? Would you rather live in a beautiful house, looking out onto an ugly view, or in an ugly house looking out onto a beautiful view? I can never remember which is the right answer to that (people say there is no right answer but of course there is, there always is). I wouldn't have said that the cottage was ugly but it had a self-conscious austerity about it and an energy that I could only describe as dour. It had previously served as a farmhouse, which is why there were several voluminous outbuildings behind it, dwarfing it, filled with defunct farming vehicles caked in rust.

The cottage was made from grey brick, not a monochrome grey, but a spectrum of greys that gave it some dimension and character. The protrusion of chimneys from certain points along the building and the ornate lightning conductor topping the central mini tower gave it a flavour of the gothic. It was a miniature castle, certainly more castle than cottage. I could not put my finger on why it made me shudder.

Hannah had driven us to King's Cross, where I took the Caledonian Sleeper overnight, reaching Dunkeld and Birnam station at just after six the following morning. If I could, I would forever sleep on a train. It must have been one of the few nights that the baby slept right through. I can only imagine that it was the rocking of the train that ensured such a restful sleep. I didn't sleep a wink, however. I sat at the window, watching England become Scotland. And as we rushed along the line one city seemed to morph into another, spires and domes, concrete monoliths, neon signs. I reflected that cities were all the same basic idea.

I had departed the life I knew, which must have looked so small and inconsequential from the outside. My little life with its routines and habits meant everything to me. I had clung on to it for longer than I should have. Staring out into the rushing darkness from my cabin window, I knew I could not return to it. I had no idea what I was heading towards, and I worried that I wouldn't be able to fulfil what was expected of me. The only person whose expectations I cared about were the baby's, and the baby had no expectations. That's why I loved the baby so much.

We were met at the station by Kelly, the housekeeper, who took us straight to the cottage in an enormous truck type of vehicle that she called the Defender, a sensible choice given that the track leading up to it was inhospitable and vertiginous. Grouse ran insanely about, careering off to the sides of the track and then straight back into the track again, without a clue as to their own idiocy. I had no idea how I would traverse this on my own when my turn came. I tried not to show my consternation, which took all the energy I could muster.

Kelly apologised that Mark, the estate manager, hadn't been there to greet me but something had come up, she said, and I wondered if something bad had happened to the marquess in a coma. I had to make sure that I did not reveal what I already knew about the family in case I blew my cover, in case the twins, Biddy and Morwenna, somehow found out that I had run away and taken the job of chauffeur for their sister-in-law, the marchioness: the job that they had inadvertently advertised to me and which, potentially, had enabled my liberation, delivering me from Hilary and from James. I made up a new name for myself and I think it suited me.

Kelly was not at all what I had imagined the housekeeper of a Scottish country estate to be. I had expected someone older, in her sixties, perhaps dressed in a tweed suit, someone stern and cold, a bit like Mrs Danvers in *Rebecca*. But Kelly was the opposite. *Bubbly* would have been the best word for her, although I don't much like that word. She must have only been a few years older than me and wore metallic leggings with a hot pink polo shirt. She was sweating heavily and given that it wasn't at all hot outside (if anything, it was bracing), I guessed that she was going through some major hormonal event because she kept fanning her face with her hands and it seemed to be doing little to help. Beads of sweat sat on her upper lip, refusing to budge, and they clung onto the hairs up there. That would be me in a few years, I reckoned.

The other thing about Kelly was that she wasn't Scottish, but from the South like me, and I must admit that I was disappointed because I would have liked a more immersive Scottish experience, but beggars can't be choosers. I just didn't want to be reminded of where I had come from.

Kelly hadn't expected that there would be a baby and appeared to be mystified by the sight of it glaring at her from the pouch as we stood on the empty station platform, tall evergreens looming over us. It was almost as if she had never encountered a human infant.

'What have we got here?' she said, her face mooning into the baby's.

'It's a baby,' I said. 'It's my baby.'

It had been Hannah's idea not to disclose the existence of the baby. She wanted to get the job done, so to speak, which meant impersonating me during the telephone interview because she knew that I hadn't the stomach for subterfuge. She justified not mentioning the baby because no one had specifically asked her if there was one.

'So technically it's not deceit. It's just an omission.'

Hannah said that, in her experience, employers tended not to like babies anyway, which is something I knew only too well, as did Hannah, evidenced by what she called the negative correlation of her colleagues' entry into motherhood and her ascent up the corporate ladder. I had no idea what I would do with the baby while I was working. Hannah told me to cross that bridge when I came to it.

'We need to ascertain two things,' she stated, looking up

from her laptop and showing me two of her fingers. 'Firstly, the salary, and, secondly, whether you can be paid in cash.'

'Cash?'

'Yes, cash. I'll explain later,' she said. 'But I'm going to ask them because I know what you're like. I can talk money. You can't. I do it for a living. You'll end up offering to work for free rather than even broach the subject. But the fact is that you need money, lots of it, and fast.'

I must admit to having felt pathetic at that moment and considered overruling her just to prove that I had some fire in me, but I also had to tell myself that this was no time for heroics and that I should preserve my courage for what was to come.

According to Hannah, it wasn't much of an interview anyway, not particularly probing. I wouldn't have known; I had been hiding in the loo at the time, refusing to bear witness to the reality unfolding in the room next door. Hannah said there were no hard questions. Just 'is your licence clean?' and 'when can you start?' And also to check that I was a woman and not a man pretending to be a woman to get the job.

The job advertisement was precisely where the twins had said it would be, in a magazine called *The Lady of the House*. It was a window into a world I never knew existed: features about etiquette, 'A Guide to Modern Manners', recipes for dishes straight out of the 1970s, 'The Five Best Winter Hats'. This was where aristocrats posted jobs. Housekeepers, cooks, butlers, live-in nannies, companions, carers; jobs I didn't know people could do – live-in house parents in boarding schools. If it weren't for the baby, I might have applied for that. We hunted through the job section until we came across an advert that read:

LIVE-IN DRIVER (F) FOR A PRIVATE ESTATE IN PERTHSHIRE

We are looking for a full-time driver (F) for a large estate in Highland Perthshire. Immediate start.

Someone who has high standards, discreet, self-motivated with a positive attitude and ability to be flexible. Previous experience preferred. Duties include daily driving. Must be able to work on your own and as part of a team. Not averse to hospitals.

We offer a lovely self-contained cottage and competitive package according to experience. Must be fluent in English. Non-smoker. Interviews commence ASAP.

'Bingo,' Hanna said, gazing at the screen on her laptop, her face misted by vape steam. 'Although I've no idea how they got away with stipulating the applicant must be female.'

'Positive attitude, self-motivated, high standards . . . Hannah, this isn't me.'

My brow was furrowed.

'Well, it's going to have to be.'

Hannah went silent and pressed a finger against her lips. She pointed towards the front door. 'Shh.'

It was James, banging – yelling at me to give him the baby. He must have returned with Anya from rehab to find that I was no longer at home and had taken the baby with me. And he must have realised that I had fled to Hannah's flat (where else would I have been?). We ran to her back bedroom and hid. He sounded drunk. He had managed to get himself drunk again.

'This is why you have to leave,' Hannah said.

Hours passed. The banging receded in rhythm, now

becoming sporadic, like a heart giving up. James had tired himself out. Soon the banging stopped altogether, and we took our chance to leave, stepping over his reeking, near-lifeless body in the hallway.

And that was how I came to be standing at the little doorway to the cottage, the lovely self-contained cottage with the sinister aura, on top of the hill, looking down to the valley. Kelly had entered first, simply by opening the door by the handle, using no key as if it was just another room in a house.

'Do you not need to lock it?' I asked. 'Do you just leave it open?'

'Why would we need to lock it?'

'Isn't it safer to lock it? In London, I wouldn't dream of not locking my front door.'

'But we are not in London anymore, my lovely,' Kelly said and she chuckled merrily, using her forearm to wipe the moisture that had gathered around her eyebrows. 'Can I call you Cam? Or Millie? What do your friends call you? I'll call you that.'

I had decided to call myself Camilla after the treacherous bitch who stole my livelihood. I wanted to be reminded of my reams and reams of failures, and my unwitting usurpation was another one of them. I wanted to jam my thumb into the wound that was my life. I had failed at everything! And I didn't know what my friends called me, this being the first outing with my new name. I tried to think fast. It was so hard. Kelly was eyeballing me. She was witnessing the laborious trudging of my brain. It was either that or my facial asymmetry that was causing her to gawp. She was looking too much at my funny eye. I wanted to tell her that it was rude to stare.

'Well,' she said, less merrily, 'no rush. I'm sure it'll come to you. Unless you don't have any friends!'

She laughed. At first, I didn't laugh because she had touched a nerve and then I did laugh, seeing that it was essential to the security of my future to laugh at that moment. I wasn't keen on either Cam or Millie. I had made a grave error with the name I had chosen and wished I could have retracted it.

'This is the kitchen,' Kelly said, standing in the middle of it with her legs quite far apart. 'That much is probably obvious. We've just had it redone. What do you think? Nice, isn't it? You should have seen it before. I won't even try to describe the state it was in but all I will say is that it was grim. Gur-rim.'

The kitchen didn't look redone. I was trying to see what in it had been redone, but it was hard to tell because the flooring was a retro dappled brown Formica made to look like terracotta tiles and the worktops were white and grey granite-effect vinyl, which gave it a clinical feel and jarred with the floor's pseudo-Tuscan aesthetic. It was a galley kitchen, like the one I had at home, but out of every window I could see nature, trees and other green things and the wooden fence that ran around the perimeter of the cottage to keep sheep out. I was aware of the absence of noise outside, and it almost had a sound, or perhaps it was just the novel sensation of silence on my ears. There was a hob with four induction rings on it, an oven, a dishwasher and a little counter by the window with two wooden chairs pushed underneath that Kelly called the 'breakfast bar', which made the place sound cosmopolitan. I wasn't sure that I would ever eat my breakfast there, looking out of the window at the enormous tractor shed.

'I've put a few things in here for you, just to keep you going,' Kelly said, opening the fridge. 'The village shop is four miles away and I thought you'd probably like to get settled in before you start work tomorrow.'

I nodded and looked inside the fridge. There were two bottles of milk, a loaf of white bread, a pack of butter and a Victoria sponge. 'Thank you,' I said. 'It's so thoughtful of you.'

Kelly closed the fridge. She looked forlorn; I think she wished she could have stood in front of the opened fridge forever. 'I can show you around the rest of the house if you like,' she said, fanning her face. 'God, it's hot in here.'

'That's fine,' I said. 'I'll be fine. I've held you up long enough.'

'Okay, then,' she said. 'Just a couple of things before I shoot off. The estate manager will be coming by later in the afternoon to brief you about tomorrow. Torches are in the cupboard under the stairs. We get a lot of power cuts out here. We even had one that lasted for a week, can you believe it? You'll soon get used to it. The key to the gun cupboard is in the tractor shed behind the cottage.'

'Gun cupboard?'

'Yes. Gun cupboard. For shooting grouse. This used to be a shooting lodge.'

'Oh, right,' I said. 'Not any more then? Why is that?'

'The marchioness doesn't agree with shooting, so they don't do it.'

'That's great,' I said.

'Not for Mark,' Kelly added.

'Mark?'

'The estate manager. He's the one who interviewed you.'

'Oh yes, of course. Of course.'

'Mark's old-school. The marquess trained him up,' Kelly said. 'Doesn't like the no-shooting rule one bit. Neither did the marquess for that matter. Says that's why the place is now overrun with grouse. Mark's got a pole up his arse, quite frankly, and could do with chilling out.'

It was hard to know how to respond to that because I didn't know the man, but I sensed there was merit in ingratiating myself with Kelly so I smiled and said, 'I'd probably better put the baby down for a nap. It's been quite a morning.'

I pulled the baby out of the pouch but remembered that I didn't have a cot or anything to put the baby in – apart from the car seat, which was in the other room and I didn't feel at liberty to get it – so I just held it and rocked it in my arms. The baby was using its stomach muscles to try and sit up, but I preferred the baby to be horizontal at that moment and we appeared to be having a bit of a tussle.

Kelly watched the whole thing. I'd gone quite far down the road of not knowing what I was doing with the baby, so I decided to try and style it out, behaving as if there was nothing unusual going on vis-à-vis my care of the baby.

'Where will the baby be when you're at work?' she asked. She looked concerned. It was imperative that I improved the impression I was making. Things were going downhill. 'You know,' she continued, 'when you're driving the marchioness to and from the hospital.'

'Can I ask what the marchioness's name is? Do I call her by her name or do I call her 'Marchioness'? I really don't know.'

'Didn't Mark tell you? What has he told you? Sometimes that man can be a bit light on the old detail. Us girls need to know these things, don't we? Details.'

'Sure,' I said. 'Sure. I know about the driving. Driving to the hospital, waiting at the hospital and driving back again.'

'Right,' Kelly said. She hoisted up her silver leggings. They were ruched around her knees.

'I was thinking about having the baby in the front of the car with me,' I said. 'The baby loves cars, any transport really. I don't think it will be a problem.'

When Kelly made a disapproving sound I knew I was in big trouble.

'Oh, my love, the marchioness won't be too happy about this,' Kelly said. 'I think it might be an issue, you know.'

'A big issue or a little issue?' I asked.

'On the biggish side,' Kelly said. 'It's just that she's got this policy about children on the estate. No one under the age of eighteen anywhere near it. I'd go as far as saying no one under the age of twenty-five. You're going to have to tell Mark. I'm sorry, my lovely, but I don't see how this is going to work.'

'But I've really got to make this work,' I said. 'I really need this job. Really need it.'

The baby, who sensed my jitteriness, began to cry.

'Oh dear, oh, you poor love,' Kelly said, approaching the baby. She stroked the baby on the chin. The baby smiled at her.

'Are you in some sort of trouble?' she asked, looking at the baby, not looking at me. I felt that she was beginning to like the baby.

'No,' I said. 'I'm not in trouble. But I do need this job.'

Kelly tilted her head to one side. She crossed her arms over her body. And then she stroked her chin with her hand. 'I've got some things I need to be getting on with at the castle,' she said. 'But leave it with me. I think I might know someone who can help you with this.'

She turned to leave the cottage. As she held the door open, she said, 'But whatever you do, don't tell Mark about the baby.'

Chapter 12

I did as Kelly had told me and left my childcare conundrum with her. There was no alternative, as far as I could see.

I hadn't moved from the kitchen, hadn't attempted to look around the rest of the cottage, because it was possible there might have been no point, that I would be given my marching orders, sent packing. The baby had fallen asleep in my arms, so I sat down at the breakfast bar and stared out at the tractor shed which was in essence an enormous barn without a door, a gaping black rectangle where the insides were.

I was anxious, but I told myself to eat anyway and so I made myself a cup of tea, but only because there was no coffee, and slowly I worked my way through the Victoria sponge. It was mad to have come all this way without considering the baby. I hadn't been thinking straight.

The day I fled London, Hannah told me about an article she had read a long time ago in *The Economist* titled 'How to Disappear'.

'The best way to disappear is to pay for everything with cash because no one can track you if you are paying cash,' she explained. 'If you use a credit card you can be traced immediately. They'll follow the money. What you are meant to do is begin withdrawing money a long time in advance and then hide it until you have enough to bolt and then you can run away to, like, Brazil or, wherever.'

'But I don't have a long time,' I told her. 'I have the very opposite of that. And I don't want to go to Brazil. I'm too flat-chested. I'd be a social outcast.'

'Brazil is just an example.'

We had gone down to the High Road and taken out as much cash as we could. Hannah withdrew £200 and I did likewise. We made sure to withdraw it in Chiswick so that no one would be able to 'follow the money'. In all I had £400, which I knew would not last long, even if I refrained from buying nice coffees along the way, but, from my initial observations of the local area, I could see that there was little by way of temptation where nice coffees were concerned. I cut myself another slice of cake and ate that almost all in one go. My leg was doing that thing where it wouldn't stop shaking.

I was tiring from holding the baby, so I went upstairs to the first floor to look for somewhere for it to go. I made a pillow fort on one of the beds, and after lowering the baby down into it and seeing that it was safe, I made my way back down to find that there was a person standing in the hallway.

I had assumed that it was Kelly returning from whatever mission she had set herself but soon realised that it wasn't Kelly. It was someone else – a man. What a relief that the baby was safely tucked away in another part of the house, out of sight. I could only hope that it would stay asleep.

Intuitively, I stood to attention because the man was tall and something about the way he held himself seemed to require it of me. I wondered if he had been in the army at some point in his life.

'Mark,' said the man. 'Mark Young.'

He was looking down at me from his six-foot-something inches. I must have looked quite flustered because he said, 'Are you alright there?' He was surveying me and my general area.

'Yes,' I said.

'You start work at the castle tomorrow,' he said. 'Is everything in order?'

'Yes,' I said.

He looked at me and said nothing.

'Yes, everything is in order,' I echoed.

I don't know how to describe his manner apart from to say that I felt he didn't want to be standing in that little kitchen with me. He looked as if he wanted to be outside, shooting something or plucking its feathers out, hooking something through the face or clubbing it to death. I thought about mentioning the gun cupboard to break the ice, to put us on the right footing.

'I see there is a gun cupboard here,' I said.

'Do you have your paperwork with you?'' he asked, evidently not acknowledging the gun cupboard stuff. 'Passport, driving licence. You know, the ID we discussed over the phone.'

'Oh,' I said. 'Right.'

Hannah had been a bit scant on this part. In the mayhem, she must have forgotten to tell me. Perhaps she had. Perhaps I hadn't been listening.

'Can I see it, then?' he asked. 'Your paperwork.'

'Yes,' I said, 'of course.' But I was making no attempt to retrieve the thing I did not have.

He looked at me oddly. He reminded me of Captain von Trapp from *The Sound of Music*. It was his silent outrage. He did look a little like Christopher Plummer.

'We have to keep everything above board,' he said.

'Yes, absolutely,' I said. 'What ID did you say you wanted?'

'Passport, driver's licence.'

I had neither. Disappearing was proving testing.

I could see that Mark was getting suspicious. Things were going wrong. But I detected something else in his tone, something akin to relief that he was trying to suppress, as if this whole job idea had not been his.

He was exactly how I would have expected an estate manager to be. There was tweed with elbow patches, corduroy trousers. As much as Kelly had defied my expectations, Mark had been resoundingly confirmatory.

The gravel crunched outside the cottage. I looked out of the window. The Defender appeared in front of it, and for a moment I thought it would drive straight through the wall, right into the kitchen. I wished it had because it might have solved the ID problem I was having.

'I think that might be Kelly,' I said.

Mark was not looking out of the window, despite my best attempts to distract him, to displace him from his train of thought.

Kelly bounded into the kitchen, red-faced. 'I left my phone here!' she panted. 'Got all the way to the castle gates when I realised I didn't have the bloody thing.'

She saw Mark in the darkness of the doorway that led to the little dining room and seized up. I sensed an animosity that I wished I'd had the intellect to exploit.

'Mark,' she said frostily. Frosty Kelly was endearing. 'I thought you were still at the hospital. I didn't think you were coming till later.'

'Back early,' he said. 'We thought things had taken a turn

for the worst but thankfully not. I'm currently driving the marchioness.' He was addressing me now. 'But I can't continue to do so. For one reason and the other.'

Kelly looked as if she wanted to add something to this because she opened her mouth slightly and then closed it again.

'Which is why you're here,' he said. 'That was the plan at least. But sadly it looks like it's not meant to be.'

'What do you mean *not meant to be*?' Kelly was foraging about the kitchen for her phone. 'Where is it?' she asked me. 'My phone. Have you seen it? Can't for the life of me remember where I've put it.'

I began to look too. But I wasn't looking so much as finding a way to avoid dealing with Mark.

'Paperwork,' Mark said. 'We were discussing the fact that I'll need a form of identification for my records.'

Kelly was opening and closing cupboards, banging and clattering. She dashed to the loo and looked in there. 'What if I've flushed it?' she said. 'What if I've flushed it by mistake, without knowing. Honestly, I am so forgetful these days.'

'Do you remember when you last had it?' I asked. 'Is there a chance it's not here at all? I can't see it.'

'Do you not have a driver's licence or passport or anything like that with you?' Mark persisted.

I kept my head inside the cupboard I had planted it in. Then I was struck with an idea. Kelly's quandary had given me inspiration. 'Of course,' I said coolly, emerging beatifically from the cupboard. 'Let me just get my bag.'

I moved to the breakfast bar and began to look about in my bag, taking my time, affecting an air of certainty. 'Hmm,' I said. 'That's odd.'

'What is it?' Mark asked.

Kelly stopped searching and turned to me.

'I could have sworn they were in here,' I said. 'My papers. I mean, I had them with me on the train because I wanted to double-check everything was in order.'

Mark nodded. This sort of talk seemed to appeal to him.

'Are they not there?' Kelly asked.

'No,' I said. 'How strange. I wonder if I've left the copies of my ID on the train.'

Fortuitously, Vanessa's Companies House documents were still in my bag, which lent my lie some credence. I flicked rapidly through them, like a filing clerk, all the while making sure the content of the papers was hidden from view.

Kelly peered into the bag. I drew up the sides. 'God, look at the pair of us,' she said. 'Losing things left, right and centre.'

'Leaving your ID on the train is very worrying,' he said. 'Very careless. You have no idea whose hands it will end up in. It'll be in Inverness by now. You'd better notify the relevant authorities.'

'Yes,' I said. 'I will. I will do that immediately. It's so unlike me. I mean, I wonder if there was a chance it was stolen from my bag while I was sleeping. I mean, how difficult would it be for someone to just come and take something so valuable from passengers while they are fast asleep?'

'That would never occur to me,' Kelly said. 'But, now that you mention it, a sleeper train would be a prime target for thieves and fraudsters and, well, all sorts of criminal offenders.'

'Is there a way for you to get hold of another copy?' Mark asked.

'Give the woman a break, Mark,' Kelly shouted, having surrendered the search for her phone for a moment of activism.

'She's just had her ID nicked off her while she was sleeping on the train.'

'I'm not saying that's what happened,' I said.

'Well, you're not saying it definitely didn't happen, are you?' she said.

Mark uncrossed his arms and said, 'Just make sure you secure some ID as soon as possible.'

'Yes, I will do so,' I said firmly, believing that I was consolidating the terms of his departure, which I was more than ready for because I had been desperate to check on the baby. While no noise came from upstairs, it was only a matter of time. But he didn't go and instead strode into the dining room next door, went over to the window and stared down at the valley below. It wasn't clear what he was looking at.

I did not like that room at all. The air in there felt full of something, of a presence, some darkness, like my loo back home. In the centre was a table with four chairs around it and behind it, against the far wall, was a black leather sofa, and seeing it, all I could think of was my husband. The walls were decorated with brown and green striped wallpaper and a solitary portrait of a man. He was sitting in a chair, holding what appeared to be a gold medal in his hand.

'Who's that?' I asked. 'On the wall.'

Kelly stuck her head around the door. 'That's the marquess,' she said woefully. 'The late marchioness, his mother, commissioned it when he won some award or other for science. It would have been a few years ago that was painted. He doesn't look like that now, sadly. You'd get a fright if you saw the man he is now compared with the man he was then.'

'Was it the Nobel prize?' I asked, pointing at the element of glinting gold on the portrait.

'You're asking the wrong person there,' she said. 'I wouldn't have a clue.'

'Yes,' said Mark. 'It's the Nobel prize.'

'Gosh,' I said. 'Why is such an important painting in this cottage? Do they ever stay here? The marquess and marchioness?'

'There are so many artefacts of the marquess's considerable achievements,' Mark said, 'we had to find space for them somewhere.'

I made sure to nod appreciatively at the portrait, thinking to myself that I would take it down as soon as Kelly and Mark had left. It would trouble me to be so constantly reminded of someone else's achievements.

'The flooding's subsided,' Mark said, looking out of the window again towards the valley. 'I'll be able to head back through the fields. Unless you can give me a lift. I need to leave the car here for Camilla.'

'I would, my lovely,' Kelly said disingenuously. 'But I really need to track down my phone.'

Mark glowered. He turned to me and said, 'The marchioness is expecting you tomorrow morning at nine a.m. and she will tell you herself the demands of your job. I had expected to do it, but the marchioness wants to see to it herself. I've come to hand over the keys to the car you will be driving.'

'I just wanted to confirm one thing,' I said.

'Yes?'

Mark had moved away from the window and was now back in the kitchen, making his way to the front door. I had unintentionally unearthed a couple of nappies while I was fiddling about with the paperwork in the baby bag. I prayed that he hadn't seen them poking out from the opening.

'What is it?' he asked wearily.

'It's about the money. I just wanted to make sure that it was cash.'

'Cash?'

'Yes,' I said. 'Cash. I must have cash.'

Kelly and Mark both turned to look at me, oddly unified in their expressions.

'It's just that,' I said, modifying my stance, 'I've been having some trouble with my online banking. I've been locked out of my account by accident and I'm really struggling to find anyone who will help me with it. You know, at the bank. I wish you still had banks on the high street.'

This seemed to placate them both.

'Tell me about it,' Kelly said, returning to the fridge to stand in its chill.

'I don't think I've ever known anyone with such a series of administrative problems,' Mark said.

'So would that be okay?' I asked. 'Cash?'

'Until you get your account sorted,' he said. 'But as I said on the phone, we like to keep everything above board here.'

'Right,' I said. 'Everything above board.'

'There it is!' Kelly said, triumphantly pulling her phone out of the fridge.

Chapter 13

I had imagined that I would be driving something stately and spectacular like a Bentley or a Rolls-Royce, perhaps a Range Rover. I could never have expected the car I was given, which Mark described as the marquess's pride and joy.

It was a massive Volvo limousine, about twenty years old. It was more of a vessel than a car. In essence, it was a boat on wheels.

'If the marquess had been driving this the day of the accident,' Mark said, 'I'm pretty sure he wouldn't be in the hospital now. And you wouldn't be here either.'

'What had he been driving?' I asked.

'A Rolls-Royce,' he said.

He asked if I'd ever driven this type of Volvo before and I said yes, which was an outright lie. I'd never even seen one of those cars, let alone got myself behind the wheel of one. He handed me the keys before heading off down the drive by foot. He couldn't have been happy that I'd rendered him a pedestrian but, despite the cold weather, it was a sunny day in the valley so he didn't have to worry about rain or snow.

Kelly had spoken to her hairdresser, who had spoken to her sister-in-law, who had spoken to her best friend, who said that she had space for the baby in her childminding operation in the village of Grandtully (pronounced, I noted, *Grahntly*), four miles away. She relayed all of this in a note to me which she had considerately slipped through the letterbox later that evening while I slept upstairs. She must have seen how tired I was after the journey. In the note, she wrote the address of the childminder and the time at which I should meet her the following day, charmingly dotting her Is with hearts.

And so, first thing the next morning, after a fretful sleep, the kind I used to have before a big presentation or if I had said something ridiculous to someone the previous day, I entrusted the baby to Shona, a knockout blonde in a pink velour Juicy Couture tracksuit, and went straight to my new job at the castle.

Chapter 14

My first day was not what I had expected. Right off the bat.

I was on time, reasonably well dressed, well groomed (I had brushed my hair and my teeth). I had deposited the baby with a perfect stranger who seemed nice enough, nice-ish at any rate, and I vowed to say no more about it while I was within those four walls, although there were far more than four walls in that castle. There must have been hundreds of walls.

There was no sign of the marchioness when I arrived. As I had understood from Mark, she was to brief me at 9 a.m., but 9 a.m. came and went, and then 11 a.m. came and went. The day was ebbing away. I could only hope that I was getting paid for just sitting there. I really hoped that I was.

I was seated in the baronial entrance hall, which is what Mark called it. It seemed important to him that I was aware that that was the name of the room I was in. It was dark inside and wood-panelled, as you might imagine a baronial entrance hall would be. On the walls were ancestral objects, swords, portraits, crests, that sort of thing. The swords had been arranged in an elegant crisscross formation across the cherrywood panelling. Sitting there, it occurred to me that it was possibly the most efficient way for aristocrats to show

how many battles they had won without having to keep telling everyone, which must have been an occupational hazard. It differed from similarly grand rooms I'd seen on the television in that there was no taxidermy on the walls – no stuffed animal heads, tiger skin, game trophies – but then I remembered that the marchioness had instated a hunting ban so that explained things.

The hall was north-facing and looked onto the drive I had just driven down, which went on for miles and miles. As I made my way towards the castle, apprehension was swelling inside me and it occurred to me at that moment that long drives such as this, lined with tall trees and flanked by acres and acres of parkland, and deer running wild and free, was a guaranteed way to make a person feel like an impostor, if that was the desired intention.

I assumed that the rooms at the back of the house looked onto the gardens I had seen from the car and that might have been a more pleasant vantage point from which to start my new job, but perhaps that decision had also been intentional. All the doors to those rooms were shut, keeping the light out. It was a dark day, so dark, the sky heavy with cumulonimbus clouds, and so there was little reason to sit a person in one of the south-facing rooms because the day was not offering anything spectacular. I had a lot of time on my hands to consider this. Perhaps I had too much time. That was the problem with being punctual and without a baby. Time: it allowed thought to creep in and take hold. There was a danger that all this time would make me mad.

Kelly, who had initially greeted me at the front door (telling me next time to use the staff entrance around the back by the stables), was to hand me over to Mark, and said I could sit on one of the tall Jacobean chairs until the marchioness appeared. I noticed that something had changed in Kelly, something almost imperceptible and to do with her erstwhile bubbliness. It was gone, had been popped. I was dealing instead with a different version of that same woman and I had to adjust. But being a woman myself, I was used to the abrupt and unexplained altered states of other women, so I did not find it too hard.

She was a wearing a tabard. In that garment, she reminded me of the dinner lady at school who used to dole out the roast potatoes, taking one or two for herself, putting them into her mouth and sucking on them. She had no teeth.

'Fetching, isn't it,' she said, fanning out the sides of the tabard. 'I'm polishing the silver. Silvo stains like a bitch.'

I laughed, cheered by her ribaldry. I wanted to thank her for helping me with the baby but knew that it was not the time to start that conversation.

I sat in the chair as instructed. I did not feel at ease. I had the car keys in my hands, waiting for the marchioness to enter so that we could go to the hospital and I could start to be of service. I was terrified about driving the car because it was so enormous and chunksome and the other people driving around the estate drove like maniacs. I think because everything was spaced so far apart, if you didn't drive like you were escaping the fires of hell, you wouldn't get anywhere and you wouldn't get anything done.

Before making my way to the estate, I had studied the route to the hospital in Dundee using an old map I had found in the glove box of the Volvo because, to my dismay, there was no sat nav system in the car. It was too old for that. I couldn't remember the last time I read a map, but the route appeared to be straightforward and therefore I believed that I had everything in order. I was apprehensive of course. I had never driven anyone before and I was unsure as to the level of scrutiny I would be under; would I be allowed to get on with it or would my every move, every decision, be watched and judged?

I felt at sea to have left the baby with someone I didn't know. I had taken a leap of faith and had to keep overriding a fierce impulse to retrieve the baby from the pink velour stranger. I found myself alone for the first time in months. I didn't know how to be on my own anymore. It was a feeling I was not used to. It was not the same as being on my own before I had the baby. Now, being alone felt as if something had been excised. What a wrench it was to be away from the baby. What a wrench it was, but what an audacious freedom!

Sitting in that dark, echoey hall, with all the liberty of not being shackled to anything, I noticed that my nails could have done with a paint. I did not want the woman, who clearly commanded considerable power over the people who worked for her, to see my lack of self-care so I sat on my fingers. The green silk damask of the upholstery was heavenly against my skin. This was a sensation that I had been unprepared for. The chair was another level of luxury and, I'll tell you what, I wanted it for myself.

At intervals, Kelly appeared and set about directing people around the castle: the florist (who had entered with a procession of stark white, almost funereal, arrangements, depositing them into a variety of rooms) and the cleaners (a small band of them, glassy-eyed, marijuana-fragrant, and innovatively tooled out in belts bulging with eco products). There was some gesticulating to the gardeners at the window, motioning either to get a haircut or prune the roses. Someone had come to empty the cesspit, arriving at the front door by mistake because, according to Kelly, he was a 'new one' and didn't know to go to the entrance by the stables, a misunderstanding which appeared to be the bane of her existence. I asked her what a cesspit was and she said, 'You don't want to know,' even though I did. It seemed to me that Kelly's job involved delegating jobs and I figured that hers was one of the best jobs in the world.

It was almost midday by the time Mark appeared again. I was starving and I needed the loo. He entered from a far room as if he were a ghost, footless, sort of floating in from the shadows. He was wearing the same clothes he had worn the previous day and I wondered if he'd gone home to sleep, if he even had a home, a family, somewhere to rest his head. He didn't look like much of a sleeper. He looked as if he'd spent his entire adulthood on vigil.

'The marchioness is feeling under the weather,' he said.

'Oh,' I said. 'Is she?'

'Yes,' he said.

'I'm sorry to hear that,' I added. 'Please pass on my good wishes.'

I had never said anything like that in my life. I wasn't sure what had come over me. A baronial entrance hall could make a person become a stranger to herself.

'Yes,' he said again. 'Well, it happens from time to time that she takes herself to her bed. Life gets too much for her. I think the marquess's sad condition has taken its toll on her nerves.'

Mark was making the marchioness sound like Mrs Bennet. I would have told him to suggest to her on my behalf that she gave Sertraline or Citalopram a go, if it was nerve-easing she needed, but I could see there was only danger in exposing my own mental health trials and tribulations.

I nodded and said, 'Of course. I can't even imagine what she must be going through.'

He nodded too. We both nodded. I'm not sure we meant our nods. We were behaving as if we were appeasing an eavesdropping, truculent queen.

'The marchioness has asked that you go upstairs and talk to her from outside her bedroom,' he explained.

'What, right now?' I asked.

'Yes.'

'Right.'

I got up off the Jacobean chair and followed Mark upstairs to the marchioness's bedroom suite, surprised that he hadn't simply decided to send me back to the spooky cottage on the hill so that I could sit for a while without the baby amid the ghosts and ghouls and perhaps have a cup of tea and polish off the cake.

•

'Hello?' I said.

Mark had left and I was standing in the corridor by the marchioness's bedroom. I couldn't see into it because of the darkness. The marchioness had kept the curtains closed. She must have had blackout blinds. The silent woman languishing in the daytime blackness reminded me of Mum when she was alive because she suffered from terrible migraines and spent days in bed. We'd bring her food but she wouldn't eat because everything made her sick. And then, suddenly, she would be fine again and life would go back to normal. But the marchioness wasn't having a migraine. I had no idea what was wrong with her.

'Hello.'

The voice that returned to me was soft. I couldn't place the accent. It wasn't English and it wasn't Scottish.

'Are you okay?' I asked.

There was a silence. I thought I had blown it. Any fool could say hello. And I knew she wasn't okay. Mark had said she wasn't okay.

And then: 'I am not.'

'Is there anything I can do to help?' I asked.

I heard a sigh. I was boring her to death. I was the most boring person in the world. I was aware that Mark was listening to me from down the hall, judging me on my ability to commune with the voice in the darkness.

'Can I ask you a question?' said the voice.

'Of course,' I said.

'Am I hideous?'

'Hideous?'

'Yes,' she said. 'Hideous.'

I was silent.

She added: 'You know, hideous. Monstrous.'

'Monstrous?' I asked.

She was silent. Soon she said, 'The word monster comes from the Latin "to show". Did you know that?'

'No,' I said. 'I didn't. I never learnt Latin. I wasn't taught it at school.'

Then she was silent again. She wasn't showing me. How could I know if she was monstrous if she wasn't showing me?

'Do you use collagen?' she asked.

'Collagen?'

'Do you answer every question with a question?'

'No,' I said.

'Well?' she said. 'Do you?'

'No, I don't.'

The next silence throbbed. I had never wanted to leave anywhere so fast.

'But I know people who swear by it,' I said.

I didn't know anyone. I had seen people on Instagram talking about it, and that is what I meant. I wanted to try it, but I didn't believe in things like that, things that could make things better without pain.

'Can I see your face?' said the voice.

'Okay,' I said reluctantly. 'Do you want me to come in?'

I heard the creaky click of a bedside lamp switch. A warm orange light shone onto the short entrance corridor.

'You can come in,' she said. 'Close the door behind you. I don't want *him* coming in.'

I took *him* to mean Mark. I walked into the room. It was different from the baronial entrance hall. The floors had been stripped bare to reveal the floorboards that would have been unpleasant underfoot were it not for the heat emanating from beneath. On the walls were panels of the most unusual panoramic wallpaper – giant sepia images of Greek and Roman antiquities, pots and urns – their outlines daubed with thick black ink. A tall, cast-iron chair sat in one corner. In the other was a giant misshapen object in a large black casing. And a bed, four-postered, with what appeared to be a bear skin covering the duvet but couldn't have been. A little head poked out from a trench of pillows.

I stood on the other side of the bed from where the head was, about two metres away. I could see only a dome of shiny black that fell down the forehead to form a fringe. And there was a spray of black eyelashes that met it, like brushes moving in an automatic carwash.

'I like your wallpaper,' I said.

The head rose, jacked up by the elbows. She hoisted herself into a sitting position. She turned around and stacked her pillows into a tower. She turned to face me.

The woman was objectively beautiful. The closest comparison I can think of is Elizabeth Taylor – in *Cleopatra*, not *Who's Afraid of Virginia Woolf?*

'I like your wallpaper,' I repeated.

She looked at the walls and then said, 'It's Pierre Frey. Have you heard of him?'

I nodded. I had not.

'I have begun to tire of it,' she said. 'In my dreams, I am ripping it off the walls. Do you ever get that urge?'

'To rip off wallpaper?' I asked.

I wanted to tell her that I used to have the urge both to rip off my wedding ring and throw it out of the window when I drove down the M4 to visit Mum and also to lob Hilary's spectacles off Hammersmith Bridge.

Hilary . . . I dispensed a thought for Hilary. I wondered how she was doing, Hilary and her rotten-tripe blood vessels.

The marchioness's head moved from the walls to me and she narrowed her eyes, reaching over to her bedside table, where she fumbled for her glasses, a pair of black horn-rimmed spectacles with round frames that made her eyeballs look enormous, like peeled and painted lychees.

'Come over here,' she said. 'Come over to my side. I can't see you very well in this light.'

'I could open the curtains if you like,' I offered.

She shook her head. 'No.'

I did not want her to examine my face. I was only too aware of its shortcomings: the thick trenches on my forehead from raising my eyebrows in repeated expressions of shock and outrage over the course of my life. My ragged jawline. The broken capillary on my left cheek. The ptosis in my right eye.

She was itemising my face in the same way and what she saw seemed to cheer her up.

'How old are you?' she asked.

And when I did not reply immediately, she said, 'Am I not allowed to ask that? Don't be coy. It's just us girls.'

She sounded like the meanest girl in school.

'I'm thirty-eight,' I said.

'Thirty-eight,' she replied, not being able to reconcile the number I had given her with the age I obviously looked.

'How old do you think I am?' she asked.

There was no way of knowing. There was just no way. I wanted to ask about the car and driving to the hospital. This definitely felt like the worst kind of trap. All traps are bad. But the 'how old do I look' trap was by far the most perilous.

'You are a very beautiful woman,' I said.

'Yes,' she replied. 'But how old do I look?'

'How old?'

'Yes,' she said. 'It's not that difficult. You just look at me and then you tell me how old I look. So I look at you and I think, okay, her hair's thinning, her skin is sagging, there are quite deep wrinkles in the skin, some sun damage, that red thing on your cheek . . . What is that? I've never seen one of them before.'

'It's a broken capillary,' I said. My voice had become very fragile at this point. I was going in on myself. 'I was going to get it burnt off but the baby–'

'Baby?' she said. 'What baby?'

'My sister's baby,' I said quickly. 'My sister needed help with her baby. Her husband was in hospital.'

The marchioness leant over to her bedside table, a structure fussily trussed in silk with fringing and tassels, and picked up a framed photograph of a person whom I now understood (from the dozens of portraits that lined the baronial entrance hall) to be her husband, apparently photographed in a desert, or some other arid place, and he was wearing the sort of helmet you'd wear if you were at risk of stepping on a landmine. She stroked the glass.

'Snap,' she whispered.

She blew the image a kiss.

Chapter 15

I had promised Hannah that I would call her once I had settled into my new life in Scotland. I supposed I had settled in, to a certain extent. Although I've discovered that it is hard to settle in fully when you are on the run. At first, I missed my phone; my instinct in any kind of new and frightening situation was to send Hannah a text. Even in moments of lethal boredom at home with the baby, I would want to tell her about it.

Initially, I felt cut off from her, from everything, but soon I enjoyed the freedom I had without my phone. I'd heard people say that before about being phoneless and I had dismissed it as lies, but in no time I found myself fully endorsing that view. And I knew that it was for the best because of the dangerous tracking capabilities of phones about which Hannah had warned me. My phone could have been my downfall. It always had that potential.

The landline phone in the cottage did not work; Mark said he would get someone to look at it, but I didn't have much faith in that. Getting a replacement was something I shouldn't expect any time soon.

I hadn't even considered using one of the many phones in the castle. I was scrupulous when it came to pushing my luck, given the strangeness of my first day.

Ultimately, the marchioness had seemed content with being told that she looked thirty-two. It was a number I pulled out of the air at random, but on reflection I recalled reading an article in *Vogue* where some celebrities were asked which was their favourite age and thirty-two had been the resounding reply. Old enough to gain some experience and sense of self, young enough for the face not to have collapsed. But if I were to be honest with you, I'd say that the marchioness was in her mid-forties. Easily. Her thick black fringe hid a multitude of sins. The light in the bedroom had been sympathetic, and given that she had not ventured out into the daylight – the harshest of skincare critics – I could not get an accurate reading. But it was her hands that gave it away. The outlines of veins were beginning to protrude, the skin was creping.

I explained all of this to Hannah on the payphone in the village of Grandtully. I had half an hour to kill before collecting the baby and surprisingly I did not feel like collecting the baby early. I parked the Volvo outside the village shop and I could see that it wasn't the best idea because people stopped to stare at what they must have regarded as an automotive antiquity, looking in through the windows, so I had to shoo them off from the payphone by waving my hand about. When I did that, I was appalling.

'What a madwoman. A proper fruitcake,' Hannah said. 'Is that how you spent the day? Lying to a mad aristocrat about how old she looks?'

'I did other things,' I explained to her.

'Like what?' she asked.

'She wanted me to scan her legs for varicose veins. She said she finds it hard to look at the backs of her own knees.'

'Jesus.'

'It is hard,' I said.

'Is that it?'

'She wanted me to google photofractional lasering near the castle.'

'I want your job,' Hannah said. I heard wine glugging into a glass on the other end of the line followed by a thirsty swig. 'What happened to driving her to the hospital to see her dying husband?'

'I think I still have to do that,' I said. 'But she was having an ugly day and she doesn't go to the hospital on ugly days.'

'Ugly day?' Hannah said. 'What's an ugly day?'

'When she feels ugly.'

'By contrast then,' Hannah surmised, 'when it is not an ugly day, is it a beautiful day?'

'I think so.'

'Wow,' she said. 'Just wow.'

'Essentially, she is very beautiful,' I said. 'It's hard to empathise.'

I sensed that, on the other end of the phone, via telepathy or some similar hocus pocus, Hannah's eyes were rolling.

'How's it going otherwise?' she asked.

'It's fine,' I said. 'The cottage is a bit scary. The bedrooms all have shiny leather headboards.'

'Grim.'

'The sheets are thin and bobbly, as if a million people have slept in them, because they've been washed a million times. The floors are uneven and sloping so it makes me feel dizzy. Also, the bathroom has this strong melamine smell. It's really pervasive. You can smell it in the kitchen, it's so strong. And it's haunted. It's properly haunted.'

'Have you seen a ghost?'

'No,' I said. 'But it's only a matter of time. I wish I could see something rather than just sense it.'

'Maybe it will feel a bit more homely once you've settled in and can put your mark on things.'

'And that's another thing: there's this guy called Mark, the estate manager, and I don't like him. He's hostile and a bit frightening. Honestly, I don't know how I'm meant to do this. These people are so strange.'

'You'll be fine. Keep your head down. Keep at it. One day at a time.'

'Okay,' I said. 'Keep at it. One day at a time.'

I took a deep breath in. For a moment, Hannah was silent.

'Before you go,' she said, 'I need to talk to you about something.'

I didn't respond.

She continued: 'I got a call from the police last night and they want to talk to you.'

'Why?'

'It's James. He's saying you've abducted the baby.'

Chapter 16

'I'm sorry about yesterday. Deeply. All the nonsense.'

The marchioness was up, dressed and in the back of the car. We were on our way.

'I'm not sure I know what you mean,' I said, looking in the rearview mirror.

'All that drivel about the collagen,' she explained, gazing out of the window at her parkland. 'And the how old are you and the general vanity.'

I had a stranger in the back of the car. I did not know this person. This was so unlike my prior experience with the head in the bed. This woman was up, fierce. I was palpitating. She sat in the back like Julia Roberts in *Pretty Woman* – once she has shed her Hollywood Boulevard aesthetic and is finally allowed to go shopping after those women have been so mean to her. (*Big mistake. Huge.*) She had incredible knees, I noticed. She wore a short black wool dress, black tights (I assumed they were tights; they may have been stockings), black patent stilettos. I was certain that I would find a red sole underneath, certain of it. She had a Birkin, a real one. I'd never seen a real one before.

'Oh,' I said, 'that's okay.'

But it wasn't okay. After I picked up the baby from Shona's house, I went back to the scary, lovely cottage and cried while I looked at myself in the bathroom mirror. I tried not to spend too long doing that because I worried that if I lingered too long I might see a ghost looking back at me and I wouldn't have been able to unsee it.

'I'm so sorry if I pushed it too far. You have very good skin – you do. It's Mark,' she said. 'He listens in. I don't want him to know that I know when he thinks I don't know what he knows.'

I had no idea what she was on about. I did not know where this was going. We reached the end of the drive, and before moving onto the road she said, 'We're not going to the hospital.'

I was confused. I had been expecting either to take the marchioness to visit the marquess at the hospital in Dundee or, if I was lucky, have another Ugly Day back at the castle – a gentle browse on the internet, perhaps for local suppliers of filler and Botox.

'We're going somewhere else.'

Because I was at a junction, with no clear idea of where to go next, I had to ask: 'Is somewhere left or right?'

'It's left,' she said. 'Somewhere is Edinburgh.'

Edinburgh! I knew that Edinburgh was one and a half hours away. It was already 1 p.m. There was no way that we would make it there and back in time for me to collect the baby at half past four. And I'd just been sitting mindlessly in the baronial entrance hall for most of the morning, waiting for the marchioness to get ready, believing that I'd be able to go home early. I wondered what it was that she had to do to herself that had caused such a lengthy delay. I did not know how long we would be staying wherever it was we were meant to be going and I had to get the baby. I could not be late for the baby. I could not leave the baby, and because there was now a notion in circulation that I had abducted the baby (rather than free it from an unhappy home), I could not do anything injurious to my reputation as a mother were I to appear in a court of law for stealing a child from its father, even though he was a philandering good-for-nothing. And because my efforts to disappear required me not to have a phone I could not call Shona the childminder.

Panic gripped me in its calloused claw!

'If you just follow the signs to Edinburgh, that's fine. I can give you more detail when we get closer.'

'Okay,' I said.

But it wasn't.

•

Time was ticking. We got held up. A tractor with a line of around twenty cars behind it blocked the road ahead of us. I tried to crane my neck to see the front of the queue but I could not. The marchioness had no clue as to my anguish, sitting in the back doing the crossword on her iPad, without a care in the world. I hoped that the clues were particularly cryptic that day.

Suddenly, she looked up and announced that she needed the loo.

No, I thought. *No loo for you. You're a grown woman. Hold it in.*

We were near Loch Leven. I told her that we were only half an hour from Edinburgh if she could wait, but she said no, and I imagined that she didn't want her beloved Volvo to smell of wee if she pissed herself. She didn't say 'pissed herself', for the record. To my knowledge, she hadn't any children so

I couldn't understand the grounds for her incontinence. We drove through a village called Kinross and I noticed a little café on the high street.

'I think they'll have a loo,' I said, hoping that, if this was to be the end of everything, the end of my new start, of my new life, I might as well score a latte while the marchioness drained her bladder.

She lowered her window as I slowed down. There were several people on the street and all of them, all of them, stopped to stare at her. I wasn't surprised; she was a sight for sore eyes.

'Sure,' she said. 'Looks darling.' I pulled up right outside on the double yellow lines. Devil may care! I had no time for parking regulations. If the woman had enough money for a Birkin, then she could surely afford the odd penalty charge notice.

I got out of the car and opened the door, and she took my hand. I held it. I wanted to yank it. The bones in her fingers were slim, the skin that covered them was soft, unaccustomed to things like Viakal. She stepped out of the car holding on to me. I wanted to pull her out, to say 'chop, chop we haven't got all day', but I was certain those were words she'd never heard before in her life.

'Is it push or pull?' she asked, tottering up behind me.

'Let me try,' I said.

I pushed. The door did not yield.

'It's pull,' we said in unison. I mainly shouted it like I was on *The Crystal Maze*.

There was a person working behind the counter wearing an apron, the sort of serious black apron you might find in a London coffee roastery, and it reminded me of my favourite place on Turnham Green Terrace that ground my beans for me when my grinder broke.

The marchioness said, 'Would you like something while we're here?'

'That would be lovely,' I said shrilly.

She inserted a hand into her Birkin and then into her wallet, out of which she pulled a crisp fifty. 'Here you go,' she said. 'Could you order me a hot chocolate? Whole milk. Whipped cream. Marshmallows if they have.'

A hot chocolate. Marshmallows if they have. I had not expected that. I stood at the counter thinking of all the drinks she might have ordered and that was the last thing I could have imagined her choosing. I was sure it would have been a flat white. Skinny milk. Or oat. An oat milk flat white. I would have put money on it.

I handed over the fifty and the person behind the counter looked at me as if I was Marie Antoinette or Kim Kardashian. But I didn't mind, because I knew I wasn't. I was a chauffeur now, in the driving seat but also not. It had always been my fate. And I didn't feel the need to apologise. I just stood there and smiled until she handed me my drink and I sipped it as if it was the blood of Christ and it made me forget about the time I didn't have, the time that was running out. I could not remember the last time I had enjoyed a coffee that much. I looked at my watch. It was 2 p.m.

The marchioness ran out of the toilets straight towards the door. She said, 'We have to go. Now.'

I turned to look at her. 'But your hot chocolate,' I said.

'Fuck the hot chocolate,' she said.

When she said *fuck the hot chocolate*, I swore I heard a different accent; there was a guttural, phlegmy emphasis on the 'ck' sound that for a moment I thought sounded Scouse. I still couldn't place it. I was useless with accents. But it wasn't the one she had previously been speaking. I knew that for sure.

•

She was on the phone making frantic calls to this person and then that person.

'What do you mean, you don't know? How is that possible? We had a plan. Why isn't the plan happening? It absolutely must be today. This has been booked for months.'

The marchioness shot me a look from the back seat. She then edged closer to the door. I must have been watching her too much. I kept my eyes on the road.

She made another call, this time to someone who was familiar to her. I could tell because whoever it was had managed to console and calm her. She was talking in a whisper. Before hanging up she said, 'Okay, I'll eat it. I promise. Thanks for making it for me.'

I could hear her rummaging about in her bag. She pulled out a container – an ornate silver tiffin box – and when she opened it an aroma sprang out and filled the car with the scents of Southeast Asian cuisine: lemongrass, coconut, lime. With a fork, she dug about in the box and stuffed mounds of leaves into her mouth, as if she was packing a suitcase in a hurry.

I wanted so much to know who she had been talking to, what had been said. In another life, we might have been friends (although I was never very good at making friends) and I would have asked her, but in my new capacity I was too scared to ask. I was scared even to ask which way to drive so I kept going towards Edinburgh until she said (through a muffled mouth), 'Where are you going?'

'To Edinburgh,' I said.

'No, no, no,' she said. 'Turn around now. This is all wrong.'

The relief I felt! We were going back. All would be well. I would be able to get back to the castle to drop off the marchioness and head straight to Grandtully to get the baby she didn't know I had.

But it was not easy to simply turn around on the M90. We had to go all the way to a town called Kelty, where I got lost and we suffered a twenty-minute detour because I had been reading the map upside down. This was testing the marchioness's patience; I could tell because she put her sunglasses on and, very faintly, I could see her eyeballing me from behind the blacked-out lenses. I was getting so angry with myself.

We wound up in a council estate and she said, 'Slow down, will you? Can you pull up here for a moment?'

I did so, and her window lowered, and she looked around outside.

'I won't be long.'

She discarded her lunchbox, half-eaten on the seat beside her, released herself from the car and strolled away like Holly Golightly up Fifth Avenue, her black wool silhouette singing out against the concrete terraces. I looked at my watch. It was half past two. I had only two hours to get back, drop the marchioness off, then drive another four miles to collect the baby from Shona. I looked in the back of the car to see if she had left her phone in her bag. I might have been able to use it to call Shona but I remembered that I didn't have her number. How many childminding Shonas could there be in Grandtully? But her phone wasn't there. She must have taken it with her.

The marchioness disappeared. She was gone for ages. I panicked again, worrying now that she had been kidnapped because then, not only would I be late for the baby, but I would no longer have a job. I felt hot and scared. I had lost my boss on our very first outing. I had misplaced an aristocrat. Who would reprimand me? Mark? He'd send me packing. I couldn't think of anything he'd like more than to see the back of me. Suddenly, the bobbly sheets and the ghosts didn't seem so bad.

And then the reality of things hit me: I was in a strange town in the middle of nowhere. The baby was miles and miles away from me with a woman I hardly knew. I was a fugitive from the police, an abductor, a criminal. I was spiralling. I told myself not to, yet it was fruitless; I was at the mercy of my own mind. I should have just stayed at home with Hilary and James and his new girlfriend. I should never have left. All I needed to do was make a bit of dinner for a few people once a week and put up with my cruel and heartless husband having a lover (better her than me!), Hilary would eventually recover and return to St John's Wood. I could get the baby and just take the next train home and pretend none of this had ever happened.

There was a knock at my window. It was the marchioness.

'Haven't you always wanted to see one of these?' she said.

I must have looked confused because she went on to say, 'You know, this sort of place? What would you call it?'

'A council estate.'

'Yes,' she said. 'A council estate.'

And then she stood silently outside the car for a few seconds looking in while I sat inside. It took me some time to understand that she had been waiting for me to open the door for her.

Chapter 17

Shona was unhappy. When I arrived at her cottage, she was standing at the window, so I waved at her, making a plaintive, apologetic face.

'You should have a phone, you know,' she said. 'For emergencies. Personally, I don't think it's right that you haven't got a phone when you have a baby.'

I half expected her to say, 'What kind of mother are you?', but she didn't. She didn't have to.

The baby was crying and appeared to be clinging onto Shona, who on this particular day was wearing another velour tracksuit although this one was black, not pink. The baby did not want to come to me. I was wounded psychologically.

'It's Friday night,' she said. 'I have plans. I have an online lecture in ten minutes. I was nearly late for it. And then I'm dyeing my eyebrows.'

'Oh wow,' I said. 'What are you studying?'

'Business Management.'

'Wow,' I repeated, examining her eyebrows. I wanted to tell her that businesses were bad. 'That sounds interesting.'

Her eyebrows looked dark enough. There was a danger she was heading into Groucho Marx territory. I wanted to ask her what kind of plans she had because I had no plans and I would have liked a plan that wasn't going back to the spooky cottage on the hill with the baby.

'Again, I'm really sorry. I'll get a phone over the weekend.'

That seemed to appease her. She softened her stance, so I asked, 'Do you know where I could get a phone around here?'

'Closest place is Perth. About forty-five minutes' drive from here. Head toward the A9 and at the end turn right. There's an O2 in the shopping centre.' She looked at her watch. 'It'll be closed now though,' she said. Spitefully.

I did not like this version of Shona. I liked the one I got when I was punctual. 'I'll go tomorrow,' I said.

'Make sure you do.'

She closed the door on me.

•

Friday night in that cottage did not feel like a Friday night. I had managed to get a few bits and pieces from the village shop in Grandtully, including a bottle of Wolf Blass Chardonnay, a family pack of Wotsits, some Super Noodles, yoghurt (alas not Greek), a punnet of strawberries (off season), a packet of cheese slices and box of Ritz crackers. I was very pleased to have strawberries. I had eaten too much cake over the course of my first three days in Scotland.

They sold Aptamil, Pampers and baby food in the shop so the baby was taken care of. I had been running very low on baby supplies. The man in the shop was friendly, seeing me as a friendless newcomer, and said he had a Facebook group that I could join if I wanted to know more about the community. I thanked him, but what he didn't know was that I didn't let myself go on Facebook anymore because I once befriended everyone on the 'People You May Know' list without any recollection when the baby was around three months old and I had hit the metaphorical wall.

The baby was asleep in the bedroom upstairs, ensconced in a pillow fort again because I still didn't have a cot. I reckoned it was safe there, and I put my social services/health visitor hat on, assessing the risk to the baby in that location. I judged that it was good enough. So I was now alone in the living room downstairs, a small room furnished with brown leather sofas that were slippery and cold when you sat on them, and made you shiver, and which were occupied by salmon-pink corduroy cushions.

There was a stone fireplace and chintzy curtains at the windows. There was a picture of a forest above the fireplace and a trio of wooden birds on the mantelpiece, one which was pecking the wooden sill, another pecking its tail feathers and the last, a duck, sitting as if on water. I found these mesmerising. And I realised that, in the event of a power cut, I could burn them on the fire because they were wooden. There was a television in the corner which I found to my delight had Netflix and therefore promised that there was some Wi-Fi connection in the house, which I planned to locate once I felt less scared about wandering into the other rooms without the baby as my human shield against things I could not see but believed were there. I assumed that the baby possessed a sixth sense and would be able to pick up on bad energy, so I stared at it when we went into the rooms I deemed to be 'hot', figuratively. Hot with ghosts. But the baby showed no signs of gauging this, and if it did, it certainly was not letting on.

I had my Wolf Blass, and it was giving me some comfort, as well as a small headache, but I could just about live with it. Sadly, white wine did that, but there was no alternative in the shop because all they had in the reds was a Shiraz, which made my belly hurt. I did feel pleasingly woozy though.

The night drew on. I had no idea what I was watching. One show turned into another, I could not follow any of them, but it was good because as long as they continued to do that, I was no longer thinking about the abduction I had done and the marchioness I couldn't figure out and the faff of having to go to Perth in the morning to get a phone. I'd lulled myself blissfully into a wine sleep and was dozing off when I was awoken by a loud noise outside the cottage. A bang – something breaking, falling, a smash. I opened my eyes and could have sworn I saw a figure swaying about in the darkness outside. My head told me it was the gentle motion of a tree, but my heart thought not and was trying to crawl out of my chest to find a home in a calmer land. It was unbearably loud. I had never heard my heart make so much noise. I could hear it in my head. It was likely that the alcohol had had something to do with the racket it was making. And then there was another sound, coming from the kitchen. It was the front door. The envelope flap had been opened and closed.

I was paralysed. I could not move. I wanted so much to close the curtains but I could not get up from the sofa. My body was now a prime environment for a stroke or cardiac arrest. My fingers were gripping the brown leather. I lifted them up for moment to see that I had deposited a sweaty trail across it, as if snails had been massacred at my hands.

By the front door, I saw a piece of paper written with the words: *I know about the baby*.

Chapter 18

'What does this mean, Hannah?' I wailed. 'What does this mean?'

I had my new phone and I was calling Hannah on it. It was a pay-as-you-go Nokia that I bought from the O2 shop in Perth with the cash remaining from my withdrawal in Chiswick. I was running out of money so I went to the Ramsdens on the High Street and sold my engagement ring, which felt both final and liberating in a way that I hadn't expected. The remorse and sadness I had anticipated were stifled by the revelation from the man behind the counter that the ring was a fraction of the value James had told me it was (and he would tell me this regularly) and it further confirmed to me that our marriage had been nourished by a stream of lies.

'It means,' she said, 'either someone knows that you've run away with James's baby–'

'It's my baby too,' I said.

'Or they know you have a baby and you're not meant to because your boss hates kids. It reads to me like a threat.'

'But I've only been here four days,' I said. 'How can I have messed this up already?'

'Look,' she said. 'I've got to go. I've got a lunch with some new clients.'

'Oh right, sorry,' I said. I had to be mindful of my pernicious self-absorption – Hannah had a life with things going on in it that had nothing to do with me.

'I'll call you later,' she said.

I read the note again. It was handwritten, but it was not handwriting I recognised. The clipped, detached lettering set it apart from the cursive form I was familiar with. I made a mental note of it, should I at some point encounter it again and expose its writer. I could not think who it might be. I had discounted Mark immediately, because if he had known about the baby he would have simply told me to leave, likewise the marchioness. I couldn't imagine that they would engage in this kind of cloak-and-dagger activity. And it couldn't have been Kelly because she of course did know about the baby. I had also seen her writing, with its signature hearts over the Is and circles instead of full stops.

I spent the rest of the weekend with the curtains closed, hiding in the living room. I wouldn't go into the kitchen at night because it was too dark outside and there were no curtains on the windows and I wouldn't have been able to see faces if they were looking in at me, watching me as, unaware, I was going about my business. I bet I looked stupid while I did it, a true victim, eminently killable. But, luckily, fear of what was happening outside made me less scared of what was going on within. I saw no ghosts, heard nothing internally either, apart from the heating turning on and off (how I missed the reassuring clatter and rattle of the Tube crossing the bridge on Acton Green) but I remained on high alert, hardly sleeping at all on the mattress in the bedroom next to the baby in its pillow fort because it was so uncomfortable and I was so terrified about being murdered or, worse, found out.

The note, I secreted in the freezer for the time being, convinced that it was the most suitable home for it.

At 3.20 on the Sunday morning, as I was lying awake in the darkness, I texted Hannah: *Any update? Any news from James?*

The message did not get delivered until 8.30 a.m. She must have turned her phone off.

No. Try and get some sleep. Tiredness can kill.

At the castle on the Monday morning, after I dropped off the baby with a much more amenable Shona (having waved my new phone theatrically about in front of her) I looked at Kelly with consternation as we sat at the kitchen table with our morning coffee, which she had made from the Sage machine with Nespresso capsules and was a little piece of heaven.

I was undecided as to whether to tell her about the note. James had always told me not to trust anyone, to enter all relationships with distrust. But look where that had got me. I missed all the friendships I didn't have, the fun I might have enjoyed had I been allowed to let more people into my life.

I picked the note out of my bag and slipped it over to Kelly.

'What's this?' she asked.

'I don't know,' I said. 'I found it on the doormat on Friday. Someone posted it while I was watching the television.'

'What does it mean? *I know about the baby.*'

I shrugged. 'You don't recognise the writing, do you?' I asked.

'No, I don't, sorry, lovely.'

She pulled the piece of paper away from me, scrunched it up into a ball and threw it in the bin.

'I wanted to keep that,' I said. 'You know, as evidence.'

'Evidence?'

I nodded.

'You don't want to keep hold of that,' she warned. 'It's giving bad energy. Can you feel all the bad energy coming off it?' She recoiled as if she had been scorched. She stood up and pushed her chair into the table and glanced at the giant clock above the cooker. 'The plumber will be here any minute,' she said. 'The marchioness's loo's blocked again. I bet he goes to the wrong door. Honestly, that man . . . it doesn't matter how many times I tell him.'

'What do you think I should do?'

'About what?'

'The note.'

'I wouldn't worry about it,' she said. 'But I can ask around. We're a small community here. I'll get to the bottom of it.'

And I believed that she would, if her childcare-arranging skills were anything to go by. Sporadic brain-fog aside, Kelly seemed to be dazzlingly competent. I wanted so much to know what had brought her to the castle. It was hard to make sense of it; her capabilities exceeded the requirements of her role.

The bell rang. Kelly scanned the switchboard.

'It's coming from the hall,' she said. 'She must be ready.'

•

I was keeping my eyes on the road, trying not to look too much in the rearview mirror because I sensed that the marchioness didn't like to be looked at. I wasn't sure whether it was by everyone or just me – a thought even crossed my mind that she might have regarded me as a sort of deviant. I had to reassure myself that I was not one. Rather, I was a woman, just like she, finding her way in the world, earning a living (although

I suspected that this applied only to me). Yet I was more than aware of how unappetising I was as an employee in my jeans and jumpers, my white high tops. It was an unremarkable outfit, yet a uniform of sorts. I wished I could have afforded a suit, a tuxedo or smoking jacket, something that would have matched the vim the marchioness was bringing to our dynamic. At least I did not have to wear a chauffeur's hat.

That day, there was a deliberate pop of colour in her attire. It was a red coat. Blood red. If I squinted, she looked like a haemorrhage. It was fitting for a trip to the Intensive Care Unit. What a sense of occasion she had.

'Can I ask you something?'

'Of course,' I said.

'What made you decide to take this job?' she asked.

I was not prepared for the small talk. I was unnerved by the normality of her tone.

'I only ask because it is an unusual job for a woman to apply for,' she continued. 'You were the only applicant. Did you know that? I wanted a woman. I didn't want a man. I do not like being on my own in a car with a man. Do you?'

Before I had the chance to reply she continued: 'Any moment he could just decide to stop the car, jump in the back and try to violate you. And who's to stop him from doing that if he is especially strong? It is only the slimmest veil of civility that stops a man from doing that. It is the most fragile veil in existence. Gossamer, I would say. I was lucky to get away with asking for a woman. Mark said it was unfair. He was saying that it wasn't an equal opportunities thing.'

Luckily, very luckily, we passed a castle to our right, just as we were leaving a town charmingly named Inveralmond. I asked, 'What's that?'

The marchioness shrugged. She was examining her cuticles. 'Some old monument. A castle. This country's full of them. Belonging to this family or that family. Usual story. Do you want to stop and look at it?'

Tick-tock.

'That's very kind of you,' I said. 'But I can go another time.'

'How do you like driving the car?' she said.

'Fine. It's in good condition for its age.'

That wasn't enough of an answer for her. It wasn't the answer she wanted.

'It's really stood the test of time,' I added, tapping the steering wheel with my right palm. 'Volvos. They're meant to be very reliable cars, aren't they?'

'My husband loves this car,' she said. 'He wouldn't dream of driving anything else. He's had it for twenty-five years. Twenty-five years, can you believe it?'

'I can't,' I said.

'It has a lot of sentimental value,' she said. 'Can you guess why?'

I shook my head. The clutch was rattling.

'Guess,' she said.

I gripped the steering wheel. Flecks of leather were peeling off it.

'Oh, I don't know,' I said. 'I really have no idea.'

'Guess.'

I didn't want to have another guess. She was trying to make me do fun and games and I hated fun and games.

'I really have no idea,' I repeated with my teeth jammed together.

'He got it when he was working for NATO,' she explained. 'It was gifted to him by an American diplomat. The marquess was instrumental in brokering the Dayton Treaty, you know, all that dreadful stuff in Bosnia back in the 1990s.'

'Oh right,' I said. 'Do they give you a car for doing that?'

'Brokering treaties?' she said pityingly. 'No. They don't. David was accompanying this diplomat to a meeting one afternoon. They were in Ohio. That's where all this happened. This particular diplomat was a woman and she was heavily pregnant. I mean about to pop.' The marchioness formed a great invisible dome over her stomach. She puffed out her cheeks. 'They were stuck in traffic on the way, I don't know, perhaps there had been an accident or something. But the traffic wasn't budging, I mean, not at all, and they were on the freeway at the time so there was no pulling off and, this is the crazy part, her waters broke. Right there in the back of the car.'

'This car?' I asked. 'In this car?'

'Yes,' she said. 'In this car.' She stroked the seat next to her. 'She told him: "The baby is coming. The baby is coming."'

I slowed right down. Cars overtook me.

'And, of course, he delivered the baby,' she said breezily. 'Breech.'

'That's incredible,' I said. 'I had no idea he was a doctor too.'

'Oh no, no, no. He isn't a doctor.'

'Then how did he know what to do?'

She shrugged and then she sighed and twiddled the stack of diamonds on her wedding finger. 'That's the kind of man he is,' she said. 'As a gesture of gratitude, the diplomat shipped the car back to the UK, wrapped up in a big red bow. I thought it was perhaps a bit unnecessary, but I suppose what do you give the man who has everything apart from a diplomatic services Volvo executive limousine with an extended wheelbase in which he saved the lives of both a mother and a baby on the way to brokering an international peace treaty?'

She winked at me. At least I thought she did. It might have been an involuntary spasm, a tic, a statement of madness. She went quiet and gazed out of the window. I was silent too. I was wondering what to say. I couldn't think of a single thing to say. Something about her made me forget all my words.

'He calls it David,' she said.

'What?' I said.

'What?' she echoed.

'Pardon,' I said.

'Yes,' she nodded. 'The car. After the baby he delivered. The baby was named David after my husband. Isn't that a riot?'

'That's a riot,' I said.

The conversation stopped there. We were approaching the city centre. I followed the signs to Ninewells Hospital. I didn't have much faith in the rickety sat nav Mark had given me that was now plugged into the car's quarter-century-old cigarette lighter.

'Did you know I used to be a racing car driver?' the marchioness asked.

'No, I didn't,' I said.

'Of course you wouldn't. Why would you?'

'Mark said that you liked cars,' I said.

In the rearview mirror I saw her raising her eyebrows. 'I do. He is correct,' she said begrudgingly. 'I had a very nice car. But it's a write-off.'

'Can't you get a replacement?'

'I would prefer to take this one. It makes me feel closer to my husband. Mark has tried to get me to buy a new one but he doesn't understand me. He never has. He never will.'

I wanted to ask why she couldn't simply find another estate manager if she disliked this one so much. She wouldn't be the only beneficiary of his dismissal.

'Was Mark driving you to the hospital? Before me.'

'Yes, a few times. It doesn't work for either of us. He's busy. That's that.'

'When did you stop racing cars?'

'When I married my first husband. That was the end of the car racing.'

'Your first husband?'

She did not reply.

'You must miss it,' I said, changing tack. 'The car racing. It sounds thrilling.'

I watched her, thinking she would say more about the car racing, perhaps even the first husband. I didn't want to push her on it. I didn't want to pry. It's blurry, the line between curiosity and intrusion. Her head bent forward to look at the iPad and continued to do so until we arrived at the hospital in Dundee.

Chapter 19

'I will be one hour. No more, no less. You wait here.'

Over and out. I could do that. I could follow that simple instruction.

I closed the door behind the marchioness and watched as she walked into the drab, brutalist building through the revolving doors, a vanishing red blood cell. I checked the time on my phone (I had left my watch at home that day) and decided to move to the car park, where I would wait for her. It didn't feel right to be parked on the zigzag lines by the main entrance in that gargantuan vehicle.

I found a space that looked onto a swathe of grassland with what appeared to be a crop circle in the middle. I considered its incongruity for a minute or two before moving my attention to my phone and to Spotify to see if there were any podcasts I liked the sound of. I had so much leisure! I spared a thought for the baby but retracted it in case I went too far down the road of worrying about how it was, how it was feeling, whether it was happy, whether it was safe, whether this childcare provider was right for it, if all this commotion would have an impact on it. I shook my head, ridding it of troublesome thoughts, and listened instead to a socialite talking about the benefits of leaving her banker husband for a post-pubescent Portuguese footballer and telling her listeners to do the same. But the thought of getting *in flagrante* with a twenty-something footballer had the same effect on me as thoughts about Steven, James's arresting officer.

In no time, an unsettling awareness came over me that I needed a wee. I looked at the display on my phone. Only fifteen minutes had passed. I reckoned I could safely leave the car in search of a toilet and be back in plenty of time to meet the marchioness. There would be no possibility of stopping on the way back to the castle.

I got out of the car and made my way into the hospital. It was enormous. Its many wings stretched out for miles and miles, like an eagle on a rack. I followed the signs to the loos but the first set I found were out of order, so I took the stairs to the floor above and went in search of another batch. The smell in that place was unbearable – boiled vegetables, disinfectant, human secretions. I was not happy there. I was not happy at all.

Eventually, I found an operational toilet on the second floor near the radiology unit. It was standalone and, I assumed, because it was off the beaten track of the main hospital, was for use only by staff. I felt guilty for using it, but I was sure my bladder was about to burst and reasoned that I would save a lot of manpower in A&E were that to happen. It must have been those coffee capsules. I should have remembered that caffeine was a potent diuretic. I went and was relieved, washed my hands repeatedly as per the instructions above the basin, and with an overwhelming awareness of the scale of superbugs there might have been present, but found that when I tried to open the lock (after drying my hands on my trousers) it would not budge. The lock was stuck. My hand became sweaty with panic. I wrapped my sleeve around my hand to absorb some of the moisture, hoping it would give it some purchase on the hardware but nothing was happening. I reached inside my pocket for my phone but could not find it. It was in the car where I had left it, playing that woman and her toyboy on Spotify, gobbling up my tiny ration of data from my Ramsdens sale.

I knocked on the door, quietly at first. 'Hello?' I said meekly. 'Is anyone there?'

There was no answer. I tried again. And again. I heard nothing. I heard no movement outside: no squeaking tread along the floor, no voices being cleared, no shunting of elevator doors. I was in the remotest part of the hospital and there was no one around to help me. The walls in the radiology department were purposely thick.

I continued to bang for what felt like an eternity. I screamed and shouted; I became hoarse, hideous in my wailing. Nothing was happening. No one was coming to save me. No one knew where I was. And there was something else at work, some long locked-up distress which I identified as a memory of being trapped in a loo when I was five and Mum having to kick the door down.

Someone would have to kick the door down.

I told myself to breathe. I breathed in through my nose and out through my mouth but this was resolving nothing. Panic felt more productive. The marchioness! Where was she now? Outside the hospital, no doubt, wondering where I was. I had only one job – to wait for an hour – and I couldn't even do that. The baby. I was going to be late for the baby again. What if no one found me and I died in the loo. Who would tell Shona? Kelly was the only person who knew about Shona. She would have to tell her that I had disappeared – and I had given no contact details of anyone I knew in this scenario. The baby would be handed over to an orphanage and live out the rest of its life like that girl from *Les Miserables*. And then the irony hit me – my fabricated disappearance had transformed into my genuine disappearance.

•

A new psychological development – I had reached the point of hopelessness, having exhausted myself mentally. I had given up all hope. I was without resilience or tenacity. I was slumped on the loo with the seat down, staring at the wall.

Please wash your hands.

I had no idea how long I had been in that loo. Minutes, hours, days. All was lost. I had reached the nadir.

And then, suddenly, there was some movement outside, as if someone was trying to get in to use the toilet for themselves. I stood up sharp.

'Hello!' I shouted, my voice scratchy from the screaming.

'Heh?' was the answer.

'Thank God,' I said. 'I'm locked in here! I've been in here for hours. Can you help me get out?'

It was a man's voice and he was speaking in a language I couldn't understand.

'Help!' I said. 'Help! Help!'

I banged on the door with my fist.

Then I heard footsteps walking away. I had been abandoned. Left to rot. The irony of festering away in a place that could offer immediate medical relief was not lost on me. The baby would never know its mother. Would never know how much its mother loved it. An exceptional dizziness came over me. All the blood in my body drained from my brain.

I heard another voice, this time English. 'You know the lock works the other way,' it said.

I had been suspended in a strange survival-mode spell. I came to.

'Huh?' I said. 'Hello? Help!'

'The lock works the other way,' the voice repeated. 'It's counterintuitive. Try it now.'

I walked up to the door – my jailer, my nemesis – and I turned the lock in an anticlockwise motion. Immediately, I heard a click. My freedom was granted. A constellation of junior doctors peered in at me as if I were a specimen warranting close examination. They must have been students doing their rounds, because there was an older one who looked serious, like a surgeon, observing me from over his spectacles.

'There you are,' he said. 'Not that difficult in the end.'

I emerged from the room, hot, red-eyed, drenched in sweat, parched of mouth, my lips stuck to my gums.

'Thank you,' I croaked.

'Thank Markus,' he said, pointing out the hospital porter. 'He's the one who found you.'

•

The marchioness was crouching down in front of the car. She was pulling at the big yellow clamp with her hand, trying to yank it off. She stood up, stood back and looked at it from all the angles. There was a ticket on the windscreen. She peeled it off and turned it around in her hand, flapping it about. I had never seen that scale of confusion on a face before.

I watched all of this from the rotating door. I was just going round and round. I couldn't face breaking out of its orbit. I was safe in that rotation.

She looked up and around herself. I could see that she

was hoping for someone to appear and help her, and then the parking warden, who had been checking the registrations of the other cars in the car park, came over to her and she started talking to him, pointing at the new addition to her car. Then she turned to look in my general direction and said, 'Camilla! Camilla! Camilla! Where have you been? And what is this?'

She pointed her foot at the clamp.

I had no idea who she was talking to until I remembered that Camilla was my fake fugitive name.

Chapter 20

'How do *you* think things are going?'

Mark was emphasising the *you* to demonstrate that my version of reality was likely to be different from his.

'Good,' I said. 'I think they're going good.'

'Well,' said Mark.

'Well,' I repeated. 'They're going well.'

It was unclear from the way he was behaving whether the marchioness had told him about what had happened at the hospital and whether any explanation had been given as to our lateness, for which Shona (when I went to collect the baby) simply responded by saying, 'That's strike two by the way.' So I then had to ask, 'How many do I get?' and she said, 'Three.'

Perhaps the marchioness hadn't given him any explanation. Explaining things was something she would probably not feel any necessity to do. *Never complain, never explain*. I bet that was her school of thought and I appeared to be its indirect beneficiary. Mark seemed to know nothing. Nothing at all. I hadn't seen the marchioness that day. I hadn't seen her since we got back from my hospital loo and car-clamping disaster. I had no idea where she was.

Mark nodded defeatedly. He peeled his sleeves over his

elbows revealing his forearms. That bit of flesh under the elbow was shapely with a crop of fine brown hairs all pointing in the same direction. He had a thick neck. I thought how I liked thick necks generally but that Mark's was a bit too thick. His baby blue and white gingham shirt offset this thickness but not entirely, not enough anyway. He pulled something out of his jacket, which he had hung neatly on the back of the chair he was sitting on. We were down in the kitchen. It was getting late. I needed to get the baby before strike three and I didn't want to test Shona's veracity.

'Here you go.'

He slid an envelope across the table. I picked it up, noting its formality: windowed, my name in print centred with painstaking accuracy.

'It's your pay,' he said.

I felt unbridled joy. I hadn't received a pay cheque since I left my old job at the magazine five years previously, before I started the business with Vanessa. I was overcome with excitement for how I would spend it, and then I remembered that most of it would be on Angry Shona.

'I have been instructed by the marchioness,' Mark said resentfully – relating this to me clearly irritated him – 'to tell you to be ready in the hall at eight o'clock tomorrow morning, and to pack an overnight bag because she will be staying at her destination – wherever that is – returning the following day by the evening.'

'Overnight bag?' I said. 'Overnight?'

'Yes,' he said. 'Is that going to be a problem?'

'No,' I said. 'No problem.'

But it was a problem.

He was gauging my reactions, waiting for me to crack. He

had every expectation that this would be my downfall. Maybe it was. Perhaps it was all over. I had nowhere for the baby to go. My adventure had run its course.

'Well,' I said. 'I'd best be getting off.'

'See you tomorrow,' he said. 'Bright and early.'

'See you tomorrow,' I said.

But I knew I wouldn't see him tomorrow. I wouldn't see him again.

He stood up from the kitchen table, lifted his corduroy jacket from the back of the chair and put it on. He tucked the chair under the table and briefly looked out of the window and up towards the sky. I didn't know where he was going, how he was planning to spend his evening. Sleeping standing up somewhere, most likely. The man was a mystery.

Chapter 21

As with everything in my life so far, I planned to defer to Hannah so that she could tell me what to do. I kept trying to call her but she wasn't picking up, either on her mobile or her landline, which was unusual because she was a hawk with her phone. I left plenty of messages and texts but I'd heard nothing back. She might have had a client dinner, I reasoned. But without her, I did not know where to turn. I had no next move. I couldn't think.

After collecting the baby from Shona (who, by the way, point-blank refused to be the solution to my childcare problem), I went straight to the village shop and picked up the fanciest items I could find including an Arctic Roll and a bottle of Freixenet, giving myself a little payday treat and also some items of comfort for my last supper as I had begun to regard it. I could not leave the baby on its own and I had nowhere else to take it. There was no alternative but to go. I decided that my exit would take place early the following morning. I felt flat. I wanted to weep. I had no choice but to return to London, to Hannah's. I had wanted so much to make her proud, to show her that I could go out into the world and fend for myself, just as she had done.

I reflected on the fact that I'd got this far, that I'd managed to keep my job despite getting locked in a hospital loo for two hours, leaving my boss, a feckless aristocrat, unattended for an hour in the car park, and for incurring hundreds of pounds in parking fines. I had no idea how I hadn't yet been sacked.

After I put the baby to bed, I sat in the living room with the curtains closed. I had a glass of cava and a slice of my ice cream cake. I put something on Netflix, the show where things are either cake or not cake and a panel of American judges decides which is which. It seemed like an appropriate thing to watch at the time. I had also bought a tiny Brie that was a little on the cold side and ate it with a trio of Ritz crackers. I wondered how it would taste with a glass of port. I'd never tried port. I bet the marchioness drank port. I bet she had cupboards of the stuff. Alas, the cheese was not sitting so well with the cava.

Then I thought about what I would do next.

But my thinking was interrupted when, from outside, I heard a crunching sound. There was the sound of something trudging over the gravel surrounding the cottage. I wished there had been a floodlight outside so that I could have seen what was going on, but there was nothing, no security whatsoever, and I reproached my employers for leaving their female employee so vulnerable to intruders. The crunching continued until it stopped at the window I was hiding behind. I wondered if they'd seen my silhouette projected onto the curtain. I wished I knew how lighting worked. I looked about myself for my phone. I could not see it – it must have been upstairs with the baby, playing lullabies.

Instinctively, I ran up the flight of stairs to the bedroom, feeling that it was safest to be with the baby rather than not.

What kind of mother would I have been if I had left the baby all on its own while under invasion?

A noise downstairs. Louder. Creaking. Someone was entering. I hadn't locked the door! I had become complacent in my rural way of life. That would be the last time I ever listened to Kelly, I told myself. And then the door slammed. I was catatonic, rendered immobile. I looked for something in the room to throw at my assailant but there was nothing that could be weaponised. There was only the bedside lamp, but I worried that this could be used against me by my prospective attacker were they to prise it from me after I'd spent some time twirling it about. James was right; I had never been able to think on my feet. I was powerless, defenceless. Crouching behind the bed, my hands pinning down the slumbering baby, I awaited my fate.

The light turned on.

'Surprise!'

Chapter 22

'I know I should have told you I was coming.'

Hannah had her feet up on the coffee table in the living room. She unscrewed the bottle of claret parked in between her legs that she had brought with her from London. I held out two glasses. She poured in the wine. We clinked. The glasses chimed.

'But I couldn't resist.'

'Honestly, I thought it was a murderer,' I said. 'I really did.'

'Who on earth would want to murder you?' Hannah asked.

'I don't know,' I said, scrabbling about in my mind for a candidate. 'James. James might want to kill me. Or someone might be spying on me. I'd have no way of knowing if someone was spying on me or stalking me. It's so dark out here. What if there's a local maniac who's decided that they don't like the look of me and to kill me because, you know, why not? They fancy going on a killing spree and I'm first on the list. You have to start somewhere. If you were to stop and think about it, there are many, many possibilities. And there was that note someone posted through the letterbox. What if sending that was a precursor to murdering me?'

Hannah had zoned out. She must have been tired from the

journey. She was watching my Netflix show, eating a packet of Monster Munch and shouting, 'That's cake' and 'That's not cake' and 'There's no way that's not cake' at the television. I thought that I should have provided her with a meal of some sort. I offered her some of my tiny Brie. It had stiffened at the edges and lost some of its appeal.

'I don't know why you're so scared of this cottage,' she said, looking around the room. 'It's very sweet. Very cosy. A bit twee, yes, but I'm not feeling the whole sinister thing.'

Then I looked around to see if I could see what she was seeing. I scrunched up my face.

'It's just got this energy,' I said.

'Energy?'

'You know how Mum used to talk about energy,' I said. I was feeling quivery. My eyes burned. 'Do you remember? Things having good energies and bad energies. And energy is transferred. It doesn't just stop or die.'

'You mean the crystal stuff.'

'I'd forgotten about the crystals,' I said wistfully.

'Before I forget,' Hannah said, sitting up abruptly. 'I've brought you some things. Some of your things, actually. Let me get them.'

She went into the kitchen and returned with a bag which she placed on top of the coffee table. I peered inside and saw that it was filled with some of my favourite items, the things I could not take the night I left London: my beloved skincare products and my laptop.

'I've missed these so much!' I said. 'How did you get these?'

'Lies and subterfuge,' Hannah replied. 'I went to your flat.'

'When?' I asked. 'How?'

'Hilary called. God, she's an unpleasant woman, isn't she?'

'Yes,' I said. 'Why didn't you tell me she called you?'

'I didn't want you to worry,' Hannah replied. 'I knew how upset you were when I told you James had accused you of abducting the baby. I didn't want to give you another problem.'

'What did she say?' I asked. 'On the phone.'

'She wanted to know where you were. She assumed I knew,' Hannah said. 'She was right about that.'

'And what did you tell her?'

'Huh?'

Hannah was pulling out jars and bottles from the bag, lining them up, and sampling the contents. She released a spume of self-tan into her palm which she slathered over her face and neck, before appraising my eau de toilette, spraying it onto her wrists and rubbing them together, sniffing her skin the way she used to when we would go to Selfridges with Mum and spend hours in the fragrance hall while Hannah tried everything and Mum and I withered with fatigue from the heat of the lights and the milling crowds.

'Where did you tell her I'd gone?' I asked.

'I didn't say anything over the phone, of course,' she said. 'I told her I'd meet her in person and that I'd come to the flat. I thought I'd try to tell her to leave you alone, to give you some time, at least while you get yourself sorted out here. I also tried to show her your point of view, to see if I could get her to empathise with how difficult it has been, especially the last few weeks. Also, I knew how much you would have wanted your things but had had to leave without them, so while she took herself off to the loo, I grabbed as much as I could. She didn't notice. At least, I think she didn't.'

She flicked a monster foot into her mouth and crunched. I lined up the contents of the bag on the table. I didn't realise how important those things were to me until I was reunited with them. I had previously supposed that I was above the pull of earthly goods but that seemed not to be the case.

'You know, I don't think Hilary told James that I was coming, because he wasn't at home when I was there. I wonder if she'd made sure of it.'

'Where was he?' I asked. 'Isn't he meant to be looking after Hilary?'

No matter how hard I tried, I could not imagine James looking after himself, let alone anyone else.

'No idea,' Hannah said. 'Apparently his relationship with that woman, Anya, didn't work out. This is according to Hilary, by the way. Reading between the lines, it looks as if she stole a load of Hilary's jewellery and then bolted. I had to pinch myself to stop myself from laughing. Hilary's Rolex. Her Krugerrand. She was livid. And then she told me that James is coming to look for you, that on top of alerting the police to your disappearance, he has hired a private investigator. That is also why I came in person. I was under the distinct impression that I was being bugged. I might be paranoid though. That reminds me. Look at this.'

Hannah went onto the Missing Persons website on her phone and there I was, moon-faced, glaring into the camera with the baby in my arms. It was a terrible photograph. Hilary must have chosen it. She was right; I was gormless. Gormless and ungainly with a creepy eye. I had a reference number, where I went missing from and when, and my age at disappearance which I think was a cruel and unnecessary admission. There was a link that read 'Report a Sighting'.

'Should you be using your phone?' I asked. 'If you're being bugged, won't they be able to trace you?'

'Oh yes,' she said. 'Good point.' She turned the phone off at the switch and its face turned black. 'Hilary said that hunting you has given James a renewed sense of purpose in life. She seemed almost proud of his determination.'

'Determination?'

'Her word, not mine,' Hannah insisted.

'Any determination he has is bound up in his fear of losing,' I said. 'I know him. This is only a game to him. He doesn't want me. He doesn't even want the baby. He just wants to win, and to him winning is about me losing.'

'I know that,' Hannah said, squeezing my arm. I wrapped her hand in mine. 'I do know that.'

'How do you know no one followed you here?' I asked.

'I don't,' she said. 'But I was super careful. I changed trains three times. I stayed at a friend's house in Clerkenwell the night before I came. They live in one of those flats with an underground car park so she drove me out through there and I lay down in the back, making sure I couldn't be seen. I tried to take every precaution.'

'James is looking for me? And the police? And a private investigator?'

Hannah nodded. She downed her glass of wine and poured herself another. She went to fill up mine but I put my hand over it. My head was beating like a heart.

'I sensed that there is a plan between them,' Hannah said cautiously, finely tuning her delivery. 'And I think that the plan is to discredit you. I'm not saying necessarily to paint you as a lunatic but that you might not be that stable, that you might be unfit to mother so that they can try to claim custody.'

'But I am fit to mother. I am completely fine. I'm the most

stable I have ever been, probably,' I said. 'Do they have any idea where I am?'

'I don't think so,' she said. 'I didn't get that impression, but it's possible that Hilary was playing me, lulling me into a false sense of security so that I would divulge. But I wasn't born yesterday.'

'Good,' I said. 'That's good.'

Hannah leant forward to get the remote control from the coffee table and turned the television off. She put it back with a studied meticulousness. She took her time to assemble the following question: 'Did anything happen in the early days, when the baby was tiny, that would give James any leverage?'

'Not that I can think of,' I said. 'It was all a haze.'

'Think,' she said, with some urgency. 'Because it looks as if he has something on you.'

I could not think of a single thing. I thought I had been an excellent mother and if not precisely excellent then certainly quite good. I nodded my head. It felt so full, as if it was choking under a dense fog, almost flooding.

Hannah ran her finger around the rim of the glass. I didn't look at her face. I decided it was best not to.

Chapter 23

I slept like the proverbial with my sister in the room next to me. What comfort her presence brought me. We were a house of blissfully sleeping people but naturally I woke with a fright, remembering that I was now the focus of a major search operation.

Hannah had agreed to look after the baby so that I could go on the overnight excursion with the marchioness. I could not believe how things were falling into place, at least in the work arena of my life. I couldn't wait to see Mark's face when I turned up in the hall at 8 a.m. sharp.

'Keep the curtains closed at night,' I told Hannah. 'And lock the door.'

'Okay,' she said, through a colossal yawn. She was sitting up in bed. I had given her a cup of coffee. She took a sip. 'Yuck,' she said. 'What is this?'

'It's instant. It's all they have in the village shop.'

'Well, maybe we can go to an M&S on the weekend. Where's your nearest one?'

'Perth,' I said.

'Well, then, we shall go to Perth.'

I took my overnight bag (the baby bag), waved goodbye

to Hannah and kissed the baby, who was still asleep. What a serene pleasure it was not to have to deal with Angry Shona that morning.

I left the cottage with a renewed vigilance.

•

Mark was not at the castle when I arrived so I did not get to see the look on his face after all. It had surprised me not to find him because I was sure he'd want to be the first to witness my absence and to see the marchioness's chauffeur project unravel. It was not to be.

Kelly was there, however. She was hanging around the hall with a purposelessness that I hadn't seen on her before. She had a puzzling expression on her face. I wondered if she was under some hormonal siege or, perhaps, someone she had hired to do something hadn't done it to the required standard, which happened regularly. I recalled how ruffled she was when, earlier that week, the plumber had failed to adequately unblock the marchioness's loo, so he had to return the following day to do it properly and he still came to the wrong door, which meant that she had to run from one end of the castle to the other to get him before he left, having assumed he had been called in error. Keeping a castle was hard. Kelly kept saying, 'Keeps you fit!', which I took to mean that she was exhausted – or run ragged as my mother used to say.

She looked as if she had been crying – the skin under her eyes was puffy and her eyeballs were red. Perhaps it was just from the early start – I can attest to the ravages of the night on the morning face as you approach middle age – but I don't remember her looking that way when she came to pick us up at dawn from the Caledonian Sleeper at Dunkeld and Birnam station.

'She won't be long, lovely,' she said. 'I've just taken her hot chocolate up.'

'Are you okay?' I asked.

'Me?' she said self-effacingly. 'Of course. Why?'

'Nothing. Just checking.'

'Right as rain, my lovely. Right as rain.'

She smiled at me and moved towards a chair that looked like a throne, which she adjusted into the same position it had just been in.

'Right,' she said, at last breaking away from the chair's gravity. 'Got a pile of stuff to get on with downstairs, so I'm going to make a start on that.'

She slapped her hands together as if she was ridding herself of something.

'Do you know where we're going?' I asked. 'Has she said? I didn't really know what to pack. It would be good to have some idea.'

'I think she would prefer to tell you herself,' Kelly replied, looking at my face and mirroring its expression. 'You look worried. Try not to worry. There's nothing to worry about.'

At that moment, the marchioness appeared at the top of the stairs and made her way down slowly, clutching the banister. I could see why: on her feet she had on a pair of black suede Alexander McQueen pumps, the ones with the heels that curve inwards. She held the tiniest handbag I'd ever seen. Across her shoulders she wore a black woollen cape that would have made freeing her arms in a tumble-down situation troublesome. I wasn't sure why she hadn't waited until she was downstairs to put her cape and shoes on, given the hazardousness of the interior architecture, but, while I knew almost nothing about the marchioness, one thing I understood was her distaste for practicality. Kelly and I were both looking up at her; both of us getting on, tired, puffy-eyed, drying up at the edges like sandwiches, like brie that's been left out, in comfortable shoes. (Kelly wore Nike Air Max – you would too if you had to go up and down those stairs all day.)

'Are you not waiting in the car?' the marchioness asked me, upon reaching the bottom step. She put her bag down in the middle of the sideboard in the hall, equidistant to two sprawling silver epergnes.

I was not waiting in the car. 'Mark told me to meet you here,' I said.

The marchioness nodded. 'Of course,' she said. 'He's wrong. I'm almost ready to go. There is something I need to get first. Wait here, will you?'

'What do you need?' Kelly asked.

'My thing.'

'I'll get it for you,' she offered.

'No, let me,' the marchioness replied.

But before she could say another word, Kelly headed upstairs, saying on the way, 'What are you like? There's no way you'll get it down the stairs in those shoes.'

Kelly was struggling with the ascent; I could see that. The marchioness saw it too because she looked down at her shoes crossly and, I believe, if I hadn't been there at that moment, she might have told them off.

'I like your shoes,' I said, filling the silence now that we were alone together in the hall.

'How sweet of you,' she said, and then she looked down at my feet and seeing a pair of Converse peeping out from under my trousers, clammed her mouth shut, lifted her head and looked out of the window.

'You know, Camilla,' she said, 'I don't think I will ever acclimatise to the darkness of these Scottish mornings.'

A magpie landed on the external stone windowsill and stared into the hall at the two of us. The marchioness gasped and leapt towards it. The bird flew away and landed on the lawn outside the castle. Its motion activated the floodlights and lit up the garden. Two others touched down beside it.

'One, two, three,' she whispered.

I watched her at the window, staring out. She was transfixed by the birds.

There was great noise overhead and then, moments later, Kelly reappeared, wheeling a gigantic thing across the floor. There was some resistance between it and the carpet. It was a vast misshapen black object and it loomed over her like the remnants of a nightmare. I had no idea what it was or how it would get down the stairs. I had only expected a small suitcase, one of those little wheelie ones.

'That's my harp,' said the marchioness.

'Harp?' I asked.

She nodded furiously. 'Harp,' she repeated, wrestling with the H. 'We are going to the loch house. I've always felt that what the loch house needed was a harp. There's a trailer on the back of the car. It's a horse box in fact. But it will work perfectly well for the harp. We are going to take it there. I have arranged for some people to come. We are going to have a little recital, a little soirée.'

'Soirée?'

'Yes. Soirée. I haven't had a soirée for such a long time and I think it might lift my mood.'

Kelly stood at the top of the stairs and began to negotiate the transit of herself and the harp case down them. I knew I had to help her, as any decent person would.

From behind the case, I saw Kelly's face, glowing pink like a siren, pink as her polo shirt. I ran up the stairs with my arms out, palms aloft. I could no longer be a bystander to what I believed was an imminent disaster so I stood on the other side of the case, lowering it backwards, inch by inch, step by step.

'Okay,' she said. 'And now, down now.'

'Now?'

'Now.'

She was trying to direct me, but I found that she was not moving in synchronicity with her instructions. Down a step, thud, and the object landed on my foot heavily, on the same spot on the same toe I had twice broken.

'Hang on,' I said. 'Not quite ready. Hang on.'

It was so hard to carry a harp case backwards down the stairs! It was so hard not to vocalise all the things I was saying to these women in my head; these women whose existence and needs had led me to this moment of peril. We must have been two-thirds of the way down by this point. I should have made sure that I was the forward-facing one, the one with vantage point and the purchase. And then, in a split second, the case slipped from Kelly's sweaty grip. The weight of it fell on me – I stepped back, lost my footing, my left ankle buckled. But my right foot, by some celestial intervention, stood fast. I held up the case with both hands and in that position, I must have resembled the man who held up the sky, sort of godlike, spectacular. I revelled in my moment of heroism – even if it was accidental. I was adding value by catching falling harps.

The marchioness trotted over to me and propped up the other end of the case. She turned and looked at me in a way I cannot articulate. She showed me all her teeth.

Chapter 24

Hand on heart, I had never seen anywhere quite as beautiful as Loch Tay. It must have been the captivating alchemy of water and mountain that stirred such emotion in me – the sheer sight of it provided respite from the chaos of the morning at the castle. It was reassuringly self-contained, no unknowable depths, no surprises.

The house was only an hour's journey in the car. It didn't feel to me like a far enough distance for a second home, but I still wasn't thinking like an aristocratic millionaire. I supposed the thing that was important was that the house was on the loch, and that was something that could not be attained at the castle, unless a loch were somehow manufactured or dug out.

I later discovered that the reason for leaving so early that morning, even though the event planned was a soirée, was that the marchioness had intended to stop somewhere on the way. She gave no other details. I couldn't understand the gratuitous secrecy, and it was beginning to frustrate me. It felt egotistical in its contrivance, even narcissistic. But the plan for the diversion, whatever it was, had to be shelved, because of the delays incurred back at the castle. We had to get to the loch house in time to let in and brief the catering staff.

I had navigated the journey well with the harp in the horse box. The marchioness said to take the Defender because it was a better vehicle for that type of travel, although it had occurred to me that the harp would have fitted perfectly well in the back of the car and that the stipulation of a horse box was another of her unchallenged foibles. I didn't know what state the harp would be in when we arrived at the house but, given the heft of the case it was in, and the knocks it had already taken that morning, I thought it would most likely be intact.

After my triumph in the hall earlier that morning, I had been left in considerable pain, so I had sat on the floor and tried to rest my foot while the marchioness (to my confusion) lavished her attention on Kelly, who, on releasing the harp from her grip, had somehow lost her balance and fallen backwards on the stairs. The marchioness was asking her repeatedly if she was okay, if she was *absolutely sure* she was okay. I regarded this as a disproportionate response. She seemed not to care how I was, which was viscerally wounding given that I was the one who had been on the receiving end of Kelly's magnificent blunder.

Then Mark appeared from nowhere and stood over us all. His corduroy trousers were muddy, as if he had been wading through a bog. He was confused by the scene. He held out his hand and I took it. He pulled me up. His hands were surprisingly clean given the state of his cords and they were much softer than I had expected them to be. His hands must have been where all the Molton Brown hand lotion had disappeared to because Kelly refused to use it owing to her contact dermatitis and the marchioness only ever went to the loo in her bedroom suite for reasons I didn't understand.

The marchioness insisted on calling a doctor to examine

Kelly, who told her not to, reassuring her that she was fine and would be 'right as rain after a cuppa and an éclair'. And then Mark told the marchioness to carry on with her plans and that he would arrange for the doctor to come if Kelly's predicament (whatever that was – I still didn't know what was wrong with her) worsened. I could tell that this was preferable to Kelly because she was transparently not enjoying the marchioness's fussing, her face having turned pink as a hydrangea, pink as Pepto Bismol, and I also felt that Mark wanted the marchioness gone.

'You saved the day,' the marchioness said to me later in the car. She was perching on her seat, so far forward that her nose practically grazed the windscreen. 'What was I thinking, letting Kelly bring the harp down the stairs? It's my harp. I should have done it.'

She had chosen to sit in the front with me – I have learned that the backs of Defenders are uncomfortable places.

'Thank you, sincerely. I don't know how I will repay you, but I will.'

'That's alright,' I said. It wasn't alright. I was driving on a sprained ankle, and the pain was searing. I was changing gears only when it was necessary, which made the gearbox screech and caused my passenger to wince. That brought me some comfort. I needed some Ibuprofen. Something even stronger would have been welcome. Like fentanyl.

'Would you like something for your foot?' the marchioness asked. 'I have a number of pills, you know, painkillers, at the loch house.'

'That would be great,' I said. 'Thank you.'

She sat back a bit, not all the way, and said, 'What use is a micro-pharmacy like mine if you cannot dispense its pleasures?'

And then, after a pause and a brief scan of the countryside beyond the window, she said, 'Do you know that "harp" means "pluck" in Old English?'

'I didn't,' I said.

'It's true. It's true. No word of a lie,' she said.

'You know a lot about words,' I said. 'Monster.'

'Pardon?'

'Monster,' I repeated. 'To show.'

'Yes, monster,' she said. 'What excellent recall you have. I like etymology. I like to know the origins of things.'

I gripped the steering wheel. I put my right foot down. The gear box howled.

'It helps to gain a better understanding if you know where something has come from,' she continued.

'Etymology,' I said. 'I wonder what the etymology of etymology is.'

The marchioness laughed uproariously and when her laughter petered out, she said, 'Do you think it's strange that I am not seeing my husband today?'

'I don't think that's any of my business,' I said.

'What we are doing here is kind of related – to my husband.' She looked down and fiddled with the diamonds on her tennis bracelet, one by one, as if they were prayer beads. 'I want to tell you a secret,' she said. 'You saved the day, so I can tell you a secret.'

'I don't know about that,' I said.

'You did, you did, you did.' She put her hand on my hand, held it there for a few seconds and then removed it, returning it to her lap. It felt odd to have another woman touch me like that and to have her sitting in the front with me. I couldn't get a sense of demarcation.

'Do you want to know why I don't drive?' she asked. 'You must have wondered. How I used to be a race car driver, how I love cars, but I don't drive. Have you stopped to think why that might be?'

'It's really none of my business,' I said. She was eyeballing me from behind the slick black wall of her fringe. 'I thought that perhaps your husband's accident had made you nervous about driving. That's understandable. Maybe in time you'll feel like driving again.'

And then I shut up, pressing my lips together. I was at risk of talking myself out of a job.

'A few months ago,' she began, 'David and I were at a dinner party. After the dinner we all went into the drawing room – is that what they call it? Drawing room?'

I said I thought so, yes, but that I wasn't much of a drawing-room person.

'We went there and there was this lady in the corner of the room who was doing fortune telling, you know, with the tarot cards. Have you ever tried that?'

'No,' I said.

We were driving along a very thin track of road on the lochside, and I was worried that the car would lose its grip and plunge us into the water, that gravity would stop working, or that the harp would come loose and run off down the steep bank. And it didn't seem like the right time to tell her that I had always been terrified of knowing my ending and would do everything I could to avoid it.

'It was my turn,' she continued. 'I was reluctant because I haven't done things like that and I don't believe in the occult and, you know, dark things. I suppose I am superstitious. I have suffered great sorrow in my life, and I think it's better not to dabble in case it unleashes past pain. But, I had had a few drinks by then and whatever else over dinner and I thought, okay, why not? I had nothing better to do and no one at the party was particularly interesting and I was quite curious, you know?'

'Sure,' I said.

'I sat down, and she held out the cards, and she started to tell me this and that: this card means this, this card means that, and it was fine, entertaining, but, you know, nothing exciting, and then she pulls out this card, the Death card, and her face changes and she gets very serious and looks at me like I have the plague. And then she says, "This card can also symbolise change, the death of an old life and the beginning of a new one, but I am sorry to say" – she said it just like this – "for you this is not the case. For you it means death. And, most specifically, death at the wheel of a car."'

She turned her entire body towards me. I could feel how desperately she needed a reaction from me so I gawped.

'Gosh,' I said.

'Right,' she said.

'And did you believe her?'

The marchioness shrugged. 'I asked her to explain it to me, and all she said was this: *and if you don't die at the wheel of the car, but happen to survive any accident, then you will be rendered hideous*.'

'Hideous?'

'Yes,' she said. 'Hideous.'

'It must be quite frightening to be told you will be hideous if you are beautiful.'

'Exactly,' she said. 'I suppose for some people this wouldn't be so much of a problem, because you can't lose what you never had.'

I was one of the 'some people' she was talking about.

'It's quite specific, isn't it? To be told that you will die at the wheel. And the hideous stuff. That sounds odd to me.'

'I realise that,' she said. 'Which is why, at first, I dismissed it as some light entertainment. A joke even. There was something funny about the hideous part at the time, something disarming.'

'Could it have been a metaphor? It could all be a metaphor. Don't these things have huge margins for interpretation?'

'That's what I thought.'

'So did you stop driving then, after you had heard that?'

'You know what? I asked David. I told him what this woman had said and he said "claptrap". Claptrap. He said she was only a prop, not a genuine person, and that his friend, the Earl of This and That, had hired her and she was just an actress and told me to forget it. And I thought, okay then, even though she looked so *real*. And I put it right out of my mind, and I was driving here, there and everywhere and I wasn't dying or being rendered hideous so I guessed my husband was right.'

We reached a junction. 'Which way?' I asked.

'You have to go down there. Turn left. The house is down there.'

I did as she said and turned left off the road into a smaller, narrower track that I could see led directly to the loch.

'And then, one day, it was a Thursday, we were supposed to be going to a charity gala in Edinburgh, but I couldn't go – I can't remember what the reason was, some medical thing – so David went on his own.' Her speech was stalling and stammering. 'The next thing I know,' she continued but slower, much, much slower this time, 'he is in the hospital in a coma. He is barely recognisable. And the worst thing is that it should have been me. I'm the one who should have suffered that day, not him. He is much more vital to the world than I will ever be. It's the injustice of it. I can see it; everyone can see it. *Everyone knows*. I know people see how unjust it was that it should have happened to him and not me.'

We pulled up to the house and a light turned on that illuminated it like a forgotten tomb. What I saw I had not expected.

'People?' I said.

She shrugged. 'People. They think I don't know what they're thinking. They think I'm stupid and ridiculous. I know exactly what is going on in their heads. They think, if only *she* had been driving that day, if only . . .'

'I don't see how you could have controlled the outcome,' I said, addressing the house ahead of me rather than my passenger. 'Accidents happen. I don't think anyone can predict them.'

I didn't believe a word I was saying. I was the most superstitious person in the world. I believed with every atom of my being that the fortune teller had been right about the whole thing.

She opened the tiny little bag that had been sitting obediently on her lap and took her phone out of it. On the screen was a picture of her husband. He was dressed like Peter O'Toole in *Lawrence of Arabia*. I wondered at first if it was for some fancy-dress thing but the more I understood of the man, the more unlikely that was. The marchioness ran her finger across the screen. She turned it off at the side.

'It was clearly meant to be me who was supposed to suffer that fate,' she said. 'And I do believe that fate is still coming for me. I need to know, and I need to know if my husband is going to survive. I don't know how I am meant to live without him.

He brought me back from the brink. From the abyss. Have you been to the abyss, Camilla? Have you ever been so far down to the bottom that you can't imagine ever crawling back up again? So far down that you are resigned to remain there.'

I calculated that it would be for the best to shake my head.

'I can't go back to the abyss. I need to know what is in my fate. I need to know.' She opened the passenger door and stepped out on the gravel. The spikes of her stilettos pierced the ground beneath. Usually, she would wait for me to let her out of the car. 'That's why I've asked the fortune teller to come tonight.'

Chapter 25

The marchioness was right. The harp was the perfect addition.

The house was magnificent – pitched directly over the loch so that you felt as if you were on a boat, but not moving, so there was no sense of motion, only calm. It was overlooked by a swell of tall mountains, dusted with snow. Scots pines shot up through the crevices and the light on the loch gave it the appearance of a windowpane – impossibly flat and broad – laid seductively on the ground, begging to be smashed.

It was a modern house, or rather it had once been an old house but had been converted to look like a new one with only the merest suggestions of its heritage – a brick or grey stone wall here and there – so that it appeared to belong to the loch, a harmony of entropy and progress. At the back of the house was one enormous sheet of glass, spanning all three floors, and it was topped with a concrete cantilevered roof that would have imposed a sense of brutality onto the building, were it not for water surrounding it and all it held in its reflection.

I wheeled the harp over to the window and then the marchioness adjusted it. She seemed certain about the angle of its position. I watched her at work, wishing that I had that kind of conviction. She clapped her hands together and she said, 'Perfect. It is like it has always been here. Like you.'

She smiled at me, her hands still suspended in the air. 'Let's have some champagne before the others come. I'm having a Beautiful Day.'

I didn't know who the others were, or how many there would be.

The marchioness drifted over to the bar in the open-plan living room, where a member of the catering staff, one of three who had earlier helped to carry the harp in from the car, was arranging glassware ahead of the arrival of the guests (the others were downstairs in the basement preparing canapés – solitary implications of food flecked with roe). I stood by the window, looking into the space. The feel of the house was so different from the grand castle rooms with their portraits and antiques, their icy resplendence.

The marchioness opened a fridge that was stocked with champagne. She pulled out a bottle, tilted and held it away from herself admiringly, as if having just produced a newborn from the birth canal. 'Do you like this one?'

'Yes,' I said. 'But I'm fine. I don't think I should drink if I'm driving. You know, if I'm on duty.'

'But we're not going anywhere now,' she said. 'We won't be leaving until tomorrow. Drink with me. I hate to drink alone. You're officially off duty.'

I was worried that if I did drink I would let out all of my secrets the instant the fizzy liquid touched my tongue, because that is what usually happened to me, so I resolved to take a glass and drink as little as possible, which went against every impulse I had.

In no time, I was relaxed, on my second glass of champagne

and had completely forgotten all my resolutions. I think I was more relaxed than usual because of the painkillers the marchioness had given me when we arrived at the house. I hadn't seen the packet they had come from, which was silly of me, but my foot was hurting so much that I took them regardless and they worked. The pain disappeared and I felt euphoric.

People arrived, perhaps ten or eleven in total, none of whom I'd met before. Not that that meant anything. I'd hardly known the marchioness long enough to understand the finer details of her social world. She introduced those people to me and what I remembered most vividly (although my recollections of that evening are vague) was that they were nondescript. This will sound odd, but there was a professional anonymity about them as if they were extras on a film set; polite, amenable, capable of making bland conversation, but, conspicuously, no one stuck out. The intention of this, I imagined, was to aggrandise the host, but I'm not sure that this effect was achieved and, if anything, there was a stiltedness about it that I didn't enjoy. I had another drink. And then another. That helped to diffuse the tension I felt, particularly when she started playing the harp. Don't get me wrong; she played it beautifully, but there was an insincerity, a fissure in her connection with the audience.

I had another drink. I should have eaten something – canapé trays sailed past me, occasionally stopping by, but I declined most of them because there was no getting away from all the fish eggs.

When the recital was over, the marchioness dismounted her instrument and headed towards the sofa, picking up a champagne flute from a waiter on the way. The person who had been sitting next to me shifted quickly, making space for her, and then milled robotically among the others, who were behaving most unnaturally, propped up stiffly against the bar in parodies of themselves.

I was ecstatic in my champagne haze, warm and cossetted. Thoughts were floating peaceably about in my mind like clouds: that of my distant child, safely ensconced in the cottage on the hill with my sister, that I was holding down a job of my own and living my life as an independent single mother with this most glamorous of employers with harps and loch houses and castles and off-duty champagne soirées. Other thoughts, those more distant, the ones I didn't like so much, kept themselves wondrously at bay.

Outside, darkness rubbed out the loch. The trees were cutouts of themselves, skeletal, occasionally shuddering. The marchioness drained her glass, turned to me and said, 'Tell me about yourself. Tell me something I don't know.'

I was ready for this moment, having rehearsed in my head a stock answer. 'Oh, I'm not sure there's much to say.'

She wasn't satisfied. 'That's not good enough,' she said. 'I know very little about you. I'm interested to know more.'

'Well, I was born in London.'

'Oh no, not that. Not the dreary stuff,' she slurred. 'Not that one bit.'

'Is there anything in particular you want to know?'

'Well,' she said. 'The obvious. Why on earth you are here – of all the places, of all the jobs. Why you are doing this. What you are running from.'

'Running?'

'Yes,' she said. 'You are running from something.'

'I'm not running from anything,' I said.

She was glaring. Her pupils were the blackest I had seen;

fronds of yellow radiated from her irises. On the coffee table in front of us was a bottle in an ice bucket. She took it, shook the water off and filled my coupe to the rim. The bubbles lurched at the precipice and then sloped back down inside the glass. Then she filled her own.

'Everyone is running from something,' she said. 'Whether they know it or not.'

'What are you running from?'

'What we are all running from. Running as fast as we can. Running as if our lives depended on it. Running, running always running from it.'

'What?'

'Well, death,' she said breathily. 'Death. Dying, ageing, decay.'

'I'm not running from death,' I said. 'At least I don't think I am.'

Husbands, I thought to myself. Husbands are a thing worth running away from, running away from husbands as if my life depended on it.

The marchioness cleared her throat and ran her finger around the rim of her glass. 'Then what,' she said, 'or whom are you running from?'

Just then the doorbell rang. The marchioness's head spun around. 'That's her,' she said.

•

There was no headscarf. No black tasseled shawl or heavy black eye make-up. Not at all what I had imagined. Or what I had seen on the television.

She must have been in her mid-fifties and said her name was Evelyn. I reckoned that she was from Newcastle or thereabouts, but, as you know, I'm hopeless with accents. She had cropped hair – the tips blonde. Purple eyeshadow on the upper lids and purple mascara. She wore a grey woollen dress and cowboy boots on her feet. She jarred with the sparkly monochrome of the party. Something about that felt intentional.

Over the course of the evening, the guests took turns with Evelyn. I watched from the comfort of the sofa, relieved that I did not have to participate. I wanted to see the expressions on the guests' faces when their fates were revealed to them, but Evelyn's table had been positioned at such an angle in that far corner of the room, and with only the feeble glow of the wall sconces to light it, that the teller and the told were indistinguishable.

I had assumed that I was safe, immune from this activity, when I noticed her waving at me. She was calling me over. I shook my head as if to say 'no, it's fine, I'm all right here'. I was worried that I wouldn't be able to get up off the sofa, if my legs would work after the quantity of champagne I had consumed.

The marchioness approached me and grabbed me by the arm. I had imagined that she would be weak, given the slightness of her frame, but it turned out that she was alarmingly strong. I got up and felt a tingle in my foot.

Evelyn pointed at the seat opposite and said, 'Sit down, pet.'

I sat. The marchioness was hovering behind me, her hand on the back of the chair. I turned around to look at her. She was watching Evelyn shuffling her cards, laying them out. I wanted her to go. My heart was beating so loudly I thought she might hear it.

One of the catering staff set a mug on the table.

'Are you sure I can't get you anything stronger, Evelyn?' the marchioness said. 'A glass of champagne?'

'I never drink during a reading,' she said. 'It clouds the judgement.'

The marchioness nodded approvingly.

'Do you mind?' Evelyn asked.

'Excuse me?' the marchioness replied.

'I do my readings privately. No spectators.'

'Oh,' the marchioness said. She looked crestfallen. She moved away from us, over to the bar.

I turned to face her. I saw only the back of her head yet sensed she was straining to hear because she was motionless, rigid, visibly disengaged from everything around her.

'Have you set your intention?' Evelyn asked.

'Intention?'

'What you want to achieve from this.'

'To be honest,' I said. 'I'm a little tired. I hurt my foot earlier and I think I could just do with a lie down. I don't really want to do this. It's my boss's idea.'

'She's your boss?'

I nodded.

'I see,' said Evelyn.

'Why don't you do her first?' I suggested.

'Later,' she said. 'I'll do her later. She wants you to go first. But if you have no intention, I could do a general reading. The three-card spread. It's the fastest.'

'Okay.'

'I am just going to cleanse the deck.'

'Is that necessary?'

Evelyn said yes and sat with the deck in her hands and took a deep breath and then exhaled over the cards. When she breathed out, I was hit with the acrid huff of stale cigarette smoke on her breath. She did this a few times before shuffling the deck. Then she cut it, separating it into three piles. She pulled a card from each pile until there were three in front of me.

'The Fool,' Evelyn said.

'Oh dear,' I replied.

'Don't worry. It's not what you think. It doesn't mean that you are a fool.'

'That's a relief,' I said.

'Yes, it means new beginnings, taking a leap of faith. The Fool card is a good card; it means innocence and a fresh start. You are a person who is willing to take risks, but it can also mean that there are new opportunities on the horizon for you that are exciting.'

Evelyn gave a winsome smile. Her teeth were yellow, grey in the cracks.

'It's a good one,' she said.

I nodded. One down.

She turned over the next card. 'Ah, interesting,' Evelyn said. 'The High Priestess.'

'Sounds promising,' I said. I was beginning to relax now. I could see that Evelyn had nothing on me. She was certainly a charlatan. If I could keep my mouth shut, I would be able to get out of this unscathed. 'What does it mean?'

'I'm just about to tell you,' Evelyn said, taking a swig of her tea. She put her palm over the card and said, 'This card represents intuition, mystery and the power of the unconscious mind. It is mostly associated with secrecy.'

'Secrecy?' I asked, my skin suddenly prickling. I looked around, making sure no one had heard.

'Hmm,' Evelyn said. 'Yes. It is to do with inner thoughts and feelings. Do you trust your intuition? I'm sorry, I've forgotten to ask your name.'

'If you're psychic, shouldn't you know that?' I quipped.

Evelyn looked at me stone-faced, appalled. 'I'm not a psychic. I just read what is on the cards.'

'It's Emma. No!' I shouted. 'Camilla! My name is Camilla.'

'Camilla,' Evelyn said, her eyes narrowing to the thinnest slits, 'this card indicates that you should trust your intuition and listen to your inner voice when making decisions. Are you a decision maker? Or do you find it hard to trust your own judgement? To take control of your life?'

'I haven't really thought about that,' I said. 'But, yes, I think I do.'

'What this card is telling me is that you need to do that more. Have more faith in yourself, listen to what your intuition is telling you.'

My intuition was telling me to get away from Evelyn.

'There is one other thing,' Evelyn said. 'There is an alternative reading to this one, which is that you should be aware of hidden influences or information that is affecting your situation. There could be hidden information that needs to be uncovered or acknowledged in order to fully understand a situation.'

She sounded as if she was reading from a textbook. And then I thought that, instead of being a chauffeur, I could be a fortune teller instead, just like Evelyn. There seemed to be nothing to it. I could clean up.

'Maybe that's got something to do with my internet banking,' I said, proud of my improvisational skills. 'I still can't access it.'

Evelyn looked at me nonplussed and then turned over the final card. I was relieved. It was not the Death card.

'The Tower.'

I looked closer at the card. On it was a picture of a tower in flames with plumes of smoke snaking out of it and bodies falling from the battlements.

'Oh. That doesn't look good.'

Evelyn's expression changed. She was losing her poise.

'What's wrong?' I asked. 'I thought Death was the bad one.'

'I'm afraid it's definitely not good,' Evelyn said, taking a deep breath. 'Chaos. Destruction. There is a signal here of unexpected and dramatic change, brought about by external forces or circumstances. You should be prepared for upheaval and chaos. Or it might mean you are currently going through a difficult and chaotic period. You must be aware of the potential for destruction and take steps to protect yourself.'

My mouth dried up. My lips clung to my gums. I couldn't draw them over my teeth. 'Protect myself?'

Evelyn nodded.

At that moment, the marchioness ran over to me, phone in hand, and said, 'Mark just called. He's saying the cottage is on fire.'

Chapter 26

Hannah and the baby were not there. They were nowhere.

I had received no calls from her on my phone, and I had been checking on it regularly throughout the evening at the loch house. There had been no reason for me to worry. That's what I had thought.

But now I was calling Hannah frantically, over and over again from the back of the car. Her phone was ringing and ringing, going through to her message service.

'My baby,' I screamed. 'My baby and my sister are in the cottage and she's not picking up. I can't get through. Is Mark there? Can I speak to Mark?'

After Mark's call, we raced to the estate. I was over the limit and naturally the marchioness refused to drive, so Evelyn took us in her Nissan Qashqai.

The marchioness was fumbling about on her phone, attempting to call Mark, saying all the while, 'Baby? Sister? Baby? In the cottage?'

I was so wracked with terror that I had forgotten all about the secrets I had been guarding. They came out, unremittingly. None of it mattered now.

'Hurry!' I screamed. 'They are all I have. They are my whole world.'

Then the phone was handed to me and Mark was on the other end. He was saying things to me like 'the firefighters are here', 'they are putting out the fire', 'there doesn't appear to be anyone here' and 'are you sure?' and 'are you certain?' and I had to say, 'They are in there. Find them. My sister is there. And my baby. My baby will be upstairs in the bed. Please, I'm begging you. Please look.'

I could not contain what was happening in my head. I could not be in my head for one moment more. I wanted so much to get out of my head that I thought getting out of the car would help. I could throw myself out of it and into the road and hobble back on my own. I should never have left them alone in that cottage not knowing who or what was out there. I had failed to protect them.

The Qashqai crawled up the hill to the cottage, its tyres hitting every rock and boulder along the track. I am sorry to say that a number of those hapless grouse lost their lives in our haste to reach the summit of the hill on which the cottage stood. I flung the door open, nearly falling out of the car, and staggered over to where a cluster of the firefighters stood. There appeared to be a man in a chief-type function, with his elbow wrapped around his helmet and he was saying to Mark, 'Most likely it's a plugged-in hairdryer. If I had a penny for every fire that was started by a hairdryer–'

'My baby and my sister are in there!' I screamed. 'Get them out.'

'Madam,' the chief said. 'Madam, I would ask you to calm down. It is clear you are under the influence of something. But I would urge you to take a deep breath.'

I told him I couldn't do that until I knew that my baby and my sister were safe.

'The cottage is empty,' he said. 'There are no casualties. We know what we are doing. The first thing we do is check for people and there are no people here.'

The marchioness appeared, having struggled to eject herself from the car. She teetered on the grass in her stilettos, soon opting to remove them altogether to prevent herself from getting stuck in the mud. She swayed, watching the cottage and the smoke billowing out from the central tower. It looked just like the image on the tarot card.

'What happened?' she asked. 'What on earth happened?'

The chief firefighter with the helmet under his elbow relayed his hairdryer hypothesis.

'But we had all the electrics checked during the refurbishment. We had the building inspector come and it was all passed.'

'Who are you, madam?' the firefighter asked, as if she were a tourist wandering cluelessly into the carnage.

'I am the owner,' she said.

He looked at Mark, and Mark nodded.

'Who called you?' she asked. 'Who raised the alert?'

'That's the thing, madam. We don't know. The call came through anonymously. And it would have had to because there are no other properties for miles around. If we hadn't had the warning, the place would have been razed to the ground.'

'Impossible,' she said. 'It's made of stone. That can't happen to stone, surely. Can it?'

It appeared that the chief thought better of engaging with the marchioness on the physics of fires because he turned to me and said, 'Have you got anywhere to stay tonight?'

I was confused, rattled. Accommodation was the last thing on my mind. I said, 'I have to find my family.'

Mark said, 'You can stay with me.'

The marchioness turned to me and said, 'Why didn't you tell us you had a baby?'

She was barely comprehensible; she was mangling her words. There was a chance that she'd forget all of this in the morning.

'Perhaps this is something that should be discussed tomorrow,' Mark said.

I knew he was talking, but I couldn't hear what he was saying. I couldn't compute any of it. I kept dialling Hannah's number. I could see on my recent calls list that I had tried calling her 103 times. The calls were now going through to voicemail and were not even ringing. Something was terribly wrong.

'It's late,' the marchioness said. She yawned and wobbled. She had to steady herself. Reflexively, she grabbed hold of Mark. She must have had more to drink than I had because she seemed not to be able to absorb the gravity of my plight. 'It's very late. It's been a strange evening. My cottage has no roof. It had a roof this morning and now it has not. I need to get back to the castle. I am feeling wildly off colour. Mark, will you take me?'

Mark propped her up. He looked around himself apologetically at all the people who had gathered in the garden before the blaze, the chief of the fire brigade, the other firefighters and me. 'I'm not sure I can leave yet,' he said, smiling awkwardly at the chief. 'I'm not sure when I'll be able to leave. But could your friend not take you? The person who brought you here.'

'Evelyn?' the marchioness asked. 'I sent her home. You know she charges by the hour.'

On hearing this, the chief raised his eyebrows. He turned to Mark and said, 'You can go, Mr Young. I can see no reason for you to stay. The fire is extinguished, and we can deal with any paperwork in the morning. I can see you have your hands full.' He aimed his big yellow helmet at the marchioness.

'Right,' Mark said, gruffly, so gruffly. 'Of course. We'd better let the firefighters finish up here. I think it best you come with us, Camilla. And then after that you can stay in the spare room in my cottage. It's on the estate not far from the castle.'

The marchioness's head swivelled towards me, like a melon on a pin. I wondered how someone so expressive could still be so inscrutable.

Chapter 27

We were in Mark's kitchen and I was on the phone to the police. I was on hold.

'Where do you think they could have gone?' Mark said.

I could not understand the change in his approach to me – the reason for his kindness and hospitality. I had expected him to be gleeful, having at last found cause to get rid of me. If I hadn't been so disturbed by events, I would have been suspicious.

'I have no idea,' I said. 'It makes no sense. When I left this morning, everything seemed fine. I had no reason to be worried.'

Then I remembered the note and, after weighing things up in my mind, I decided that I would tell him about it because I saw that I had nothing to lose.

'There was a note posted through my door a week or so ago. I don't know who sent it.'

'What did it say?' he asked.

'It said: *I know about the baby.*'

'Do you still have it?'

'No. Kelly got rid of it.'

'Kelly? Kelly knew about this?'

'Yes. I told her the day after I'd received it.'

'And she got rid of it?'

I nodded.

'Why?'

The police came back on the line. They told me that they had tried to call Hannah, but that her phone went straight to voicemail.

'Is there any chance her phone isn't turned on?' the officer asked.

And then I recalled telling her to turn it off when I thought she was being followed by the private investigator, but I couldn't disclose that for fear of revealing my circumstances.

The officer told me that they would send a car out to drive around the area. That if Hannah was on foot, she couldn't have got far. I told them that if Hannah was anything, it was not on foot. That didn't go down well; the officer hung up.

Mark went over to the sideboard, a stout farmhouse-style edifice on which he had displayed his crockery, including the most sublime collection of blue and gold bone china. He removed two cups and saucers and placed them gently down on the oak worktop. He turned the kettle on and while it boiled took out a bottle of milk from the fridge, poured it into a little blue jug, removed a bowl of sugar from the shelf and set it down on the table.

'This will see you right.'

He was exacting in the procedure, applying a sense of devotion to it. His hands were big, the china diminutive. It was a curious spectacle, oddly riveting. I had never seen a man make tea with such a sense of theatre; James used to pour milk into his mug straight from the carton, then dig the sugar out of the bag, afterwards stabbing the wet spoon back into it and causing the granules to clump and the paper to disintegrate.

'The marquess gave me this set on my fifth anniversary of working for him,' he said, running a finger across the rim of a saucer. 'It was a gift, given to him by a monastery that he had once helped when he was a student and had been travelling around Nepal. He never told me how he had helped, what it was he had done for them, and I didn't ask. I knew not to because the marquess didn't talk about things like that, the good things he had done. At first, I kept it under lock and key in a cupboard upstairs. It was so precious to me. I'd never owned anything so beautiful in my life. But he came over one day – he used to do that, pop in for tea – and he asked me if I ever used the set he gave me. I told him it was far too precious, too special for that, but he insisted that I use it. He said that it was both useful and beautiful and it would enhance my life every day. He was right.'

The kettle boiled and Mark poured a little water into the teapot, swirling it around its china walls and then, having assessed with the back of his hand that the pot was adequately warm, emptied it before dropping in a couple of bags followed by a steaming stream of water.

After a while of waiting for it to brew, watching the water turn brown, swirling a spoon around in the pot, and me watching as he watched the water, he brought the pot over to the table and poured the tea into the cups. The spout was a good distance from them and the water ran like a waterfall, trickling hotly. I felt comfortable, so comfortable, I thought that I'd like to watch him make me tea again.

'I suppose it explains a lot,' he said.

'What do you mean?'

'I mean, your behaviour. I found you to be a jumpy person, nervy, and I wondered what it was. I thought it was a London thing. Now I know. I suppose it must have been hard to keep the baby a secret.'

'Yes, it has been,' I said. I sipped. The tea was hot and strong. Mark was right; it was seeing me right.

'I have to warn you,' he said. 'I'm not sure the marchioness is going to be particularly sympathetic to this.'

'Sympathetic to what?'

'To your having a baby.'

'Well, currently I don't have a baby.'

Mark laid his cup down into its saucer, warming the tips of his fingers against the sides. It was a cold night. And he had been standing out in it, watching the cottage burn. It was the coldest night yet.

'You must be exhausted,' he said. 'Let me show you the spare room. Go and lie down, even for a little while. You should rest. Keep your phone on loud.'

He got up from the kitchen table and walked up the stairs to the first floor. I followed. I was so tired. My champagne haze had faded and had given way to a low-grade headache. He bent his arm around the door and turned the light on. The room was beautiful. Twin beds with blue Toile de Jouy wallpaper on the wall and headboards. Crisp white linen with plump cushions. A basin in the corner with a bright white towel wrapped over the rail.

'This is lovely,' I said.

'It used to be my daughter's room. The marchioness decorated it.'

'I didn't know you have children.'

'Had,' he said. 'I had a daughter.'

Chapter 28

It turns out that Hannah had left burning the scented candle that she had salvaged from my London flat when she went out in a taxi with the baby to the shop in Grandtully to get more formula because she had accidentally spilt the container I had left her all over the kitchen floor. By the time she returned, after having dinner in the village pub, the baby napping in the car seat beside her, and having acquainted herself with the owners, a couple recently moved up from London, the cottage was a smoking wreck with only one or two firefighters left to impart to her the bad news.

I had fallen asleep in Mark's spare bedroom but woke up two hours later in a disembodying panic.

There were dozens of missed calls from Hannah on my phone. I seized it, my eyes wide and pulsing in its stark glow against the pitched blackness of the bedroom. I had to close my funny eye. I was one-eyed, glaring at the screen. It was so dark there. The Scottish countryside must be the darkest place in the world at night, almost as dark as the very bottom of the sea.

'Hannah!' I shouted. 'Hannah! Where are you?'

She told me that she and the baby were in the police station in Pitlochry and the baby was hungry and ratty because she still hadn't managed to feed it since her expedition to buy more formula.

'I've got the formula,' she said. 'But I don't have the bottle or the sterilised water. I'm a bit stuck.'

'You burned the house down,' I said.

'Yes,' she said. 'Absolute disaster.'

'We don't have anywhere to live now, Hannah.'

'I'm so sorry, Em. Look on the bright side: at least I've exorcised the ghosts.'

Mark knocked at the bedroom door and entered. 'Are you okay? Is that your sister?'

I nodded. I still had the phone to my ear.

'Where is she?'

'Pitlochry. In the police station.'

'Tell her to speak to Malcolm,' he said. 'Malcolm Stewart. Say Mark Young says to bring her back to the Gamekeeper's Cottage on the estate. There are some pheasant in it for him.'

I did as he told me and relayed that message to Hannah. She told me that she would call me back as soon as she knew what the plan was vis-à-vis Malcolm and the free fowl.

•

It was now 2 a.m. Hannah and the baby were on their way to the cottage. Malcolm Stewart clearly liked his pheasant. Mark was sitting with me in his living room while I waited for them to arrive.

'Would you like some more tea?' he asked.

'No, thank you,' I said.

He sat back in his armchair and crossed his legs. He closed his eyes.

'Thank you,' I said. 'Thanks again. I really can't thank you enough. You have been so kind.'

'No problem,' he said, narrowly opening his eyes and smiling.

I looked at the time on my phone. It was 2.02 a.m. I kept watch at the window for any sign of a car. I could not imagine what sort of state the baby would be in, having been up all night.

'Can I ask,' he said, 'what's going on?'

'What do you mean?'

'All the secrecy, you know. I still haven't seen your ID. What you said about leaving it on the train. Or it being stolen. Whatever it was, it's not true, is it?'

I shook my head. 'No,' I said. 'I didn't bring it with me. I left it in London. I had to leave quickly. I just didn't have time to get it.'

'Why didn't you tell me that?'

'Because you were adamant about having it,' I said. 'I didn't want to give you a reason to turn me away. It seemed at the time that it wouldn't take much for you to tell me to, you know, just turn around and go home.'

'You're right,' he said. 'I probably would have. It's better in those sorts of situations to just call it rather than waste everyone's time. The other thing is that it can be a hassle taking on new people and, if I'm honest, I'm jaded by it. We've had people come to work here and they either love it or hate it. Well, mainly they hate it. They leave pretty much as soon as they arrive. They don't like how isolated it is up here. They don't like the cottage. They find the marchioness demanding.'

'But you and Kelly have been here for ages. There must be a reason you've stayed so long.'

'We have our reasons.'

'What about the marquess? All I hear is what an amazing man he is.'

'But he's away a lot,' Mark explained. 'He's a very busy man. Or was, at least. Running the castle is the marchioness's job. And mine. And Kelly's.'

He battled with the last word.

'I suppose it's all academic now, the ID stuff,' I said. 'I think I've probably run out of lives.'

Mark didn't say anything. I supposed there was nothing to say.

'Your daughter,' I said. 'What happened?'

Mark looked down at his hands. He was pulling his skin away from the edge of his thumbnail using his other thumb. Mum used to do that. She used to do that all the time and I had to tell her to stop. I had to stop myself from telling Mark to stop.

'I'd rather not talk about it if that's okay,' he said.

'No problem,' I said.

A beam shone through the living-room window. A car pulled up. I ran to the front door and I let my baby and my sister into the cottage and I held them for the longest time.

Chapter 29

'The thing is,' said the marchioness, standing in the hall in a twinset that I assumed was Chanel, with no shoes on, just tights, 'is that if I were to lose you now, I would have no housekeeper and no driver. I would have no one. Well, no one except Mark.'

I wasn't sure what to say; if it was better to keep my mouth shut and listen or to fight to keep my place.

'Hmm,' she said ponderously.

'How is Kelly?' I asked.

'Kelly is taking a leave of absence,' the marchioness replied abruptly. I got the impression that I was infringing some jurisdiction just by asking. 'Her fall on the stairs was more serious than we thought. She is out of action for the foreseeable future. She's going to stay with her parents in Hampshire. I'll have to find cover for her.'

'I could arrange that for you if you like,' I offered. 'You use that magazine, don't you? *The Lady of the House*.'

The marchioness tapped the buttons on her jacket. It was the most pleasing sound, the collision of pearl and shellac. 'I feel conflicted,' she said, ignoring my offer. 'Because on the one hand you lied to me, to all of us in fact, and omitted a vital piece of information, knowing full well that it went counter to my stipulation about requiring my staff not to have dependents.'

'Dependents?'

'Yes.'

'And on the other hand?'

'On the other hand, you burnt down my cottage.'

'I would have thought that that would have been on the same hand,' I said stupidly, mindlessly. 'I'm so sorry but I can assure you it was an accident. I really don't know how it happened because my sister is usually so careful, so cautious. She's the clever one.'

'I thought we had a connection,' the marchioness continued. 'I thought we had an understanding and I thought you could be someone I could come to rely on. Yesterday, with the harp, you really stepped up, quite literally. '

'That could be a thing for the other hand,' I suggested.

Just then, Mark came through the door. The wind blew it shut behind him.

'I've just finished up with the police,' he said. 'It looks like it wasn't the candle after all. It may have been burning, yes, but they seem to think it's somehow foul play because the fire didn't start in the living room where the candle was. It seems to have started in the kitchen. They're not sure what caused it; they don't think it is any of the appliances. They're not ruling out arson.'

'Arson?' gasped the marchioness, pressing a palm against her chest.

'Yes,' Mark said. 'Arson. And they're saying that the biggest issue with arson is that any evidence is usually destroyed by the actual fire so it's almost always impossible to prove.'

'So it wasn't the candle?' I said.

'Doesn't look like it,' he said.

Mark was much stiffer in her presence, I noticed. Knowing him better, I felt his response to her was the work of something that went beyond formality, but I could not put my finger on it. The marchioness adjusted her stance. I could see that she was telling herself something in her head because she had that curious look about her that I had come to recognise as thought.

'Who on earth would want to burn the cottage down?' she asked.

Mark shrugged. 'There was one more thing. The police said that whoever raised the alert was a man saying that the cottage was on fire, and he had seen it because he had been driving past at the time. He spoke with an English accent, by all accounts. But the thing is that you can't see the cottage from the road, even in the daytime. And I noticed that when I went this morning there was a car parked in the lay-by opposite the entrance to the drive.'

'What kind of car?' I asked.

'I'm not sure. It was a small silver hatchback. Nothing remarkable really. But it struck me as odd because you never just see cars parked like that around here.'

'Was there anyone in it?' I asked.

'Not that I could see,' he said.

'So what happens now?' asked the marchioness.

'I'm not sure,' Mark replied. 'Continue their investigations, I imagine. And they mentioned something about insurance. You'll need to speak to the insurers.'

'Can you not speak to them?' the marchioness asked. 'I just don't know how to deal with that stuff. You're the estate manager. You should manage it.'

Mark flared his nostrils.

The marchioness turned to me and said, 'David used to do all that stuff. He used to organise it all. I don't know what's happening. It all seems to be unravelling. Everything seems to be falling apart.'

I cleared my throat and addressed the marchioness: 'I'd understand if you would like me to leave. I'm sorry that I've let you down. Sadly, I just didn't have a choice. I'm sorry that it's ended this way.'

The marchioness nodded and looked down at the floor with a sheepishness that did not become her. I turned to go, casting my eyes once more across the baronial entrance hall, knowing it was a place I would never see again.

I caught sight of Mark on my way out and he offered a consolatory smile. Then he said, 'The police want to talk to you about the fire. It's just a formality. To see if you'd seen anything suspicious in the days leading up to it.'

•

It was a short walk back to Mark's cottage from the castle. Hannah would be there waiting for me with the baby when I arrived. I had no idea what I would tell her and what we would do next. Mark had earlier offered that we could stay at the cottage for a few nights, should the marchioness decide to let me go, but, even though I was heartened by his hospitality, it didn't feel right to stay on. His life on the estate was continuing and mine was ending and I knew I would feel defeated.

I walked back with an acute sense of finality. I hadn't yet had a chance to see the grounds of the estate, but now, without a job to return to, I tried to take in as much as I could of the place, as hard as it was to be appreciative of its beauty at such a distressing time.

The route to the cottage started at the back of the castle and passed the walled garden, which, according to Kelly, was opened to the public during the summer months. I peered through the cast iron gates and looked inside. It was a paradise, a sprawling wonderland with fountains and statues, a small loch, little enclosures blooming with hellebores and winter jasmine. There was a cottage at one end, and I wondered who, if anyone, inhabited it. I broke away from the gate, having lingered long enough. From there, I went on, further across the lawns, beyond which was a spray of red and yellow in the woods, a full declaration of autumn.

It was a damp morning; the sky was peat-grey, nearing pink, 'Elephant's Breath'. The ground underfoot gave off an earthy scent of mud and rain. My Converse were taking the brunt of it; they'd never recover from this walk. I envied Mark his commute home through the woods each day. But as I walked, I was aware of a rustling sound behind me. I had that feeling I used to get if I was walking home at night from the Tube in London. My heart was beating very hard. I had nothing on me to protect myself from whoever was behind me; no keys to form a stabbing implement, no panic alarm. I was completely vulnerable. I walked faster and faster, soon breaking into a jog. My shoes were squelching in the mud. I did not look back. The rustling sound continued behind me.

I had no idea where I was. Mark had told me to follow the track for a half-mile and I would find the cottage at the end of it but there was no cottage. I took my phone out of my pocket and saw that there was no service. I kept going, but soon the track narrowed and the trees overhead drew in on me until the light dwindled. I turned around. The rustling sound had stopped. Whoever or whatever had been following me had ceased its pursuit.

My heart rate returned to a more moderate pace and I could see that probably no one had been following me, that it was an animal of some sort: a stag or even a giant squirrel, the type that the marchioness reported had laid claim to the castle attic. It was just my paranoia making me think that had been the case. And eventually I realised that I had taken the wrong track from the start. Mark hadn't sent me in the wrong direction. Once I had retraced my steps, I could see that there had been another path all along, one that I would have been able to follow had I not been so distracted by my dismissal.

In the daylight, the cottage was particularly quaint – a squat white building, with a central cylindrical part that looked like a new loo roll and two symmetrical wings on either side, two smaller loo rolls. The symmetry gave it an aesthetic appeal as did the whiteness of the paintwork and I thought how my burned-down cottage would have benefited from a similar treatment. There were two storeys and a little path that ran around the outside of the property. It was lower down, so the view onto the valley was not as magnificent as it was from on top of the hill, but you could still see the winding of the river, and it brought a sense of calm in the way that only flowing water can. The cottage stood in the shade of an oak tree, broad and avuncular, its acorns strewn across the ground all around it and they crunched beneath my feet. I couldn't put my finger on why it felt nostalgic there. I could see that the neatly clipped topiary that surrounded the cottage had been the work of Mark's hands because it was so precise, so exact.

I wondered if he ever got lonely there.

Approaching it, I noticed that Hannah was standing in the window, waving at me and pointing to the landline phone that she had pressed against her ear. She then beckoned me frantically with her hands.

'It's the marchioness,' Hannah whispered to me as I entered the cottage, extravagantly mouthing the words. 'Here, quickly.' She passed me the phone.

'Camilla,' said the voice at the end of the line. 'Camilla, I need you to take me to see my husband. It's urgent.'

'But I thought you didn't want me to work for you anymore,' I said. 'I thought you wanted me to leave.'

'Please, I need you to take me to see my husband,' she said. 'How long will it take you to get here?'

'If I run back now,' I said, examining the damage to my sodden trainers, 'about ten minutes.'

'Okay,' she said. 'I'll be waiting for you.'

I put the phone down. I couldn't understand why she wanted me to take her instead of Mark.

'What's happening?' Hannah asked. She was standing by the draining board, drying one of Mark's special cups with a tea towel. She had no idea what she held in her hand.

'She wants me to take her to the hospital,' I said. 'Will you be okay here for a few hours?'

'Sure,' Hannah said. 'Mark's so nice. So attentive. How come you never told me about him?'

She went over to the dresser and restored the cup to its shelf, positioning the handle to match the others. She flung the tea towel over her shoulder.

'If the police call or come round,' I said, 'tell them I'm out at the hospital but will be back very soon.'

'The police?' Hannah asked, panicked.

'They have some questions about the fire. Don't tell them anything. Not my name, nothing.'

'Okay. I'm not sure how that will work but okay.'

'Just don't pick up the phone and hide if you see them coming.'

The baby was sitting on the carpet in the living room, playing with Mark's Tupperware that Hannah had deployed as toy substitutes. I went to the baby and kissed it on the forehead. The baby smiled at me. We locked eyes and I could not break my gaze away. I tried to imagine the alternate reality where the baby was not sitting there, was not happily chewing on plastic, was not putting box into box into box, was not smiling back at me, where the baby had not returned the night before, had not spent the evening in the pub in Grandtully with my sister. I could not picture it. My mind wouldn't let me.

I was more determined than ever to make life as good as I possibly could for us. I ran out of the cottage all the way back to the castle. I did not get lost.

Chapter 30

'Come up with me,' the marchioness said. 'Come up to the room with me.'

We were in the hospital car park and I had successfully parked the Volvo in a nice, spacious spot overlooking the grassy patch with the thing that looked like a crop circle. Driving that car was like mooring a ship, though I have never attempted to do so. I followed her through the revolving doors of the main entrance and up to the Intensive Care Unit, where the marquess had been installed in one of its side rooms.

The marchioness went in first and walked over to his bedside, taking his hand in hers. It was limp and pallid. Tubes were attached to his face, to his mouth and nose, and he was breathing through a ventilator, the rhythm of which was soporific, oddly calming, as was the steady beep of his heart monitor. It read 85, occasionally rising to 87.

For a man with a titanic reputation, the marquess was surprisingly small. I suppose that is often the case when myth meets reality. He was small and fragile, diminutive.

'You can come in,' she said. 'Sit on the chair over there.'

She pointed to the chair in the corner of the room with a high back, the imitation leather of the covering cracked.

'This might be your only chance to meet him,' she said. 'They called me this morning. They said that he had suffered a major brain haemorrhage in the night. The damage to his brain is irreversible, extensive. They want me to turn off his life support. They are saying he will have no life now. His life is technically over.'

'I'm so sorry. Please, let me leave you alone with him.'

'Please,' she said. 'Sit.'

I sat down. She walked over to the monitor and studied it for a moment. And then she turned to me and said, 'Have you ever been married?'

'Yes,' I said.

'Well, then, you will understand what I mean when I say that a husband can be either a jailer or a liberator. An anchor or a weight.'

'I do.'

'And you will also understand what I mean when I say that you can be your own jailer or your own liberator.'

I understood.

'We find ourselves in situations we don't like and we often blame other people for putting us there. But most of the time, we have made those decisions ourselves, and if we don't like the position we find ourselves in, then it is our responsibility to get ourselves out of it. Even if it feels like the most impossible thing in the world. Even if we find ways to tolerate the intolerable.'

She sat down on the chair next to the marquess, holding his hand all the while. 'My first husband was a jailer,' she said. 'I don't mean that literally. I don't mean that he locked me up in a room with a key and that kind of thing. I mean it in a figurative sense. He was smart. Very smart. Not as smart as David, but that kind of wicked smart where he was always three steps ahead and the problem was that my brain does not work like that. If anything, I was always five steps behind. Perhaps one of the stupidest things a woman can do is marry someone smarter than her.'

'Do you really believe that?' I asked, trying to make sense of her perplexing mathematics.

'I do,' she said. 'Because some men will use their smarts for good and some will use their smarts for bad, and I have experienced both, and what I will say is that the good is good but the bad – the bad will kill you.'

'Women do it too,' I said, thinking of Old Hairy.

'Oh yes, of course, of course,' she said. 'But we are not talking about women, are we?'

'No,' I said.

'Because what I suspect,' she said, 'is that you are married to a jailer and you have recently freed yourself. That is why I have sympathy because I did the same and I am sorry that it took some time for me to see, for the penny to drop as the saying goes. I have reflected on it.'

There was a knock at the door and a nurse appeared. 'How are we today?' she said.

'We are fine,' the marchioness said. 'Well, in truth, not fine. Not fine one bit.'

The nurse tilted her head to one side and looked at the marquess. She scanned the monitor and made a note of the stats. Everything was eerily calm, which surprised me, given the seriousness of the marquess's condition. 'I'll be in soon to do his bloods. The doctor won't be long,' she said.

'Thank you,' said the marchioness.

The nurse left the room.

Once she had gone, the marchioness said, 'This is the end. We are here.'

'Let me leave you with him,' I said. 'I really think it's for the best.'

'No,' she said. 'I don't want to be alone.'

And then the doctor came in, and I thought how quickly it was that he had come. It must have been because her husband was on the brink of death.

'So, good news, Mrs . . .' he said, scanning his iPad for a name. I thought she might correct him on her title. I was surprised that she didn't.

The marchioness looked up from her husband, startled. 'Good news?'

'Yes,' the doctor said. 'Good news.'

'Good news?' the marchioness repeated.

'Yes,' he repeated. 'Good news.'

'I don't understand,' she said. 'I got a call this morning telling me to come in because he had a brain haemorrhage in the night and that he wouldn't make it.'

The doctor looked down at his notes. He shook his head. 'No. Quite the opposite. We are seeing some positive improvement in his brain activity.'

'Then what about the call? Why was I told something entirely different?'

At that moment, there was some movement on the marquess's face, some motion around his eyelids, as if they were being prised open by an invisible force. The marchioness stepped back in disbelief. She lost her footing and had to steady herself on her husband's IV stand.

I wanted to say what joyous news it was. I wanted to participate in the moment of rapture, but something was stopping me – mainly the marchioness's own reaction, which fell short of my expectations.

'It must have been some sort of error,' the doctor said. 'And if that is the case, I am very sorry indeed. That really is an unacceptable failing on our part. I will of course investigate.'

'Thank you,' the marchioness said. She was distracted, fogged.

The marquess closed his eyes again.

'It will be a bit like that,' the doctor said. 'He will drift in and out of consciousness for a while. It's normal. Totally to be expected. But you will find that the general trend is one of improvement.'

'Right,' said the marchioness. She sat down on the chair next to the bed and took his hand. She stroked it. She smiled, her mouth hitching at the edges. 'That's wonderful. I can't believe it.'

The doctor smiled and then looked at me quizzically. 'Is your eye okay?'

'Pardon?'

'Your eye. Your right eye. It's quite red. Does it hurt? Looks like a burst blood vessel.'

I stood up to find a mirror but there was no mirror. I could not imagine how I must have looked. I supposed that if the doctor had noticed my funny eye from across the other side of the room and had regarded it as worthy of comment, then it must have been a non-trivial issue. Naturally, I began to panic.

The marchioness stood up and glared at my eyeball. I had never seen her that close before. Close up, she had a human quality. I could see why she tended to keep her distance.

'My God,' she said, recoiling. 'It *is* red.'

The doctor said, 'I think you had better see one of my

ophthalmology colleagues. There is some inflammation in your conjunctiva. But I don't think it is conjunctivitis.'

'I've had this for a while,' I said. 'It doesn't hurt really. Just the light – I find the light a bit bright. I'll get it looked at.'

The doctor nodded and said, 'Good. Now I'd best move along and see my other patients, but this is really good news, Mrs, um . . .' He consulted his iPad again for a name but seemed unable to locate one. He looked up from it and said, 'Things are going the right way.'

'Thank you, doctor,' the marchioness replied.

He smiled and swung his dark grey tie back round to hang in front of his shirt because it had been sitting on his shoulder oddly, like a giraffe's tongue.

The marchioness waited until he had left the room and then she pulled her mobile phone out of her bag and began to text frantically. Her brow was furrowed. The concentration on her face was unparalleled. She looked like I did whenever Vanessa tried to explain balance sheets to me.

'Is everything okay?' I asked.

Her head spun round to face me, and she said, much more forcefully than she had perhaps intended, 'Yes. Everything is fine. Why don't you go to the café downstairs and get yourself a coffee? I'll meet you there. I won't be long.'

I did as she told me, and I left the room. I passed the toilets and thought I'd better stop in to examine my eye. I had a shock – it was bloodshot. I wondered what had triggered it. It was not painful, but I thought I would go to the pharmacy while I was in the hospital to see if there was an ointment with which to treat it.

It was heaving on the ground floor, rammed with bodies, with suffering. There was a long queue that snaked around the corner of the corridor all the way to the very back wall of the building. Desolation seeped from it, from the people languishing there, like discharge. I considered not bothering to join it, but I knew that I wouldn't have an opportunity to get medication for my eye when I got back to the world of the castle.

But while I was waiting, I had a feeling that I was being watched. There was a man, short and plump with his belly hanging over the waistband of his grey suit trousers, and I caught his eye. He hadn't intended for me to see him. He moved away. His heft made it hard for him to get much distance from me. I surrendered my place in the queue to follow him because I sensed that this was the private investigator Hannah had warned me about and I was prepared to confront him. I couldn't think why he had followed me into the hospital if that were the case. I wondered why he hadn't waited outside, what it was he wanted to see.

I pursued him through the long corridor leading to the radiology department where I had previously locked myself in the loo. He was keeping studiously to the left at all times and I could tell even from the back of his head that there was some stealth in his movement. It was possible of course that I was projecting my paranoia onto him, but there was something incongruous about the way the man was moving through the hospital, as if he was running for a train. He disappeared around the corner, and I could only hope that by the time I too met that corner I would see him, that he hadn't secreted himself somewhere – in a cleaning cupboard or fire escape.

My phone was ringing. It was the marchioness. She told me she was ready to leave and that she would meet me in the entrance by the car park. I wrestled with the choice either to delay my return to her so that I could confront this man or abandon the mission altogether and meet the marchioness where she had asked me to. I knew I was already on shaky ground with her, what with the cottage burning down and having the baby she didn't know I had. It had to be the latter option.

As we headed back to the car, having rendezvoused in the entrance hall, I noticed – at the other end of the car park – a silver hatchback, the type that Mark had described seeing in the lay-by near the cottage. I assured myself that there were many silver hatchbacks in circulation but I couldn't help wondering if this belonged to the fat man in the grey suit. I wished we could have lingered long enough to find out. But it was evident that the marchioness was keen to get away.

'Where to?' I asked. 'Home?'

'No,' she replied. 'Not home.'

She knew where she wanted to go but couldn't find a way to tell me. It was clear what she wanted; hers was an expression that I recognised, characterised by an insuppressible sense of purpose. She was trying to escape.

'Edinburgh Airport,' she said.

'The airport?'

'Yes,' she said. 'The airport.'

•

I could only assume that she always carried her passport with her because how else would she be so prepared to just catch a plane at a moment's notice? I didn't see the passport. I wished I had because then I would have known where it was she had come from, which mystical land had birthed such a creature, but it was to remain an enigma. And because Edinburgh

Airport has only one terminal, unlike Heathrow, I could not deduce where she had planned to go.

'When will you be returning?'

'I'll let you know. I am not sure exactly when.'

We said all of this to each other at the drop-off by Departures. I wanted to ask her where she was going but I wasn't brave enough. She didn't want to tell me.

'Do I need to organise any clothes or things to be sent to you?' I asked.

'No, thank you,' she said, rearranging her cape across her shoulders. I closed the car door behind her. She glanced at the terminal, scanning it for the right entrance, and on seeing it, turned to me and said, 'I'll be in touch.'

'What should I do?' I asked. 'I mean, do I stay? Or do I leave? My job, I mean.'

She shook her head in slow motion, as if she had no idea who I was or how it came to pass that I was standing there in front of her. 'Oh,' she said. 'Right. You can stay. Yes. You can stay on at least until I get back. I can't think right now.'

And then she turned to leave, and I was left standing next to the Volvo, exhausted and in the same clothes I had worn for three days.

Chapter 31

Driving back to the castle, I tried to unpick the events of the last few days now that I had some breathing space and opportunity for reflection. I assembled in my mind the fragments of my knowledge – the cottage that had been set on fire, the fortune teller warning me of it only moments before, the marquess's dramatic improvement to his health and the marchioness's subsequent and hasty disappearance. Strange and unexpected things were happening all at once. I couldn't understand it. And then there was the man in the hospital with the small silver hatchback. Perhaps this was just the nature of castle life, but everything seemed to be moving at an unsustainable pace.

I was finding it hard to talk myself out of a swelling sense of paranoia. I knew that what I needed was a day off and a good night's sleep. Having reached, in the early days of the baby, the nadir of my neuroses I was receptive to the idea that I could be fabricating scenarios that were not in reality happening and I needed to be self-vigilant.

As I approached the castle, I saw that a police car had parked directly outside the main entrance. I thought about turning around as soon as I had seen it but before I could mobilise, the officers who had been waiting inside it stepped out and watched. Clearly it was me they had been waiting for. It was too late to bolt. They were both men, both wearing dark suits.

I pulled up. They looked at the car. They looked at each other. One of them smirked. I supposed they hadn't seen a diplomatic services extended wheelbase Volvo before. I waved and smiled. I smiled a bit too much. I hoped my smile would frighten them off, but it didn't. I got out.

One of them said, 'Miss Green?'

I said, 'Yes?'

'Camilla Green?'

(I got my surname from Cluedo.)

'Yes,' I said.

'We'd like to ask you some questions about the fire in the cottage,' one said. He was sunny, beaming, portly. He had a spectacular smile. The content of his enquiry was at odds with the merriment he was bringing to our encounter. He reminded me of my old postman, who used to sign for my packages so that I didn't have to go all the way to the Delivery Office on the other side of Chiswick. This one was Good Cop, no doubt about it. I did not like the one he was with, the other one. All joy had been leached from him. 'You were living there at the time?'

'Yes,' I said, 'but only for a week or so. I'd only just started working at the estate.'

'Can we go inside?' the dour one asked, flicking his head toward the castle.

'Yes, of course,' I said. 'I think the front door is bolted from the inside. The family tends not to use that door. We all use the service entrance by the stables around the back. You can follow me if you like.'

The gravel crunched beneath my Converse. I looked down. They were crusted in mud. There were flecks of mud up the back of my jeans too. I was not happy about my appearance. I needed a wash, a hosing down.

I was trying to work out what to say to these two men but my mind was scrambled. I needed to disable any interest they might have had in me as someone whose life had suspicious things going on in it. Luckily, the detectives had been rendered mute by the sheer scale and grandeur of the castle, looking up, pointing out things to each other – gargoyles, balustrading, crenellated turrets, stained-glass windows.

'It's like a mini Glamis,' said Good Cop. 'But white. Looks a bit Swiss. Is it Swiss?'

'I've never been to Glamis,' I said. 'Would you recommend going?'

'Oh, for sure,' he replied. 'Avoid it in the middle of summer though – it's packed with tourists. The restaurant does a mean steak bridie.'

'Yum,' I said.

I would have shared a steak bridie with Good Cop any day of the week, whatever a steak bridie was. I wondered if I should ask, if it would be trivial of me to ask. Now would be the time to ask, I thought. Leaving it any longer than I already had would tell these men everything they'd need to know about the sort of person they were dealing with.

'What's a bridie?' I asked.

'It's a kind of pie,' Good Cop answered. 'Like a meat pie.'

'Like a pasty?'

'Pasty?'

'Meat in pastry.'

'Aye.'

My phone pinged. It was a text from Hannah: *Where are you. I'm going stir crazy. Need to get out.*

I wrote back: *Police here. Be back asap.*

She replied with an expletive that I have chosen not to inscribe.

I sat the officers down at the kitchen table and offered them a coffee from the coffee machine, wielding the wand of capsules. Good Cop declined and chuckled, explaining that he'd reached his caffeine quota for the day and Bad Cop said yes, nodding eagerly, conceding a facet to his personality of which I would have previously believed him incapable. Fiddling about with all the stuff bought me more time and it also allowed me to emit a sense of calm and industry.

I think they would have rather been upstairs in one of the grander rooms and I had reflected on whether to conduct this meeting in the ballroom or the green drawing room, given that I currently had free rein of the castle but thought that the formality of those spaces would create an incriminating jumpiness in me.

'So you were saying that you've only been here a few weeks,' Good Cop said.

'Yes,' I nodded.

'And where were you before?'

'London.'

'London?'

'Yes. London.'

'Whereabouts in London?' Bad Cop asked.

I placed his coffee on the table in front of him. 'West London.'

'West London,' he repeated. He wrote it down.

'And what brought you to work here?' Good Cop asked.

I thought I should offer him a biscuit. I didn't know where Kelly kept the biscuits. I wouldn't have known where to find them.

'Would you like a biscuit?' I asked.

He patted his belly and said, 'Watching the weight. But thank you.'

'No problem,' I said.

I wished he'd said yes to biscuits because then I could have gone on a hunt for them and stowed myself away in the larder with the door closed, rattling tins and jars, biding my time.

'What brought you to work here?'

'Oh,' I said, 'I just fancied a change. I've always wanted to get out of the city and live in a rural place. Get away from the congestion and the pollution. The cost of living, you know.'

They nodded and scribbled.

'And had you noticed anything suspicious on the days leading up to the fire?'

'How do you mean?' I asked.

'Well, anything at all really. I don't know, some activity around the cottage. Anything suspicious? Someone you hadn't seen before. An unknown car.'

I shook my head. 'No. I'm afraid I haven't.'

'And was it just you living at the cottage? No one else?'

'Just me,' I said. 'My sister came to stay. But it happened the night she arrived.'

'And the baby?' Good Cop asked.

'My sister's,' I said.

'Your sister's?' asked Bad Cop. 'I was under the impression that the baby was yours. The estate manager said so. What's his name?'

He started flicking through his notes. Flick-flick-flick. His fingers sprinted through the pages.

'Mark,' he confirmed.

'Sorry,' I said. 'Yes, the baby is mine. The last few days have been manic.'

'I think you'd remember whether a baby was yours or not, wouldn't you?' Bad Cop asked.

'I thought you meant who was looking after the baby at the time of the fire.'

'When I asked you if anyone else was living there, you said it was just you.'

'I thought you meant it in a married sense, like do I have a husband,' I said. The skin on my neck was pricking. I was getting hot. I was not appreciating Bad Cop's competence. 'I always see the baby as being part of me.'

They looked at me nonplussed.

'Do you have children?' I asked.

They both shook their heads.

'My partner's expecting in a few months,' Bad Cop said.

'Then you'll soon know what it's like,' I explained in the manner of one of those experts I had watched on mid-morning television. 'Your baby will feel like an extension of you. Perhaps that's just what mothers feel. Maybe it's a maternal thing.'

I felt I could talk in this way forever.

'Have you been married, Miss Green?'

'No,' I said. 'No. I'm afraid not. I'm afraid I never met the baby's father.'

The men had that look on their faces.

'I conceived through sperm donation,' I continued. 'I was getting on, and Mr Right hadn't appeared and I wanted to have a baby.'

They recoiled. I could see that they were desperate to end the interview. I had found the winning formula. I had found a way to repel my interrogators. They didn't want to talk to a woman who had not done things the way she was meant to have done them. Not in any arena. Not even in an inquisition.

Good Cop looked at the time on his phone. 'We'd best be getting off,' he said. 'Thank you for your time. If you do see anything or remember anything, please let us know. Mark has my number.'

'Thank you, detectives,' I said.

I showed them out through the service door.

•

Back in the kitchen I put the espresso cups into the dishwasher and tidied up, cleaning the surfaces and the table, before preparing to leave the castle and head back to Mark's cottage. It was a splendid kitchen, full of big machinery and the most beautiful black and gold range cooker I had ever seen. I wondered if I'd ever get the chance to cook on one, if I'd ever have one to myself. I took great pleasure in wiping the surfaces of that cooker, reflecting as I did on the deft and skilful way with which I had put those police officers off the scent of my subterfuge. I draped the cloth over the head of the kitchen tap, just as I had seen Kelly do, as if I were master of the kitchen, and was about to leave the castle to relieve Hannah of the baby when Mark appeared at the kitchen door.

'I've just seen the police car leave,' he said. 'Everything okay?'

'All fine,' I replied. 'There wasn't much I could tell them.'

He nodded. He seemed satisfied. 'Where's the marchioness?' he asked. 'I tried looking for her but I couldn't find her anywhere. I have to discuss the insurance with her.'

He was flapping some papers about in his hand. I wondered if that was why the marchioness had fled – because she did not want to deal with all the paperwork. That would be reason enough for me to run away and never come back.

I wasn't sure how to tell him that she'd gone. As Mark was looking at me, I noticed an adjustment in his expression. He knew the spirit of what was coming. He was bracing himself for bad news.

'She wanted me to drop her at the airport,' I said.

'The airport? Why?'

'I don't know,' I replied. 'Presumably to get a flight? I don't know. She didn't say.'

'And you didn't think to ask?'

It was a sad thing; kind, post-blaze Mark was disappearing. Original Mark was breaking through.

'I didn't think it was appropriate.'

'Not appropriate?'

'No.'

'So you dropped her off at the airport. Then what?'

'She told me I could stay on until she came back.'

'And when is that?'

'She didn't say.'

Mark walked over to the kitchen table, put the sheets on the tabletop and pulled out a chair and sat down and crossed his legs. He rolled his sleeves up. The hairs on his arms were all pointing the wrong way. I wanted to stroke them into the correct direction. It was bothering me.

'What triggered it?' he asked.

I stared at him, wondering whether to sit down next to him or to stand over by the sink, or maybe busy myself with wiping down the surfaces all over again.

'Triggered?'

'What happened prior to you taking her to the airport?'

'We were at the hospital.'

'Right.'

'And I thought it was good news because they said the marquess was turning the corner.'

Mark fiddled with his sleeves. He ironed out the creases with his palm.

'Because we went there,' I said, 'thinking that it was the other way. That he'd had a brain haemorrhage in the night and that it was, you know, time to say goodbye.'

'When did they tell you this?'

'They didn't tell me. The marchioness did. She said she got a call from the hospital advising her to go in because it was really end-of-life time.'

'I never heard anything,' he said.

'It doesn't matter anyway because it turns out that this information was incorrect and that an MRI had shown an improvement in brain activity. But when the doctor told her this, she looked worried and started texting someone on her phone, I don't know who, and then after that, as we were leaving and I was asking her if she wanted me to drive her home, she told me not to and to take her to the airport instead.'

'So she's just gone?'

'Yes.'

'Right. Well, I'm not sure what to do in this situation. It's never happened before.'

'This situation?'

'She's never done this before. Gone without telling anyone.'

'She told me.'

He emitted a low groan: barely audible, controlled. 'Did she say when she'd be back?'

'She told me that she'd text me when she knew.'

Mark uncrossed his legs and drew himself into the table. His elbows formed a triangle. He perched his chin on the apex. He looked contemplative. I liked the way he looked when he was thinking about things.

'Why don't you stay at the castle while she's away?' he suggested. 'As you said, she'll tell you when she's back. You could have one of the rooms in the guest wing. I can't see it being a problem. Anyway, there's no one here to tell you otherwise.'

I would have been lying if I said that I hadn't liked the sound of that. It had been a brutal couple of days and I didn't want to impose myself and my family on Mark for any longer than was necessary.

'Okay,' I said. 'Are you sure that's okay?'

'I can't see anyone disagreeing with me,' he said, consulting his watch. 'It's getting late. How about I drive you back to mine, pick up your sister and the baby and bring you back here. It won't take long to walk but it will be faster if I drive.'

Chapter 32

Hannah was in her element. I took her into the guest wing, and she inspected the suites, finally settling for what the marchioness dubbed 'The White Room', which wasn't white at all but a deep burgundy and we had a long debate over what had possessed her to call a red room white until the baby, whom I was carrying, began to protest.

I chose the room named Gemini, in which there was a large oil painting on the wall of two children sitting in a sailboat on a loch. There were two beds, and I pushed one of them against the wall by the window and built a pillow fort for the baby, which was something I was now adept at. It was about time I bought a travel cot. I wasn't sure why I hadn't already done so. When I look back now, I wonder if I had been superstitious about committing too readily to my new life: in particular, to cot-buying. Things could have changed at a moment's notice.

Hannah went down to the kitchen to see if there was a supper that could be cobbled together while I sat with the baby on the bed and sang 'Baby Mine' fifteen times. The baby gurgled back at me. Sleep was proving elusive. It must have been the relative novelty of spending time with me that was keeping her up. I saw her in a new light, brighter, clearer. The weariness and tedium of our days together in London had been obstructing the flow of my love. In Scotland, we had some time apart – I had time to work on something else (even if that work involved just driving to and from hospital). I had some space to breathe, some space to chart where I ended and she began.

I ran my fingertips across the arch of her eyebrows and down her ski-slope nose, caressing her cheeks with the backs of my fingers, and I breathed deeply, hoping that my calming rhythm would dance its way into her every pore.

I would have liked to think that this microcosm, our little world, was sacred and inviolable, but the threat of James hung over it and imperilled its sanctity. He would try to break it, to rupture it. I believed he was capable of that. And what if I couldn't keep the baby away from him forever? What if she, inevitably no longer a baby, desired a life with James in it? As much as I told myself that I didn't have to worry about that now, I understood how quickly time passed and that that eventuality might present itself sooner than I could imagine.

The baby was asleep, I put her down and laid some pillows on the floor in case she rolled out. The guest suite was so far away from the kitchen that I decided it would be wise to return to her every hour to check that she was asleep, at least while we were downstairs.

Down in the kitchen, Hannah had amassed an impressive haul. She arranged on the table a small banquet – a truckle of Stilton (it had crossed my mind that this may have been bought in preparation for Christmas), a little pot of chicken liver parfait, some cornichons, piccalilli, smoked salmon and a splay of oatcakes. It was only when I saw it all, presented so tantalisingly, that I realised how hungry I was. The last thing I had eaten were some Weetabix for breakfast in Mark's kitchen.

'Is the baby asleep?' she asked.

'Yes,' I said.

'Good.' She took two wine glasses out of the cupboard in the room next door, where the crockery and cutlery were stored. They chimed in her hand. She set them down on the table. We kept to one end.

'I want you to know that I'm proud of you,' she said, ceremoniously, her back straight, her shoulders back. 'I know that sounds patronising, but I am. I realise that some of the circumstances are less than ideal.'

'You mean the cottage burning down?'

'Yes,' she said. 'I mean the cottage burning down. But I'm proud of you for sticking with this and for not going back. It must have been tempting at times.'

'I have thought about it,' I said.

'But you didn't go back, and that's all that matters. Mum would be so proud of you too, you know. She was so worried about you. You know that, don't you?'

In that moment, I could have disintegrated at the sheer thought of her, of Mum.

Hannah dabbed the flesh beneath her eyes with a napkin. She fanned her face with her hands. 'I know you don't like to talk about it,' she said. 'But it was just after the miscarriage and James had asked you to marry him. Do you remember?'

'Of course I do.'

'And Mum told you as delicately as she could not to marry him because she knew your grief at losing the baby was so overwhelming that you would find it hard to think rationally. But I don't think you heard her. Do you know what I mean? You listened, but you didn't hear.'

'I know.'

'She tried. She really tried.'

'I know she did. I just didn't know how to say no to him. How can you when someone asks you like that in such sad circumstances? And it was the way he asked, *how* he asked. You can't say no. It sounds silly, but you can't.'

She came to me and wrapped her arms around me and held me tightly. I had been rigid. In her grip I drooped. I could have stayed in her arms. Hannah broke away, instigating a tonal shift. She shook her head comically, ridding it of her sorrow, and exclaimed, 'Booze!'

She thrummed her hands on the table. 'Any idea where it might be? Where they stash it?'

'No clue,' I said.

'There must be a cellar here. There must be a massive, massive cellar, filled wall to wall. Fully stocked, burgeoning.'

'I'm not sure I should drink,' I said. 'I feel like I should have my wits about me.'

'But it's my last night,' Hannah said.

'What do you mean?'

'I'm going home tomorrow.'

'I thought you were staying for a week. You've only been here three days.'

'I need to go back,' she said. 'A work thing has come up. Will you take me to the station tomorrow?'

'Can't you work from here? You know, remotely?'

Hannah shook her head. 'Meetings,' she said. 'Face to face.'

She smeared a nub of Stilton all over an oatcake and held

it aloft. 'Not good enough,' she said, appraising the morsel. 'Needs port. Red wine at the very least. Come on, let's find this cellar.'

Chapter 33

We found the cellar.

Oh! My head was not thanking me for finding it, that was for sure. It must have been the events of the last few days that warranted our Bacchanalian antics. We let loose, there were no two ways about it. Because of her work in private wealth, Hannah had a much better idea of the calibre of liquid we were swilling. Yet in the morning, all that was immaterial. I felt as if I had been poisoned, and when the baby stirred in the bed next to mine, I clutched my head in horror, not knowing how I would make it through the day.

I rushed down to the kitchen, the baby jiggling in my arms, to assess the damage – if any – we had left there but was relieved to see that it was spotless and I figured that it was Hannah who had ensured that. She was so good at clearing up after the party.

Hannah was in a dreadful state. I smelt vomit on her breath; I had warned her about mixing grape and grain. She said I sounded just like Mum, telling her that. She surfaced at around 10 a.m., appearing in the kitchen clutching her water bottle, her skin exhibiting a deathly pallor.

'Bacon sarnie,' she said.

'There's no bacon,' I said.

'What.'

'No bacon.'

'What are you saying?'

'There is no bacon.'

She huffed expansively and collapsed into one of the chairs at the kitchen table.

'Thanks for cleaning up,' I said.

'Huh?'

'I was so worried that we'd left it in a state, but when I came down I saw that it was spotless.'

'It wasn't me.'

'You didn't tidy?'

'No, love,' she confirmed. 'Not me.'

There was the sound of footsteps moving along the corridor, coming closer. At first, I thought it was Mark, but it didn't sound like the heavy clomp of walking boots I had become accustomed to hearing. It was the clacking of women's footsteps, not one pair but two.

I looked at Hannah in horror. She clutched the arms of her chair.

'Quick!' I whispered. 'Hide.' I seized the baby from the kitchen floor.

We dashed into the larder, leaving the door slightly ajar. The baby was making baby noises. I muffled her mouth with my hand. The baby writhed. I began to panic. I found some Carr's Table Water biscuits on a shelf and gave one to her and she sucked on it.

Voices now accompanied the footsteps. Scottish voices. Familiar Scottish voices.

'It's the twins!'

'Who?'

'The twins!' I exclaimed, whisperingly. 'The twins. You know, Hilary's twins. Her friends. The marquess's sisters.'

'What are they doing here?' she asked.

'How should I know? This is bad. This is very bad,' I said. 'If they find out I'm here, they'll tell Hilary and she'll tell James and he'll tell the police. What do I do?'

'Don't panic,' she said.

Hannah looked about herself. She focused on a door at the back of the larder. 'Where does that door go?'

'I don't know.'

She went over to it and pulled the handle.

From outside I could hear them talking, shedding snippets of conversation: *frightful mess, someone de Rothschild, indelible port stain, slattern, oak table, don't be ridiculous, Biddy.*

Behind me, Hannah was fumbling with the key in the lock. She managed to turn it. As quietly as she could, and with her back hunched, crouching, she opened the door. I followed her through it, closing it behind me. It led to another smaller room lined with stacks of golden chairs that the marchioness must have used for large dinners. At the end of the room was another door, daylight penetrating its outline. We unlocked it and let ourselves out into the stable yard where we ran further along the outer wall, away from the kitchen windows and out of the back of the house towards Mark's cottage.

'What are we going to do?' I asked.

'Why are they here?' Hannah asked. 'Maybe if you knew that, you'd know when they'd be leaving.'

'The marquess,' I said. 'Maybe they've been told he is better, and they are getting things ready for him to return. Or they are going to visit him.'

'How would they know?' Hannah asked.

'Maybe the hospital told them. Wouldn't they call the next of kin?'

'Wouldn't that be the marchioness though?'

'Maybe they can't get hold of her. Maybe they haven't been able to reach her and these people are the next contacts.'

'You don't suppose they know you're here?'

'How could they?' I asked.

'What if Mark told them?' Hannah said. 'What if getting you to stay in the castle was a trick because he knew they were coming and he wanted you to get caught staying where you shouldn't be staying? That's why he was being so nice. He was building your trust only to betray you, to lead you to the twins. Did he suggest you stay in that Gemini room? You know that means twins, don't you? In astrology.'

I was retracing it all in my mind. It would have explained his abrupt change of attitude to me that I could not account for: the kindness and the compassion. Perhaps he knew that I was on the run and had set this trap for me. I couldn't think what his motivation would be. Perhaps he regarded me as a threat.

'We can't go back to the cottage,' I said. 'We can't if we can't trust Mark.'

'What will we do?' Hannah asked.

I could see that, for the first time, she was leaning on me to solve the problem; I was someone who could produce a solution.

'We need to get our stuff,' I said.

'But then we'd have to go back into the house.'

I nodded very affirmatively. I was brimming with fortitude. 'We have no choice.'

'And after that?'

'I don't know.'

Chapter 34

I had a brainwave. It took a while, I confess. We were standing in the rhododendron dell and I was pacing around it frantically. The adrenaline coursing through my body countered the disabling effects of my hangover. That wasn't the case for Hannah, however, because she still looked green, green as the moss on the limestone walls that surrounded us. I was carrying the baby, but my arms were beginning to tire. I needed the pouch.

'Our stuff is in the castle,' I said. 'We have no alternative but to go in and retrieve it.'

'No shit,' Hannah said.

'But it's just occurred to me that Kelly is away. She won't be back for five or so weeks. We could stay in her apartment in the orangery.'

'A what?' Hannah said.

'An orangery. I think it's a building where aristocrats grow oranges.'

'Just oranges?' she asked. 'A building just for growing oranges.'

'Yes,' I confirmed.

'We were so born into the wrong family,' she said. 'How

different my perception of the world would have been if I had had an orangery in my life.'

'Well,' I said. 'What do you think? Good idea?'

'Great idea,' she said. 'Just as long as I can get a train back today. Getting a lot of angry texts from my boss.'

She scrolled through her phone and showed me the screen as proof of these texts, as if I had demanded it.

'That's Tinder,' I said. 'Why are you on Tinder?'

She glared at the screen. 'Shit,' she said.

'Do you have a date tomorrow?' I asked. 'Is that why you need to go back?'

'Maybe,' she said.

'Why didn't you just say so?'

'In case it doesn't go anywhere. Look,' she explained, 'I do genuinely also have a meeting. A big client meeting.'

'It's fine. I completely understand,' I said. 'I'm just going to miss you. I wish you didn't have to go.'

'Me too,' she said. 'I like it here. I can see why a place like this would grow on you. I like how removed it feels from everything.'

Hannah looked around the dell. She wanted to rhapsodise and I wasn't going to let her. There was no time for that.

'So what we will do is go to the orangery now,' I said masterfully.

'What if it's locked?'

'Kelly doesn't believe in locking things.'

'She doesn't believe in locking things?'

'No.'

'Okay, then. I suppose that's good for us.'

'You wait there, if you don't mind, with the baby, and I'll try and sneak back into the house to get your things.'

I got a text from Mark. *Where are you?*

'Oh God, oh God!' I exclaimed. 'It's Mark. He wants to know where I am. What should I tell him?''

Hannah seized the branch of a nearby acer to steady herself from the spins. What leaves remained fell away in a drift of amber and claret.

'Well?'

'I'm thinking. I'm thinking.'

He sent another text: *The marquess's sisters are here. They need to be taken to the hospital to see him. They want to leave here at 3 p.m.*

It was already midday. I couldn't let the twins see me. It would ruin everything. It would all have been in vain – all the obstacles I had managed to overcome to get to this moment. I read the message to Hannah.

'You can't do that,' she said. 'They'll know it's you. And you've got nowhere to put the baby.'

'Can't you? Just this last time?'

'No. I have to go. I have to, Emma.'

I wrung my hands. *Think*, I told myself. *Think*.

'Angry Shona,' I said, dialling her number with a speed that riveted my fingers.

Shona picked up promptly, and after I assailed her with apologies and explained that the reason I had not used her services for the last couple of days was not for any other reason than that my house had burnt down, she said, 'Fine. But remember you are still on your second strike.'

I texted Mark: *Just getting the car seen to in Grandtully. Needs some oil.*

The car didn't need any oil and I wouldn't have known if it did.

But the car is here?

Sorry, not clear. About to get it seen. Would you mind leaving the key in the ignition so I can do it as quickly as possible?

He replied with a thumbs-up emoji.

If I could get back to the stable block, I thought, I might be able to remain unseen while I carried out the second part of my plan.

I smuggled Hannah back into the house through the same entrance as we had left it, keeping to the servants' quarters as much as possible. Our greatest hurdle would be in retrieving our belongings from the bedrooms.

'We need to create a diversion,' Hannah said.

'Yes,' I said. 'I've got an idea.'

•

I told Hannah to dial the landline number that only rang in the library on the ground floor of the castle. The phone was answered by one of the twins. Hannah said she could hear the other twin the background.

'Are they mad?' Hannah whispered, covering the speaker with her hand. 'They sound mad.'

I nodded.

'I mean . . . box of frogs,' she said.

'Keep doing that,' I said. 'Keeping calling them. It will keep them downstairs.'

I rushed up to the guest wing and slotted the baby into her pouch, which freed up my arms. I gathered our belongings, then I headed back out to the stables and found Hannah, who had completed her telephone deception mission. We crept around the back of the castle to the orangery.

As anticipated, Kelly's apartment was open. I let Hannah in and then drove off to Grandtully in the Volvo to dispatch the baby with Angry Shona and complete the final part of my mission.

•

'Oh,' I said, 'just one more thing.'

Shona was standing in the doorway very obstructively, her foot blocking any possibility of entry.

'What?' she said. Her foot moved to close the door.

'You don't happen to have any hair dye, do you?'

She hoisted the baby into the nook of her elbow. 'Eh?'

'Hair dye,' I repeated. 'Do you have any?'

'Aye,' she said. 'Who's asking?'

'Well, I am,' I said. 'Could I borrow some? I'll pay you back.'

'Why can't you get your own?'

'Because I am in a hurry,' I explained.

'Double,' she said. 'You can pay me back double. I have to go all the way to Pitlochry for that.'

'Fine,' I said. I pulled twenty pounds out of my wallet and handed it to her.

'Wait here,' she said, and several minutes later she emerged with a pack of Clairol Nice'n Easy Ultra Light Natural Beach Blonde. They were to be my last few moments of being a brunette.

•

At this point the time was 1.30 p.m., which meant that I had ninety minutes to undergo a complete transformation. A quick scan of Kelly's bedroom confirmed to me just how organised she was. Everything was neat, so neutral in tone. I'd never been able to achieve that level of neatness, of self-discipline.

Hannah found a pair of sunglasses on Kelly's dressing table. I put them on. 'Might it look a bit strange to be wearing sunglasses in November?' I asked.

'No. Anyway, you've got that eye problem. Just say you're sensitive to sunlight.'

'Yes. I could say that and it would be true.'

'That's the spirit,' Hannah said. 'Let me see if there is anything else like a hat or something.' She began rifling through Kelly's chest of drawers until she paused and unearthed something. She held it up. 'I wonder why she's got this.'

It was a book with which I was only too familiar – *What to Expect When You're Expecting*. I released it from Hannah's grip. 'Weird,' I said.

'Right?'

There was little time to speculate although it struck me as odd that Kelly should have this book in her possession and I cogitated over its existence while I doused my hair in dye in her bathroom, making sure to saturate every inch of my scalp in the stuff. With a cotton bud I daubed my eyebrow, which I hoped would boost the credibility of my transformation. I removed the plastic gloves from my hands and set my phone timer for twenty minutes while Hannah got her things together.

'How should I get to the station?' she asked.

'Taxi?'

'Do you have a number for one?'

'No. But I think there's a service in Grandtully.'

Hannah consulted Google. There was a tremble in her scrolling fingers. 'Ah, here's one,' she said. 'Shona's Cabs.'

'Shona's Cabs?'

Hannah nodded. 'A cab to Dunkeld station, please,' she said, pressing the phone to her ear. 'How long will that be?' She mouthed 'half an hour' at me and then told the driver to meet her at the gates of the castle where she would be waiting. She hung up.

'Was it a man or a woman you spoke to?' I asked.

'A woman.'

'What did she sound like?'

'What do you mean?'

'I mean did she sound nice and friendly or really quite nasty?'

'I don't know. I can't say I even noticed,' Hannah said. 'Why? The dye is running down your forehead, by the way.'

I ran to the bathroom and looked in the mirror. A trail the colour of sputum trickled down my face, as if I had just lanced a boil. I scrubbed and scrubbed, excoriating my skin. Hannah stuck her head around the door.

She said, 'Breathe.'

I breathed – first, a short, sharp breath and then a longer one as I had seen someone do on YouTube, and it worked. It really worked. It must have been a coincidence; surely, there must be more than one Shona in Grandtully, I thought to myself, as I kept breathing. I breathed and breathed until the timer on my phone went off. And then I shrieked for it gave me such a fright.

'Time to wash it out now,' Hannah said.

•

Hannah was gone. I told her to take the bridlepath through the estate all the way up to the road. I watched as she dragged her little suitcase through the damp grass, the wheels carving out muddy divots. She said she would text me when she was on the train.

I was in the orangery. It was two-thirty. I stood in front of Kelly's full-length mirror and studied my transformation. Given the time I had allotted in which to perform it, I was satisfied and could only hope that it would be enough of a disguise. I headed out to the castle to wait in the car.

•

Mark's face . . . I'm not sure how to describe it. I had to counter his reaction to my new look by pretending that everything was completely normal.

'Camilla?' he asked, half confused, half amused. 'What's going on?'

He had seen me waiting in the car from the front entrance of the castle, the engine running, and had approached me, glaring, squinting, thrusting his head forward to get a better look.

'Oh, hi, Mark,' I said nonchalantly.

'I didn't recognise you,' he said. 'You've changed your hair. It's yellow.'

'Ultra light natural beach blonde,' I corrected.

'Your skin. It's a different colour.'

He meant the fake tan. I had overdone it with the fake tan.

'I fancied a change,' I said.

'I can see that.' And then the expression on his face switched to one of concern. 'I realise that the last few days have been stressful,' he said. 'But if you are not in the right frame of mind, then you should take some time off. Just temporarily. You've been through a lot these last few days.'

'No,' I insisted. 'I'm fine. I'm great, actually. Hunky-dory.'

'Hunky-dory?'

'Yep,' I said.

'Where's your baby?'

'With the childminder in the village. Angry Shona.'

'Who?'

'Never mind.'

He stood back from the car and turned around, distracted by some noise behind him. I saw his hands scrunch up. I looked at his face; his jaw was clenched.

'Here they come,' he said joylessly.

In the wing mirror, I saw them. The twins. Frocked in grey wool, both sinewy and gaunt, both in need of some collagen.

'Mark,' Biddy said. 'Mark, where were you? We've been waiting in the hall for an age.'

'I've been out here, Lady Elizabeth,' he said. 'Preparing the car. This is your driver, Camilla. Camilla Green.'

Biddy peered inside. She saw me through the windscreen and was visibly taken aback. I can only think it was the cumulative effect of my constituent parts; the uncanny matching of my face and hair, the decision to accessorise with John Lennon rainbow-lensed sunglasses, and my eyebrows, my incredible golden eyebrows. She was repelled, there was no doubt. The twins got into the back of the car and did everything they could not to look at me. My disguise was a triumph.

I drove off to Dundee.

Chapter 35

Rain pelted down and visibility was becoming a problem so I had to make a concerted effort to concentrate on driving, which was hard because there were several missed calls from Hannah on my phone. I could see them all coming in silently, yet I was powerless to respond. I had told her to text me as soon as she got home, so I knew something was wrong because, by my calculation, her train wouldn't have reached Edinburgh by that point. I would call her as soon as I reached the hospital, I assured myself. A text appeared. I attempted to look at it, but the twins were now scrutinising my every move, every gear change, every indication, every glance in the mirror. I felt their eyes burn into me. Their repulsion had only been a fleeting thing; the confines of the car and the tedium of the journey had seen to that. I dropped the phone in the passenger footwell. It was out of reach.

'It appears there was some sort of party in the house last night,' Biddy said. She glared at me from over her spectacles.

'You wouldn't happen to know anything about it, would you?' Morwenna asked. She removed her glasses as if she could hear better without them.

I shook my head. I realised at that moment that I would have to modify my voice. Until that point it hadn't occurred to me that they might have recognised me from the way I sounded, that they could pin me to a particular place, to a particular memory. Yet I was useless at accents; I always have been. All I could do was deepen my voice. I proceeded: 'No, I'm afraid not.'

I sounded constipated. There was nothing to do now, I could not reroute – I was stuck with the baritone. I had made my bed. The twins looked at each other and in that telepathic way they had, they exchanged reams of information using only the power of sight and hyperactive eyebrows.

'That is not a Perthshire accent,' Biddy said.

'Where are you from?' Morwenna asked.

'Peterborough,' I said.

'Peterborough?'

Morwenna narrowed her eyes until the balls were no longer visible. She restored her glasses to her face. With the mention of Peterborough, I had trapped them in a cul-de-sac of curiosity, just as I hoped I would.

'We went to our room to see that someone had slept in it and bizarrely one of the beds had been pushed against the wall and pillows placed all around it.'

'Hmm. How strange,' I mused. 'How pagan.'

'Strange indeed,' Biddy said. 'You see, it is my view that, on discovering that both my brother and his wife were no longer in residence, someone took advantage of this vacuum and had a party, also helping themselves to some invaluable wines in the process.'

'Invaluable!' Morwenna said. 'Utterly invaluable.'

'This is gravely serious,' Biddy added. 'We have instructed Mark to launch an inquiry. Unexplained parties will not be tolerated.'

'It's wonderful news that the marquess is making such a good recovery,' I yelled cheerily.

There was some nodding, once they had absorbed the shock of my assertion. They said in unison, each looking out of their respective windows, 'Indeed.'

A silence followed. It didn't last long.

'We were obviously delighted when the hospital called to tell us about his improvement,' Biddy explained. 'Although less so to be informed that his wife is nowhere to be seen. That's why we've come. The hospital could not get hold of the marchioness. After her, we are next of kin.'

'Should you really be going that fast?' Morwenna said, peering forward and glaring at the speedometer.

'You are going awfully fast,' added Biddy, 'especially in such inclement weather.'

'I can't imagine the marchioness being particularly thrilled at having to travel at such terrifying speeds.'

For what it's worth, I was going no more than 45 miles per hour.

It was the longest, most painful journey of my entire life. Once we reached the dual carriageway of the A9 I thought about putting my foot down and ramming into the central reservation, in the hope that the surface water on the road would allow me to create some fatal damage, but I resisted because of my manifold responsibilities.

•

The twins emerged from the car looking wan and bleary, and that was some consolation. They shook their hands about because they had been gripping their seats so tightly that it had aggravated their arthritis. I parked where I usually parked with the marchioness, letting them out of the car and directing them towards the hospital entrance. Rain fell relentlessly onto them.

'Are you not going to escort us up?' Morwenna said. 'It's raining, in case you hadn't noticed, and we will require you to furnish us with some protection.'

'I thought I would you give you some privacy,' I said, struggling to issue the last word. It was a hard sound to make with a low voice. 'There are some umbrellas in the boot.'

I removed the umbrellas.

'But we don't know where we're going and this is an enormous hospital,' said Biddy, who I was beginning to see was slightly less spiky than her sister.

'We are used to the Princess Grace,' Morwenna added. 'Or the Lister. Or the King Edward VIII. The Spire when we are in Edinburgh.'

'David was utterly committed to supporting the NHS,' Biddy declared. 'You mustn't forget that, Morwenna. Do you remember when he used to dress up as Father Christmas and visit the paediatric ward? With all those presents for the children?'

'I do, Biddy.'

I agreed to escort them and, after paying for parking on the Pay & Display machine, I took them through the revolving doors into the hospital. I only remembered, when we were in the lift to the fifth floor, that I had left my phone in the car. Hannah's message remained unread.

•

Judging by the look on her face, I would say that Morwenna did not enjoy the smell of the hospital. The ward itself had the most arresting funk, a heady blend of tepid, glutinous food and disinfectant that did little to mask the presence of myriad human excretions.

We reached the door to the marquess's room, and the calm and silence, apart from the beeping machines, that I had expected, was superseded by a frenzy. An assortment of doctors and nurses and other technicians surrounded him. Morwenna attempted to open the door and a woman turned to us and shut it, shutting us all out.

The twins looked at me as if I had the answer to the riddle of the swarming hospital room.

'What's going on?' Biddy said.

'I really have no idea,' I replied. But I forgot to lower my voice.

Morwenna looked at me askance. She angled one of her eyebrows at me.

'I have this eerie sense we've met.'

At that moment, the door opened. From the room came the thickest, densest silence I have ever experienced. The medics vacated apart from the last one whom I took to be a doctor, but, mercifully, not the same one as I had seen the last time I came to the hospital.

She said, 'Are you relatives of the patient?'

'We're his sisters,' Biddy said.

'Please follow me,' the doctor instructed.

And the twins followed her to a small room down the corridor, both turning to take one last look at me before going in.

Chapter 36

Angry Shona moonlighting as cab driver. She's driving around Perthshire with your baby.

I looked up from the phone. The twins were standing by the revolving door at the exit, dabbing tissues into the corners of their eyes. It occurred to me that they would stand there for the rest of their lives unless I were to get out of the car and escort them back to it. I can't deny that I was tempted to allow them to be absorbed into the workings of the hospital and not return them to the castle. I had no idea what would happen next, considering the marquess's sudden death. I was also coming to terms with the fact that Shona, despite always piling on the moral superiority, was nothing more than a racketeering moonlighter. I felt aggrieved – how much easier would my life have been had I been able to go about it with the baby by my side?

I sighed. My breath filled the deepest fathoms of my lungs. I got out of the car, flicking the hood of my coat over my head, making sure not to get it wet and thereby releasing the dye from it, opened the golf umbrella and approached the two women. They had failed to shelter themselves from the rain and were now saturated. Their hair was lank against their heads, the wool of their suits damp and matted. I held the umbrella over them.

Biddy was trying to tell me something because her mouth was opening and closing like a carp. Nothing issued from it.

'I'm so sorry,' I said.

Biddy closed her mouth and nodded solemnly. Morwenna sniffed and wiped her nose. 'We never got to say goodbye,' she said. 'And we thought we were going to say hello.'

I moved towards the car. They followed me. I opened the door. They crawled in. I observed that they were now sort of at my mercy. It was only an observation. Nonetheless.

•

'I have it on good authority that you are operating as a cab driver as well as a childminder.'

Shona shrugged. It was not the reaction I wanted. I had been so excited about displacing her from the moral high ground, about showing her that she had been caught in the act, about exalting myself by exposing her. On the way to collect the baby from her house, having dispatched the twins at the castle after a difficult drive from the hospital, I had been working on a range of reprovals. It was guilt and remorse I wanted. And some repentance. But I got none of it.

'Is that all you can say?'

'What do you want me to say?'

'Sorry at least,' I said.

'Sorry,' she said.

I was dissatisfied. She had no desire to satisfy me.

'So,' she said, 'you won't want me as your childminder anymore?'

She was woundingly unfazed.

'The marquess has just died so I can't really stand here

going over the reasons why it is unethical for you to ferry my baby around Perthshire while I'm paying you to provide an adequate level of care at the very least,' I said. 'Do you even have insurance for this?'

Shona shrugged again. 'Look, I don't know what the problem is. The baby's safe. Very happy bundled up in the car with me. I make a bit of money to pay off my student loan. It's expensive. It's the cost of living, you know?'

'Yes!' I exclaimed. 'Yes! I do know! Who do you think takes almost half of everything I earn?'

'It was your choice to have the baby,' she retorted. 'No one asked you to. No one made you.'

I was incensed. She could tell. I think she must have decided to change tack, because she looked down at the baby perched in her elbow and with the back of her palm she stroked the baby's cheek.

'The passengers love the baby,' she said.

'What?'

'My passengers. They love the baby.'

'I don't care if the passengers love the baby,' I said. 'There should be no passengers.'

'I'm just saying that people like your baby. Not all people like babies. Some babies are wee shits. I should know, I've seen plenty of them.'

'Why are you telling me this?'

'I reckon it's good to hear. It's a good thing.'

I took the baby from Shona and I scowled because I was jealous that I wasn't Shona's Cabs and I couldn't take my baby to work with me.

'Bit yellow,' she said.

'What?'

'Your hair,' Shona said. 'It's a bit yellow. Is that what you were aiming for? Yellow?'

'Yes,' I said.

And before she could shut the door on me, I grabbed the handle and slammed it shut with all my might.

•

The Saltire was at half-mast on the flag post at the top of the castle. Mark must have seen to that. There was no sign of the twins at the castle. They must have retreated to a far-flung wing to mourn their brother. Silver linings: their quest to find out who had thrown the party in the kitchen and drunk a load of the Rothschild's special wine seemed to have died with him.

I'll try to describe the sky that afternoon because it was so unusual. I was now used to the low and heavy cloud that sat above the castle most days but on this particular one it was dark grey – anthracite or gun metal – as if threatening to rain, yet the trees that lined the castle entrance were illuminated in the most celestial golden light. I looked around myself to locate the source of it but I couldn't find it.

Mark was standing by the steps outside the front entrance. There was a strange air of redundancy about him. He turned to enter the hall. I followed him. It was especially dark inside, dark and vacant.

'I'll light a fire in the drawing room,' he said. 'For the marquess's sisters. You haven't seen them around, have you?'

I shook my head.

He broke away, moving towards the corridor.

'What happens now?' I asked. The baby was in her pouch, facing out at him.

'The funeral,' he said, turning back. He was having to duck

the antlers that lined the walls because he was tall and the marquesses genetically were not.

'I mean with me,' I said.

He looked at me wearily. I had become a burden, a weight.

'I realise that sounds selfish,' I said. 'I'm sorry.'

'That's okay. You never met David. It would be impossible to mourn someone you never met,' he said, his tone elegiac. 'He was just a very good man. He was a rarity.'

Absentmindedly, he tickled the underneath of the baby's chin. The baby giggled.

'I don't even know if the marchioness knows,' he said. 'I've tried calling countless times but her phone goes straight to voicemail.'

Mark's attention was drawn to some activity outside the window. He moved closer to it. I went to look too. The view was obscured by the lattice windows. But I could see that a car was approaching from the end of the drive. As it came closer, I recognised it as the same police car that had been parked outside the castle just after the fire. Mark left the room, returning to the hall. I watched from the window.

The two detectives got out of the car. Mark approached them with an outstretched hand. They moved in turn to shake it. Mark was skilled at conjuring an air of propriety, even in the face of his grief.

I stuck my head into the corridor and could see them walking into the marquess's study. I moved closer to see if I could better hear what was happening in that room. I motioned to the baby to keep quiet by pressing my index finger against my mouth but she babbled back. I'm not sure what I had hoped to achieve by doing that. It was worth a try.

'I'm so sorry to disturb you at this very difficult time, but we wanted to tell you that we think we have in custody a suspect for the arson attack.'

I heard one of them say that from the study. I didn't know which one. I imagined it was Bad Cop.

Mark said, 'Oh yes?'

'Yes,' said Good Cop. 'Do you know a Mr James Propeller?'

'A mister who?' Mark said. He snorted involuntarily.

'Propeller,' came the answer. 'James Propeller.'

'No,' Mark said. 'Why?'

'We have arrested him in connection with the fire in the cottage.'

'God,' Mark said. 'I've never heard of the man.'

'Are you certain?'

'I think I'd remember a name like that,' said Mark.

'Is Ms Green about?' Bad Cop asked.

'Ms Green?' Mark repeated.

'We wondered if she knew anything.'

I was startled. I tried to think fast, deciding which exit to take. I went back on myself, heading down to the end of the corridor to the back staircase when a voice caught me.

'Camilla?'

It was Mark. I had been located. There was nowhere to run.

'The police are here,' he said. 'They want to talk to you. They think they found the person who set the cottage on fire.'

'Oh,' I said. 'Have they?'

Mark said yes.

'Hmm,' I said, feeling the baby's nappy with my hand. 'The baby's wet. I should probably change the baby.'

'It won't take long. Come on,' he said.

I followed him back down the corridor and considered

bolting in the opposite direction as fast as my stubby little legs would allow, but I did not.

'And who is this?' Good Cop asked the baby as I entered the drawing room.

I smiled. I was always grateful when the baby was met with warmth rather than revulsion.

'I was also about to ask who you were too,' he said. 'I didn't recognise you.'

'Oh, right,' I said, feeling my head. 'The hair. I fancied a change.'

The man looked down at his little notepad and then his feet. He didn't like my change, I could tell.

I sat down on the Eames chair by the window. I'm not sure what possessed me, given that it was the marquess's favourite chair, according to Kelly. But I was anxious and there was a chance that I had lost all sense of propriety. I would have preferred to stand with my back to the wall but I knew that would make me look shifty.

'We believe we have a suspect for the fire that was started in the cottage,' Bad Cop said.

'Oh right,' I said. 'I thought you said it was difficult with arson, you know, to find the perpetrators.'

'It is,' he replied. 'Usually. Almost impossible in fact.'

I moved the baby around on my lap and began to bounce her. There was a silence that no one attempted to break. I hated silences. Babies were usually a good way to end them.

'Do you know someone called James Propeller?'

'Hmm,' I said. I looked around the room in a quizzical fashion. I stroked my chin. 'I'm not sure I do. I think that's a name I'd remember.'

The officer was flicking through his notes. 'He was arrested in Pitlochry,' he said. 'On some other charges. Drunk and disorderly. Breach of the peace.'

I gripped the baby's thighs. I wondered which historical landmark had been creatively defaced this time.

'And while he was in police custody for that we have witnesses who say he was boasting about having burnt down a cottage nearby and we have assumed that it's the one you used to live in.'

'Why?' asked Mark. 'Why would he want to do that?'

The officer shrugged. 'That's what we're trying to find out. But we believe this confession he made to a duty officer at the time is enough to charge him.'

'There is also something else,' the other officer added.

'What?' I asked.

'It would appear that this Propeller person had hired a private investigator to spy on his wife but he couldn't pay him what he owed for his services, so this PI, according to Propeller, has threatened to break both his legs if he doesn't cough up, so he's begging to stay in custody.'

'Both his legs?'

'What was that?"

'Huh?'

Bad Cop said nothing. While I didn't like him much, I couldn't help but admire his resolve to protract a difficult moment.

'I said "both his legs". That's a pretty big threat.'

'Propeller already has a broken leg,' he said, scrutinising my reaction. 'He's limping about all over the place. God knows how he managed to set fire to the cottage in that state.'

I don't know what came over me but for some reason I couldn't help picturing the detective who was telling me all of this without his clothes on and all I could see was a shrivelled frame with a dangly phallus. I could not get it out of my head. Perhaps it was some sort of coping mechanism, my brain attempting to diminish my anxiety. I pictured the other one naked too.

'So what happens now?' Mark asked.

'We'll be working with the Procurator Fiscal now,' he said. 'But we just wanted to find out if you knew the man. He said he was looking for his wife and baby.'

Mark glanced at the baby.

I turned to face the window. 'Is that a deer?' I said.

All three men stood up to look. Their heads were moving in all directions, trying to locate the thing that wasn't there: my ingenious fabrication.

'Where?' Good Cop said.

I looked out again. 'Must have dashed off,' I said.

'What is the name of the wife?' Mark asked, retaking his seat. The others followed, doing that thing men do where they pull their trousers up by the knees just before they sit down.

'Emma, I think it was,' said the man, looking at his colleague for affirmation. 'Emma Propeller. Baby would be about a year old now, he said.'

A year. A year! James didn't even know the age of his own baby. Of course, it was fully to my advantage that he was such a terrible father.

'How old is your little one?' Good Cop asked.

'Six months,' I said. 'Coming up to seven.'

He scribbled that down in his pad.

'Emma, was it? I'll keep an eye out for her,' I said. 'But good to know you've got the culprit behind bars. Is there any chance he will be released on bail? He sounds very dangerous.'

'I doubt it,' Good Cop said. 'He's been remanded in custody until a hearing, until his intentions can be ascertained.'

'Do you mean whether he meant to do it?'

'Yes,' he said. 'And whether he knew the property was empty at the time. We think it was the drink. He's claiming diminished responsibility.'

'Diminished responsibility?'

'He's saying he's mad.'

'Oh. Right.'

Mark showed them out of the drawing room and I watched the men return to the car. There was a few minutes' worth of faffing about before they drove off and disappeared down the drive. I watched from the window.

Then came the sound of footsteps down the corridor, entering the room. I turned around.

'You're not Camilla Green, are you?

Chapter 37

'Pardon?'

'You're not Camilla Green,' Mark said.

'What makes you say that?'

'You're not though,' he said. 'They might not have put two and two together, but I have. I'm not stupid.'

'I never thought you were,' I said. 'I would never think that.'

'So it's not just the baby you were lying about,' he said.

He was standing in the doorway, half in the room and half out of it, and I did not like the way he was straddling two worlds: the world I was in and the world in which I wasn't. There was a distance between us.

'It's complicated,' I said.

'It always is,' he said, sardonically. 'We all have complicated lives, Camilla. Emma. How did you think that lying like that would be sustainable?'

'I had no choice. I had to get away,' I said. 'You can see what my husband is capable of. Although I can't believe it. I can't believe that he would do this. I can't believe that he would try to kill us.'

Mark stepped into the room. I settled.

'I don't know what to do,' he said. 'I have no idea. This is unprecedented. Our other employees have been so straightforward in comparison.'

'I'd understand if you'd prefer to let me go,' I said. 'I can see this that this whole thing is not ideal. I've brought you a lot of trouble. I'm so sorry.'

I knew at that point that I would have to go home. My new life was over. And if what the police officers were saying was true, that James was no longer to be an issue for me because he was effectively imprisoned, then my homecoming was now a possibility. But I also recognised that I didn't want to leave. I had formed an attachment. In that moment, it was clear to me that my heart was here.

Mark sat down on the chair next to the bureau. He fiddled contemplatively with a fountain pen that had been lying on the diagonal and placed it into a little cubbyhole in the desk. It rolled around for a second or two; the floor must not have been level. I supposed that was often the case with castles.

'Perhaps that is for the best,' Mark said. 'I have to do what is right for the estate. That's the basis of my job.'

I nodded, keeping my head bowed. A tear dripped down my cheek. Mark leant forward, pulling a handkerchief out of his back pocket. I took it and dabbed my left eye. I left the right one alone; I did not want to anger it. It had suffered enough.

'Stay until the funeral,' he suggested. 'I'll need your help. And then you can make arrangements after that.'

'Thank you,' I said. 'I really am very grateful.'

Mark stood up again. He was ready to leave. I didn't want to be alone with just the baby in that cold room.

'The person who alerted the fire brigade,' he said, turning to face me, 'it must have been the private investigator the officers were talking about.'

'What do you mean?' I asked.

'Someone alerted the fire brigade and no one knew who it was,' he said. 'Remember? And there was the car in the lay-by.'

'I knew someone was following me,' I said.

'What do you mean?'

'In the hospital,' I said. 'There was this man, and I could have sworn he was following me around. But I haven't seen him since. I guess now I know why. He's no longer being paid. I hope he doesn't come after me for the money.'

'That would be an irony.'

We laughed. We were finding the same things funny.

'So you weren't aware of any of this?' he said.

'No. The last thing I knew was that my husband was in London and he'd told the police that I'd abducted the baby. I couldn't use my real name because I was trying to start a new life here, away from him, away from his mother.'

'His mother?'

'You know, mothers-in-law . . .'

He prised the flesh away from his nailbeds again; evidently he had had a mother-in-law at some point in his life.

'Look,' I said, 'I know I will have to talk to the police. I'll have to come clean that I do know James and that I changed my name, but I hope they'll understand why.'

'I think you should do that immediately,' he said. 'Otherwise it's perverting the course of justice or something like that. I don't know. But whatever it is, you don't want to get yourself into trouble.'

I held the baby up, then lowered her and kissed her on the head.

'But what if they decide to take the baby away from me?'

I said. 'That's the whole reason I'm here, why I changed my name, because we had to get away from all the madness.'

'Then make that point,' he said sagaciously. 'Clearly this man hasn't a leg to stand on, quite literally too if this private investigator gets his way.'

Chapter 38

I told Good Cop, whose name I ascertained was Mo, everything over the phone and I mentioned the part about being on the run (but not in so many words) and how worried I was that I would get done for abducting my child (but not in so many words), but it turned out that there was no warrant for my arrest. Apparently, no one, apart from the PI and James, had been hunting me down. Their records stated that someone had intervened in James's accusations of child abduction, telling them that it had all been a hoax. I asked Mo who had intervened, but he would not say.

He explained that the police were trying to gather evidence that James had intended to start the fire, because he was now protesting his innocence, saying that he had been at the cottage at the time but hadn't started it and he didn't know who had. Without any evidence, the detective said that it was unclear how and if he would be sentenced – there were many mitigating factors to consider.

'It all depends,' Mo said.

'On what?'

'On what the Procurator Fiscal says,' he replied.

'What's the Procurator Fiscal?' I asked.

'Scotland's answer to the Crown Prosecution Service,' he said.

'Oh right,' I said.

Chapter 39

In the marchioness's lingering and inexplicable absence, the twins, with Mark's assistance, organised the funeral. No one had been able to reach the marchioness. No one had been able to track her down. No one knew if she was even aware that her husband had died. Morwenna was less than compassionate, flinging the word 'bolter' about on more than one occasion, while Biddy exercised restraint and suggested that something calamitous might in turn have happened to her. This thought had also occurred to me.

Mark, as ever, was inscrutable. Considering what I had understood of their relationship (or lack of it), I wondered if he didn't particularly care about the marchioness's whereabouts. I noticed however that weighty bags had formed under his eyes and his shirts were consistently misbuttoned.

In the resulting vacuum, a power struggle had emerged between the twins and Mark about the details of the funeral. Morwenna believed it should take place at St Giles' Cathedral in Edinburgh and that everyone the marquess had ever met should be invited, which, when they sat down to count, was nearing four figures. Mark, meanwhile, vexed and exasperated, produced a document from the marquess's solicitor which laid out his funereal wishes, which the marquess had had the prescience to inscribe several years before his death. It stated in *black and white* (Mark's emphasis) that his desire had been for a small funeral in the chapel on the estate, attended by his closest friends and family. He wanted a particular priest, a stoic. He wanted his wife to play the harp. The twins weren't hearing any of it.

'Well, to start with, there is no wife to play the harp. What do you suggest we do about that, Mark?'

Their harassment of him on this front was so sustained that he took to carrying that document everywhere with him as a physical reminder for them not to breach its terms, because they kept trying to.

'A big funeral is not what he would have wanted at all,' Mark told me in confidence. 'All those people. He was a private man. They know that.'

What he meant, I thought, was that the twins (Morwenna in particular) had regarded the marquess's funeral as a networking opportunity and, more specifically, an opportunity to bag a man.

Tensions ran high in those two short weeks. The twins took to drink; earlier and earlier in the afternoons I could hear the hiss of tonic and the frenzied unscrewing of the Tanqueray bottle in the library, where the twins had installed themselves. I noticed that Mark could increasingly be located anywhere the twins were not.

During this time, I kept trying to reach the marchioness, aware that if she were to return order would be restored to the castle, which felt paradoxical given the extent of the chaos that usually surrounded her.

I observed that the twins moved about the castle as if they

now owned it, commenting between themselves about the decoration in particular rooms that would 'have to come down as soon as' and I knew they were discussing the marchioness's weird Greek urn wallpaper. They hated the bare floorboards, and there was talk about Axminster carpets and tartan rugs. I imagined that they were hoping to transform the castle into their very own Balmoral.

As for me, I had come to accept that my days on the estate were numbered. After the funeral, the baby and I would be heading back to the flat in Chiswick, given that James no longer lived there, and I'd have to find a new job, doing what I had no clue.

I made sure always to look busy in the hope that my work ethic would change Mark's mind, so I took on many of Kelly's roles while she was away, which involved telling everybody else what to do, and I relished it. I told the cleaners which rooms to clean, which chandeliers to dust, which silver to polish, which curtains to take down for dry cleaning. I sent handymen to all parts of the castle to fix all sorts of things: cracked cisterns, jammed windows, bat infestations. I took delivery of the enormous Norwegian pine that Kelly had ordered for Christmas. (I wasn't sure what to do with it, whether to return it or to decorate it, so it just stood naked in the hall.) I wrote cheques and paid the household bills. The castle was running as efficiently as it always had.

Hedging that there may have been some possibility down the line that the twins would inherit the castle and consider keeping me on, I ordered food and flowers for them. (To their relief, I did not cook.) I suspected, however, that, given I was the marchioness's hire, this would be unlikely, and I would instead be just another person who had come and gone from this remarkable place.

I knew that it was only a matter of time before the situation with James came to light, that the twins would uncover my identity and Mark would only be able to keep my situation secret for so long. It would have been unreasonable of me to expect otherwise. For now, it was relatively simple for him not to mention the developments, mainly because there was no one else around to relate them to, but it couldn't last and I didn't want to burden him with the uglinesses of my private life when he didn't deserve to be embroiled in them.

The day of the funeral arrived and there was still no sign of the marchioness. We had to continue without her. And at any rate, the twins were superstitious about waiting more than two weeks after the marquess's death to hold it, especially as there was no guarantee that the marchioness would even return.

Mark had been victorious in his intransigence: the funeral took place just as the marquess had wished, in the chapel on the estate, attended by close family and the marquess's lifelong friends, of which there were many. I stood in the doorway handing out the order of service sheets and watched the guests as they entered and said 'I'm so sorry for your loss' more times than I could count. I doubted that I would be able to fill even one bench with my closest family and friends at my funeral, let alone a whole chapel. It is a serene comfort that we won't witness our own turnouts.

What I did notice was the stark difference in character between the marquess's funeral guests and the people at the marchioness's harp soirée. If I could have summed up this difference in one word, I would have said: *heart*.

The person who led the service did not look like a priest or a vicar or a rabbi or imam. She wore a red velvet cloak and a red velvet headdress with pink and purple plumes shooting out of it and read a poem that sounded as if she had written it herself because it was modern and weird and I had never heard it before – not that that is saying much – but it had that radio poetry quality that always gave me the creeps. I wondered if she was a poet or orator from the university of which the marquess had been vice chancellor. By the time she had finished reading it, I was ready to die myself. Looking around the congregation, I could see that I wasn't alone in this feeling. It struck me as an odd choice for the marquess, but I later learned that this person had been the marchioness's stipulation, because she was a humanist and the marchioness was devoutly atheistic, and once I understood that, it all made sense. It was then that I also understood just how much the marquess had adored his wife.

Then, quite suddenly, the mood changed in the chapel because there was an incredible noise behind us when the door slammed shut and who should be standing there but the marchioness.

Her entrance was met with the sound of frenzied whispering among the mourners. The twins' heads spun around so quickly that I thought they would fly off like planets from their axes. Morwenna was shooting daggers out of her eyes at her sister-in-law. Clearly, she had hoped that the marchioness had been wiped off the face of the earth.

I watched as she slipped like an eel into the pew opposite. I loved her hat! It was a black beret with a bow at the back. She wore a black silk jumpsuit, black patent stilettos. If I had to bet, I'd say it was Dior or Valentino – no messing about. That woman was made for funerals. Deep red lipstick burned on her lips. I wondered where it was she had come from. Perhaps she had been at the loch house all along. Why had no one thought to look for her there? Perhaps the whole airport thing had been a red herring.

She caught my eye and sort of smiled, lifting only one side of her mouth. I smiled back. She stopped smiling. I sensed some derangement. I had positioned myself by the entrance of the chapel so that, once the service had finished, I could dash to the castle and prepare to steward people for the wake. The baby was with Angry Shona, who I assumed would be transporting most of these people back to the station in her baby cab afterwards.

There was a tap on my shoulder followed by the sound of a throat clearing. I recognised the scratchy, hawkish sound and I withered.

'Outrageous disguise.'

Old Hairy.

I did not turn around. *Do not look round,* I told myself.

She cleared her throat again. I did not move.

No, no, no. I said to myself. *No*.

I drew breath and I turned around. 'What are you doing here?' I demanded.

'I've come to lend some moral support to my friends.'

'Friends?' I whispered. 'You don't have friends. You have accomplices.'

She was taken aback by my altered appearance, by my assertiveness, by this radical version of me. Her mouth opened, readying to make an announcement.

'This is inappropriate,' I hissed.

She sat back. Her chin retracted into the trunk of her neck as if she had been struck by a mallet.

'If you want to talk to me,' I said, 'do it after the service.'

She huffed and crossed her arms.

The marchioness shimmied along the pew and proceeded towards the altar. The harpist who was presiding intuitively stepped aside. An unwitting recruit of the Edinburgh Symphony Orchestra, whom Mark had organised in reserve, she vacated her seat and scurried into the darkness of the crypt, where she remained.

The organist approached the altar and whispered into the marchioness's ear. She whispered something back and then took her seat. When she sat, I could see that the jumpsuit had been an appropriate thing to wear, because manipulating the harp was not easy and a dress would have got in the way. She began to play. It was Cyndi Lauper's 'Time After Time'. I could have recognised that song anywhere. Even on a harp.

Come the final chorus, she nodded to the organist, who began to play the remainder of the song while the marchioness untethered herself from the instrument. She untied the black silk bow from her beret and unravelled it, swirling it around herself as she danced up and down the aisle to the song. I wasn't sure what to make of it.

Hilary sniggered behind me. I was incensed, because I loved that song and I loved the purity of the act of dancing to it. It was the song that Hannah and I promised we'd play at each other's funerals – whichever of us happened to shuffle off first. I thought that what I was watching was beautiful.

What I had come to understand about Mark, who was in the front row next to the twins, was that he was not a performance art kind of man. He turned around to look at the congregation, scanning it for someone. His eyes settled on me. I could see from his face that he wanted to do something about the marchioness's never-ending performance – either to interrupt it or let it carry on or somehow to tactfully unwind it because the mourners were wriggling uncomfortably in their seats, unsure if they were witnessing genius or mania. It was a fine line.

He stood up and moved to the side of the church. At first, he followed the marchioness around as if trying to catch a butterfly. He changed tack. He went over to the organist and made a wind-it-up gesture with his hands, but the organist, a very small individual with big glasses and an angular haircut, shook his head as if winding things up was not an option.

'I'm on a loop,' he mouthed elaborately. 'Just following orders.'

He threw his head back to signal that he meant the marchioness, who was now frolicking like Kate Bush in the 'Wuthering Heights' video. She must have been paying him handsomely.

Mark needed help.

I did what any other person would have done in that situation. I went to the marchioness, and I held her by the waist from behind. Startled, she glared back at me. She stopped dancing. All eyes were on us now.

'What on earth are you doing?' she hissed.

'Conga,' I whispered. I began to shuffle, pushing her forward with me. 'Just go with it.'

Slowly, solemnly, she began to move in time with me and, with Mark's encouragement and out of pity for the marchioness's distress, people began to join. By the time we had completed one full turn of the chapel, we were a line of fifteen people, then twenty, then thirty, and when our snake had reached a sizeable train, I steered the marchioness, amid wails and sobs, out of the doors and that was how we all ended up back at the castle for afternoon tea and champagne.

•

'Unorthodox transportation,' Mark said.

I looked at him in puzzlement.

'The conga,' he explained.

We were in the kitchen while the caterers packed up the glassware and crockery. There was an army of them, heaving crates out of the castle into vans parked outside by the stables.

'Have one of these,' he said, offering me a tray of canapés.

'I'm not that hungry,' I said. I didn't know how to tell him that I had stuffed myself stupid with them earlier while no one was looking.

'Go on,' he insisted. 'They'll just chuck them anyways.'

I took a smoked salmon blini with a dollop of unctuous cream on top and put it into my mouth. It was bigger than it looked. I was wrangling with the thing. Some of the cream oozed out. I tried to usher it back in without Mark seeing but I was not successful. I attempted to style it out. A turgid lump of blini escaped, landing on my black polo neck. I didn't know whether to pick it off or leave it. If I picked it off, I would have to put it in the bin, but it seemed like a seismic task to chaperone something as minuscule as that crumb to the bin. If I left it where it was it would make me look slovenly. If only there were a third way.

Mark took a napkin from a stack on the table. 'Do you mind?' he asked, gesturing a pincer motion with the napkin.

I shook my head. The intimacy excited me.

He removed the morsel from my chest. 'There you go,' he said.

I thanked him through a muffled mouth, ensuring that nothing else issued from it.

At that moment, the marchioness appeared at the bottom of the stairs and stood by the kitchen door. She had changed out of her jumpsuit and was back in her Chanel twinset. I wasn't sure whether she had witnessed our exchange.

'I'm sorry to disturb you both,' she said. 'But the will reading is scheduled for two o'clock. Could you take us to the solicitor? She's in Grandtully.'

For a split second I wondered if Angry Shona was also the local solicitor.

'Of course,' I said. 'I'll bring the car around.'

•

The solicitor wasn't Shona.

I know this to be true, because when I pulled up outside the office in Grandtully and let the marchioness and the twins out of the car, the solicitor, a woman who looked uncannily like Diane Keaton circa *The Godfather Part III*, came out and shook them by the hands before they all disappeared inside for three hours.

If I thought the drive to the hospital with the twins had been unpleasant and miserable, the drive to the solicitor with the marchioness and her sisters-in-law was another thing altogether. The saying was true: things could always be worse.

At first, there had been a silence. I imagined that the twins had made a pact to go nuclear on the marchioness because of her absence, her apparent unwillingness to explain it and their generalised contempt for her. It was Morwenna who cracked. She could not help herself.

'Where *have* you been? What were you thinking? You were his *wife*. You should have been here, no question. You can't *possibly* love him if you just disappeared like that.'

These were all fair points, much as it pained me to admit it. I was hoping that my curiosity would be satiated too – all the questions I had wanted to ask but dared not might be answered right in front of me (or right behind me) without any injury to myself. But that was not to be the case. The marchioness instructed me to stop the car and got out and joined me in the front. We were all none the wiser.

While they met with the solicitor, I returned to the castle where I had arranged to meet with Hilary before she headed back to London. The twins, prematurely proprietorial, had given her carte blanche to roam the castle, and I found her in one of the formal drawing rooms on the first floor that was opened to the public during the summer months. She was fiddling with a ruffle on the blouse of one of the mannequin children, used for display purposes to show what a nineteenth-century Scottish aristocratic family looked like.

'Terribly sinister,' she said, pointing at the creepy giant doll child.

'I've seen more frightening things in my life,' I replied.

'Touché,' she said.

She went to sit on a little pink silk damask chair by the fireplace, crossing one spindly stick leg over the other.

'What do you want?' I asked. 'I'll have to go back to pick them all up soon.'

'Don't worry,' Hilary said. 'I won't be bothering you for much longer.'

She swept her hands across her thighs, preparing herself to speak. 'I owe you an apology,' she said.

My heart jumped. I was in a state of hyperarousal.

'After you ran away, and I was left with James and Anya, I saw clearly the conditions you had been living under. I'm sorry that I hadn't registered it before. I hadn't realised how much you had got on with things while James did whatever he wanted and how you were abandoned by him.'

She took a deep breath.

'This is hard for me to say, but I see myself as partly responsible for what has happened.'

I didn't know how to respond. I had to fight every impulse to appease her, to put her out of her misery. To say it was okay. I had to tell myself it was not my job to make her feel better.

'You're probably not aware of this, but shortly after James alerted the police to your having run away with the baby, I spoke to the person who was dealing with the inquiry and told them that you had not abducted the baby and that it was James, not you, who was not of sound mind.'

'Not of sound mind,' I said. 'What did James tell them about me?'

Hilary shifted in the chair. 'He might have mentioned the time you went mad.'

'What are you talking about?'

'The time you ran away without telling anyone where you'd gone.'

'I didn't run away,' I said. 'I just went to a hotel, and it was only for a couple of nights. I was in the Premier Inn in Ravenscourt Park, ten minutes away, and I came back as soon as I felt better. All I needed was some sleep. James refused to do any of the nights. I did them all.'

'Be that as it may, you have form where running off is concerned,' Hilary said. 'James had to tell the authorities in case you'd done something stupid. Anyway, I now understand why you needed to do what you did. And I realise your mother passing away only months before hadn't helped matters. I phoned the police and I vouched for your character.'

'Why did you do that?'

'Because I love my grandchild and I want what is best for her.'

'Do you know what James tried to do to us?' I said. 'The fire. Do you know about that?'

She nodded and sighed. Her neck scarf fluttered in the wake of her breath. 'I do,' she said. 'That's the main reason I've come. It's a devastating day for a mother to have to visit her son in prison. Absolutely devastating. For what it's worth, he believed the cottage was empty that night. He is adamant about that. He is also adamant that he didn't mean to do it. I know he needs help with his drinking and the drugs, but I just don't believe he would be capable of attempted murder. The fact is: when he's drunk, he's a danger to himself and to others.'

Hilary hoisted herself up from the chair. 'I've settled James's debt with the private investigator. Just to make you aware.'

I wanted to say thank you. I stopped myself.

'I'd best be off,' she said. 'I just wanted to ask one more thing.'

'What?'

'Will you still let me see my granddaughter?' she asked. 'You can be there. You don't have to leave me alone with her if you don't want to, but please let me be in her life. I know that you won't want James in her life – I understand that – but I'd very much still like to be a part of it.'

'Can I think about it?' I said.

She nodded, her head bowed in chilling reverence.

'Do you know the number for a taxi?' she asked. 'I need to get to the station. I don't want to miss my train.'

•

The tension in the car with the marchioness and the twins was even worse on the way home from the solicitor's office. The sisters were stone-faced, white as swans. Even on discovering the death of their brother they had not looked as traumatised as they had after that meeting.

'We will require transportation back to Edinburgh immediately,' Biddy declared.

I looked at the marchioness in the seat next to me for confirmation. She nodded and whispered, 'Take them, will you?'

Morwenna refused to say another word for the rest of the time I spent in her company, not even as I let her out of the car at Royal Terrace and bade her farewell.

Biddy, climbing out of the car, said, ominously, 'You be careful. Things are not as they appear.'

Chapter 40

It might seem maudlin, but the following morning I took the baby with me to the walled garden to absorb as much of the estate as I could before we made our final departure. I had packed up our things in the orangery – we didn't have much stuff anyway, so it took little time – and I headed out with the baby in her pouch. I figured that I'd have to call Angry Shona to take us to the station in her cab and I wanted to delay that pleasure for as long as possible. Mark and the marchioness were nowhere to be seen. I can't begin to describe the air of desolation that had clung to the castle since the marquess's death.

The night before, there had been a storm, and I listened to the rain as it whipped the glass panels above me. The thrumming brought me comfort. It took me back to my childhood and to hearing the rain fall on the skylights in my bedroom. By the morning, the storm had passed, leaving the air crisp and the ground saturated, in parts impassable, particularly outside the orangery. I was having to wade.

I found a bench by the folly at the far end of the garden and I sat there and forced myself to make a memory of it: to consecrate my time at the castle to posterity because I had failed to do that in the past – to make a note of a moment that had been important.

The baby was silent. The sound of the water trickling ensured that. I played with her fingers, letting them glide through mine, wrapping them in my palms, jiggling them, kissing them.

But when I looked up, I noticed the marchioness at the far left-hand corner, on the opposite side of the garden from where I was sitting. She was trudging through the grass in wellies that were too big for her and made her legs look like sticks. She was wearing a Barbour coat. Her hair was tied up in a ponytail. She looked so normal.

Yet there was something furtive about the way she was moving; she looked distracted, enervated. It was such a gift to observe someone who didn't know they were being watched.

She made her way into the little cottage in the corner of the garden, the one I had noticed on my walk back to Mark's place several weeks before. I still had no idea who lived there, what was kept in there.

I considered approaching the cottage and taking a closer look but thought again. It was all over. It didn't matter what was happening there anymore, where the marchioness had been, what had happened at the will reading at the solicitors' office (although I thought I could guess). As curious as I was, as much as I wanted to demystify certain elements, it was futile. I was now an outsider.

But as I got up to leave the gardens, I thought to myself: what had I to lose? I was no longer the marchioness's employee and therefore had no requirement to be deferential. I could now talk to her woman-to-woman.

The baby began to whine. It was 11 a.m. It was time for a

feed so I knew that I didn't have long before the baby's hunger became intolerable. I made sure to take the path above the grassy bank that led to the cottage so that, if anything, she would think that I was just passing were she to come out of it and encounter me.

On reaching the cottage I knocked once, but there was no answer. I knocked again. Still no answer. I turned the door handle and felt the door yield; she had not locked it behind her. It opened fully into the blackness of the room.

'Hello?'

There was no answer.

It appeared to be a small living room with two sofas facing each other with some anodyne prints on the wall. It was conspicuously unremarkable. There was a bookcase on which stood a display of trophies and rosettes on one shelf and, below that, several framed photographs, the subjects of which it was too dark to decipher. This space functioned as a mausoleum. Yet it was casual, homely, ordinary.

The baby was whining and squirming. I knew I would have to make this diversion as brief as possible.

'Shh, shh,' I said to the baby. 'Hello?' I said to the room.

I could hear footsteps above. I considered going upstairs but felt that might have been too much of an incursion. The floorboards creaked overhead and I traced the sound over to the top of the stairs. Socked feet and then leggings appeared and then the rest of the marchioness. She yelped at the sight of me.

'God! You gave me such a fright.'

'I'm sorry,' I said. 'I was just passing and saw that the door was open so I just wanted to check that everything was okay.'

I looked at her and she looked at me. We had a stand-off

with our eyes. I smiled. She smiled. She had something in her hand that she was trying to conceal. It looked like a flashlight, one of those heavy-duty ones you use in a power cut. She did not once look at the baby. It was as if the baby wasn't there.

'Yes,' she said. 'Everything's okay.'

She made her way to the door and stepped outside, slipping whatever she had been holding into her pocket, while clutching the door handle. She did not let go until it was evident that I had taken her stance as a cue to leave the cottage. I did so. She locked the door behind me and stowed the keys safely in her pocket.

'What do you use this place for?' I asked.

'Storage, mainly,' she said.

'But the castle is so big,' I said. 'Surely there's enough space in there to store things a million times over.'

She was not used to the familiarity that I was bringing to our meeting. I elucidated:

'We're about to head off. I just wanted to sit in these gardens one more time before we leave. I hope that's okay.'

'Head off where?'

'London.'

'London? Why on earth are you going to London?' She stopped walking and started thinking. 'God. Did we make some sort of plan? Have I forgotten something? Sorry, my head's been all over the place lately.'

'No,' I said. I was affronted by her lack of consideration for my welfare, as selfish as that sounds. 'I'm going back to London because I don't have a job here anymore.'

'Who says?'

'Mark suggested it would be for the best.'

'Mark? But he answers to me.'

'I understand that,' I said. 'It's just that you weren't here and he didn't know where you were, so he had to take the decision himself.'

'Why did he have to make a decision at all?'

Judging by her reaction, it appeared that she had no idea about James's involvement in the fire in the cottage. I supposed that there hadn't been the time for all of that – she had just buried her husband.

'I've just buried my husband,' she said, as if she had read my mind. 'I haven't had the chance to think about domestic matters. Everything's happened so fast. Well, it has and it hasn't. For one reason and another, Kelly is not returning.'

'Oh. Why?'

'I'd rather not go into it,' she said and set off again. I walked alongside her.

Her wellingtons were crunching under the gravel on the path. It was a wonderful sound, satisfying, like someone eating ice. We approached the gate at the entrance. It was made from wrought iron, caked in verdigris with sublime swirls and plumes. The marchioness held it open for me as I walked through. I usually held doors open for her. I noticed that under her eyes were plump pillows of skin, edged with the darkest circles.

'I've been meaning to discuss something with you,' she said. 'I just haven't had the time. I hadn't expected this to be the case, but my husband has left the estate to me. I had assumed that because there was no heir, it would go to David's sisters as part of an entail or something. It's complicated. I don't really understand any of it, but it looks as if he changed the will before the car accident, for reasons no one knows. So I have to decide what to do with it.'

'What to do with it?'

'Yes.'

'What do you mean?'

'Whether to keep it or sell it.'

'Can you sell it? Are you allowed to?'

'I don't see why not. I can't see myself rattling around here on my own for the rest of my life. That was never something I wanted.'

We walked down the ochre avenue back to the castle, past little neglected fits and starts of topiary, where, window by window, the castle revealed itself to us magnificently. I wondered how anyone would voluntarily leave such a place.

'I need a housekeeper. No,' she corrected herself, 'I need a PA. Someone to take care of things around here for a while. Just while I get myself together. It's been a lot to deal with.'

'Do you want me to find someone for you?'

'No. I want it to be you,' she said. 'You can have the orangery. Kelly's old apartment. It's pretty there. I think you'd like it.'

I nodded. I kept my mouth shut. She didn't know that I had already taken up residence there. I knew just how much I'd like to live in the apartment in the orangery.

'And you can have the baby here with you while you work,' she said, acknowledging her for the first time. 'Or I can get someone here to look after her, whatever you prefer. I just need a friend. An ally.'

I was about to jump for joy, to offer my praises unto the heavens, when my phone rang. It was a number I did not recognise. I chose not to pick it up. Doing so would have undermined the importance of the moment. The phone continued to ring. I went to put it on silent.

'Go ahead,' the marchioness said. 'Pick it up. I don't mind.'

'No,' I said. 'it's fine. I'll get it later.'

'Pick it up,' she said adamantly and then, with a dose of restraint, 'I honestly don't mind.'

'Are you sure?'

She nodded vigorously. 'Of course.'

'Hello?' I asked.

It was a call from Hannah's neighbour telling me that as she was coming back from her morning run, she passed Hannah's flat and saw that the door was open and Hannah was lying on the floor unconscious. The neighbour then phoned an ambulance.

'Ambulance? Is she okay? What's happened to her?'

Looking back, I can see my terror so starkly in that moment. I didn't know what I was hearing. I was failing to understand what I was being told. All I could think was how helpless I was; how far I was from everything, from Hannah.

'She's on her way to the hospital,' she said. 'I found your number in her emergency contacts.'

'Yes,' I confirmed. 'I'm her sister. Where is she? Which hospital is she going to? Do you know?'

The caller hesitated and said, 'The one nearby.'

I couldn't remember having met Hannah's neighbour before, yet the voice on the end of the line was somehow familiar.

I said, 'The Queen Charlotte?'

'Yes,' she confirmed.

I hung up. The marchioness was looking at me with as much concern as she could anatomically achieve, having recently had most of her forehead paralysed.

'It's my sister,' I said, panicked. 'She's in hospital. I need to see her immediately.'

'Of course, of course,' the marchioness replied. 'Go straight away.'

'The baby,' I said. 'I can't take the baby. It's too much for the baby. I don't think I can deal with taking the baby.'

The marchioness held out her hands.

'You could leave the baby with me,' she said, looking at the baby as if it might detonate. She wasn't filling me with confidence.

'With you? Are you sure?'

'Yes, of course,' she said. 'Mark is here anyway. He knows what to do with babies.'

The thought of leaving the baby with the marchioness did not sit well with me, but neither did the thought of racing back to London with her when I had no idea what I would find when I got there.

'Okay,' I said. 'Are you sure?'

She nodded. I handed the baby over. She held the baby away from her with her arms extended. I wanted to tell her that it was an unsustainable grip. I would just have to try to let go.

'Take the Defender to the station,' she said.

'But I don't know how long I'll be gone for. I wouldn't want to leave it there if I don't know when I'll be coming back.'

'Mark could take you,' she suggested.

'Do you know where he is?' I asked.

'I make it my business not to know,' she said.

I called Angry Shona. She picked up. I told her I needed a lift to the station. She said she would be there in half an hour, as soon as her online lecture was over.

•

There were severe delays on our way to Dunkeld and Birnam. I raged against the injustice of heavy traffic in my unique state of emergency. I had hoped to catch the 12.42 from Dunkeld to Edinburgh and from there, a train to King's Cross, but it was already 12.30 and we were miles away, stuck in a contraflow on the A9 near Logierait. According to Waze, there had been an accident by the roadworks which had caused traffic to back up for ten miles. I could not understand why the other drivers around me were not as incensed as I was. Shona was refusing to beep which only poured fuel on the fire of my rage.

I asked her if it would be faster for me to walk at this point and she told me not to be ridiculous. She was chain-smoking menthols in the car.

'Should you really be doing that? I'm a passenger,' I said. 'And I'm paying you.'

I fanned my hand around and coughed demonstratively – the outraged tell of an ex-smoker – when all I wanted was to ask Shona if I could have one myself. But I'd burned that bridge with my rabid hand-flapping.

Once the traffic did ease – after a good forty-five minutes – I had missed my train so had to wait until the next one, which, infuriatingly, was not direct and required me to change at Stirling.

Dunkeld and Birnam was a relatively small station and looked more like a house with a track behind it than anything else. It reminded me of the cottage that burned down because it was made from the same sort of stone and had acutely pointed roofs. The waiting room was a glass construction on the outside of the station so I sat in there, warming my legs with my hands because it was such a cold day and I had not had the prescience to wear clothes that were warm enough.

While I was waiting, I tried to call the hospital, but there was no signal in the waiting room. I moved around, standing here, standing there – wherever I moved I could not get reception on my phone. I became increasingly frustrated and increasingly worried about my sister.

•

It was when the train was about half an hour outside Perth that I received a text message and had to do a double take.

The text was from Hannah. *How's tricks? Wanna crash at mine tonight? What time does train get into Kings X?*

I wrote: *Are you okay???*

??? came her reply.

I called her.

She wasn't at the hospital. There had been no accident. She was just scrolling through TikTok in the loos at work when she decided to text me, she said.

'But I got a call from your neighbour saying they found you unconscious in your flat,' I explained.

'Neighbour? There is no neighbour. Well, there is, but he's in Spain at the moment. He's a retired dentist. Just got divorced. Spends half the year in Marbella making up for lost time.'

'Then who called me?'

'I've no idea. What's going on?'

I couldn't understand what was happening. I was overstimulated, beside myself.

The baby. It had something to do with the baby. I was sure of it.

I stood up from my seat and ran to the train doors and pulled the emergency lever. The train alarm sounded. The train ground to a halt. The voice on the intercom told all passengers to stay in their seats, but there was no way I was going to do that. Nothing was ever achieved from being sedentary. I ran down to the front of the train and banged on the driver's door.

'Stop banging!' he said from inside his little cockpit.

'This is an emergency!' I shouted. 'I am the victim of some sort of fraud or a trick. My baby is in danger. Please let me out this minute.'

'Get back from the door!' the voice said. 'If you do not get back, I will call the transport police.'

'But my baby!' I screamed.

'Is your baby in danger?'

'I don't know!'

'What do you mean?'

'I don't know!'

'Is your baby on the train?'

'No.'

'Then what's the problem?'

'I don't know! And I won't know until I get off this train.'

'You can't get out now anyway. We're in the middle of nowhere. You can get out at the next stop. Stirling.'

'I can't wait for that!' I implored. 'I can't!'

'You can't wait seven minutes?' came the exasperated voice.

'I can,' I said. 'I can do that, yes.'

Chapter 41

I called Shona on the train on the way back to Dunkeld and explained what I had understood about the situation and that I needed to be taken back to the castle immediately because something was not right. Something was very wrong.

She laughed it off. She said it was probably some kids having a bit of fun, having a laugh.

'But it's not funny,' I said. 'How can it be a prank when it's not funny? How is it amusing?'

I was waiting for her outside the station and realised that this was the sort of conversation I should have been having with Hannah rather than Angry Shona, who appeared to have no compassion or humanity and who still wanted a fare even though I was in the grip of an enigma at best and a catastrophe at worst.

She pulled up and I got into the cab.

When I told her that I thought this all had something to do with the baby, she seized up. Her hands tightened their grip on the steering wheel.

'The baby,' she said. 'What's it got to do with the baby?'

'I don't know,' I said. 'Perhaps it's my husband. Maybe he's been let out on bail and he's tricked me into leaving the estate so that he can go in and get the baby. The person who called might be one of his friends. He might have put them up to it. I'd have no way of knowing. The marchioness has no idea who he is and what he's done. I didn't tell her. I doubt if Mark's told her either. He could just show up, say he's the father and what's to stop her from just giving the baby to him? And maybe Hilary's in on it too and because Hilary knows the twins, the marchioness will think it is all fine.'

'Hilary? Who's Hilary?'

'My mother-in-law.'

'Your family life is fucked. I mean it's really fucked.'

The headlights picked out a lonesome grouse on the road ahead. Shona mowed it down.

'Your boss. The Martian–'

'Marchioness.'

'Aye, her. She wouldn't do that,' Shona said. 'I mean, I don't know the woman, but she wouldn't give your baby away to a bunch of total strangers, would she?'

Shona turned off the A9 and onto the B road that led to the castle. Parts of it were still flooded from the night before, and I was worried that we wouldn't be able to traverse it, but, accustomed to the local roads, Shona sailed through it, carving up tidal waves on either side of her and waterboarding the sheep sheltering in the low fields.

'She's not thinking straight,' I said. 'She said so herself. You only had to see the way she behaved at the funeral. She's just lost her husband. God, what was I thinking, leaving the baby with her?'

'Aye,' Shona said, eyeballing me when she should have been watching the road ahead. 'What were you thinking?'

Chapter 42

Shona pulled into the castle, and I ejected myself from the car as it was still in motion, tripping over myself, falling and getting up again. I was a metaphor for myself! I ran to the back entrance by the stables.

From the car, I could hear her shouting that she would wait for me in case I needed to go anywhere else. It was true – she loved that baby.

I could see that neither the Defender nor the Volvo were parked in their usual places. The estate was a ghost town. I entered the castle, running through all the rooms in the basement, the ground floor and the first floor. I saw no one. I heard no one, saw no one in any of the bedrooms. Even in the old servants' quarters that were now used to store merchandise for the periods when the castle was open to the public, there was no sign. My baby was not in the castle, was not outside the castle. I ran out to the walled garden and to the cottage in the corner, but it was locked, and because it was now early evening and it was dark outside and there were no lights on inside, I satisfied myself that the cottage was empty.

I went to the orangery and that too was empty.

On my way back to the car, I phoned Hilary. I had no option. It was my last resort.

'Where is he?' I screamed. 'Where has he taken her?'

'What the hell are you talking about?' she said, sounding more like a New Yorker than I had ever heard her sound before.

'The baby's gone,' I exclaimed. 'The baby's gone. James has taken the baby.'

'What do you mean?' she said. 'What do you mean the baby's gone?'

'Where has he taken her?'

'He hasn't taken her anywhere,' she said. 'He is in prison in Perth. I spoke to his lawyer only an hour ago. Will you tell me what on earth is going on? Where is my grandchild?'

I hung up.

I returned to where Shona had parked. She was playing on her iPhone in the dark. I was entirely at a loss. My baby was missing and there was no way of knowing where she was. I was living my worst nightmare. I needed a Valium or, preferably, much heavier sedation. I was aware of the chaos brewing inside my head. It was threatening to consume me. It took everything I had to resist it.

'No one's here,' I cried to Shona hopelessly. 'No one's here.'

She looked up from her phone. 'Well, is there anywhere else they could be? Anywhere else they could've gone?'

Then, like a thunder bolt plummeting from the heavens, it struck me: there was one place.

Chapter 43

Lochs at night look like the 'abyss' you hear people talk about. Black voids. Swallowing holes.

I had imagined that it would be to our advantage that Shona knew all the local roads because it would get me where I needed to go much faster, and, to a certain extent, I was right. Shona drove so fast, we were really getting somewhere. The night had unleashed something maniacal in her – something heady and reckless. There was a drystone wall to our left that ran almost the entire route and I seized my seat as she veered closer and closer to it. We might die before we even get there, I thought to myself. The headlights of the oncoming cars blinded us, played havoc with my funny eye and, because of the surface water, the Citroën Picasso was struggling to keep a grip on the road.

I would have told her to be more careful, had I the opportunity to penetrate the density of her monologue. She was going on and on and on – she could not understand how people who lived in enormous castles could justify having second homes on lochs. I did try to tell her that water of that magnitude was not something that they could bring to the castle, which is why they instead brought themselves to the water, but she couldn't hear me; her outrage at the social injustice, at the fact that there were children in this country who spent their summer holidays starving, had overtaken her.

'Why do you think she's taken the baby there?' she asked.

'I don't know if she has,' I said. 'I've got no idea but I don't know where else to look. I've tried calling her and Mark, but I can't get through to either of them.'

We drove through the town of Aberfeldy, its main road lined with gift shops, cafés and outdoor clothing retailers, before reaching the loch and took the road that ran around it. Miraculously, I located the concealed narrow path that led down to the house from the main road and I urged Shona to proceed slowly down the track, not only because the conditions were hazardous but also because we didn't want to alert anyone who may have been at the loch house to our presence. I told Shona to turn her headlights off. We needed to be furtive, stealthy. We had no idea what we were dealing with, but as we made our way down the rocky track, a grasping beam of headlights swung towards us, and Shona swerved into a patch of woodland on my side of the track. We watched as the car sailed past us and I could see by the sheer size of it that it was not a normal car but a vessel and I guessed that it was the Volvo, driving away from the house. I could not tell who was driving and I made sure to duck down, pushing Shona down with me, in case we were spotted despite being shielded by the foliage. I could only hope that the Picasso would make it out of the copse and that we were not to be entrenched in mud.

'Turn around,' I said. 'Follow it. Follow that car!'

I sounded as if I was in a movie. It really did feel as if we were in a movie.

Shona watched as the red lights disappeared at the bend in

the track before she turned the headlights back on. She started the engine and revved up, but there was an agonising moment when the car resisted her attempt to move it and I thought that we were stuck, but soon it budged and we were out of the woods, so to speak.

We reached the top of the track where it joined the road that hemmed the loch and could see to our right those same red lights in the distance.

'There,' I said. 'Turn right.'

Shona kept back, not once getting too close to the car ahead, keeping a distance of around a hundred metres between us. 'This is what they do in movies,' she said.

'Exactly,' I said. 'Exactly.'

'Where do you think they're going?'

'I've no idea.'

By this point, we had driven for about ten miles around the loch, past the quaint and tiny village of Kenmore with its wattle-and-daub lochside cottages and the sprawling, blaring holiday resort.

'Never been there,' Shona said, her eyes gripped to the lights of the complex when I wanted to tell her to watch the road instead. 'It's got a bar – a sports bar. I've always wanted to give it a whirl.'

Two or three miles later, we noticed that the Volvo had dropped speed.

We hung back. The car crossed a small stone bridge and, through the skeletal branches of the trees on the other side, we saw the car stop.

'Wait here,' I whispered to Shona.

'Why are you whispering?' she asked. 'There's no way they can hear us.'

Shona pulled into a turning in a hamlet on the left-hand side of the road, which had a red postbox, a smattering of houses and a decommissioned telephone box next to it, now operating as a lending library, promising that other people were reassuringly in close range. There was a sailing boat attached to a car, a little further up from where we parked that must have been for use on the loch.

'Why have they stopped here?'

Shona shrugged. 'Beats me.'

On my phone, I swiped the screen for Maps and clicked the app to find our location. 'I've no idea where we are,' I said.

Shona lowered her window and stuck her head out. 'Someone's getting out of the car.' She reeled her head back in again and studied the display on my phone. 'The Falls of Acharn,' she said and pointed on the map to something that looked like a long, thin thread of water and the symbol of a chess piece – a king or a queen.

'Hermit's Cave,' I said. 'What's that?'

'Beats me.'

I wanted to throw my phone at Shona for being so flagrantly ignorant about her native environment. She opened the door. 'Where are you going?' I asked.

'To see what's going on. You coming?'

'Shouldn't we have a plan? We can't just go out there if we don't know what we're dealing with. Surely, we should have a plan.'

Shona climbed out of the car and shut the door behind her. I followed, unprepared, without any semblance of a strategy. Shona lit up the road with her phone torch and we followed its light across the bridge to where the Volvo was parked. It was shrouded in darkness now; inside there was no sign of life. Feeling reassured of this, Shona shone her torch into the windows, but I could have told her that it was pointless because all the windows were blacked out. Nonetheless, I admired her audacity.

'Look,' she said, her torch lighting up the ground, casting it in a wan light. 'That's a bootie. That's one of the baby's booties. I'm right, amn't I?'

I bent down and picked it up. I studied it in the beam of my phone, unwilling to rely on the steadiness of Shona's hand. I was so frantic that my heart began to beat arrhythmically and on the off-beats I worried that it would stop altogether.

Shona raised her torch; it shone on a sign to our left, etched in wood: *The Falls of Acharn.*

'Bet that's where they've gone,' Shona said. 'Bet you.'

She shone the torch in the direction to which the sign pointed. It was another rocky track leading to a hill. I couldn't tell from where we were standing how steep it was. I couldn't get a feel for the summit but we began our ascent regardless. My shoes were sodden. Inside them, my feet were frozen and blistered, the stones beneath them pummelling my soles. Something about this felt puritanical in the pain it was delivering, in its extremity.

We were in total darkness now, the sort of darkness that horror happens in. I checked the battery life on my phone. It read 19%. I put it on low power mode.

'How much battery do you have left?' I asked Shona as next to me she huffed and puffed, stopping occasionally to catch her breath, clutching her thighs with her hands and exclaiming Jesus Christ over and over again. And when she had done enough of that she dug inside her pockets for her Vogues, popped one out and lit up before repeating the ritual. She flipped her phone over. 'Nineteen per cent,' she said.

I nearly said snap. 'I'll turn my phone off then,' I said.

'Why?' Shona asked.

'Because I've only got nineteen per cent too,' I said.

'Snap.'

'We'll only have the light from your torch now,' I said. 'We need to preserve battery life.'

Shona was so selfish with the light. She was so selfish! I could barely see anything. I felt that she was deliberately holding her phone at an angle so that it shone more to the right than between us.

'Can you shine the light back the way we've come?' I asked. I wanted to get a sense of how far we had progressed.

Shona turned and cast the torchlight into the expanse of blackness. All I could see was the ground a metre away from me. I had no idea where we were. As long as we kept going up, as long as I felt resistance in my thighs, then we were moving the right way.

'Shh,' Shona said.

'I didn't say anything.'

'Shh,' she repeated. 'Do you hear that?'

I applied every cell in my body to locating the sound, to try to hear beyond the pounding of my heart.

'It's running water,' she said. 'Can you hear it? We must be close to the falls.'

Once she mentioned it, I could hear it. It was remote, like the sound of a tap running in an upstairs bathroom.

'What if we don't see it and we fall down into the gorge?' I asked.

'What gorge?'

'Water falls, doesn't it? It must be falling from a height. There must be a severe drop near here.'

Shona scanned the space around us, surveying it for signs of a deadly drop. The light stopped on something. It was a small wooden sign that read *Hermit's Cave*, the same one we had seen on the map. I approached the sign. It pointed to the left.

Shona shone the light in my face. I flinched. 'What are you doing?' I shouted, outraged.

'I just wanted to see the look on your face,' she said. 'I wanted to see if you're as shit-scared as me.'

I could hear something that I recognised so viscerally, the sound of it tore through me. 'It's the baby,' I said. 'In there, crying. In the Hermit's Cave. Can you hear it?' I glared at Shona, desperate for her to corroborate.

'From in there, no?' she said.

I turned my phone on again, waiting for what felt a lifetime for it to reignite. I moved to where I thought the noise was, shining my light frenziedly around me. I shone the light back at Shona. She contorted her face.

'I'm not going in there,' she said.

I had to go it alone.

The entrance to the cave was low, and I had to stoop. I stepped inside. It was dank, rivulets of water dripped from the roof of it. One drop hit my eyelashes where it stayed, suspended, refusing to release itself to the ground. I must have walked for only five metres when I came to a junction in the cave, with another tunnel leading out to where the sound and fury of the waterfall was louder and more violent. I followed the sound. A light shone on me and I looked away. It was blinding. It had come from a proper torch, a flashlight, like one of the ones on the estate, like the one the marchioness had been carrying earlier that morning.

'Go,' said the voice from which the light shone. 'Go.'

I knew it was the marchioness because of her vocal quality. That was the only clue, because the accent – no, dialect – in which she was speaking was different. For the first time, she sounded Scottish, unmistakably so, like the girl from *Trainspotting* who takes all her clothes off.

'What are you doing here?' she shouted.

I lifted my torch up to try and see her, but the glare of her light defeated mine. She could see me, essentially, but I couldn't see her.

'You stole my baby!' I shouted. 'You stole my baby!'

The baby mewled.

Behind me, I heard footsteps. It was Shona. I turned around and whispered, 'Stay back – the baby's here.'

From what I could tell, we were now in an opening – out of the cave. I shone my torch around the margins of her beam and could see railings in a semi-circular formation that must have spanned four or five metres. Beyond the railings I could only imagine was the gorge because of the sound of the waterfall thrashing the pools beneath.

'What are you doing? It's the middle of the night. The baby's tired and freezing. I don't understand.'

There was a long silence.

'This is where it happened,' she said.

'Where what happened?'

'This is where I killed Mark's baby,' she said.

'Mark's baby?'

'Not baby. His daughter. He always saw her as his baby.'

'You killed Mark's daughter?'

'It was an accident,' she replied. 'It was an accident, a terrible accident.'

The way she was speaking was new to me. This was a different person, real; complete. I could make sense of this person. The other one had eluded me.

She lowered the torch light. I shone mine on her.

From behind me I could hear Shona whispering, 'Get the baby, get the baby, get the baby . . .'

'Who's that?' the marchioness asked.

'Shona,' I said. 'She's the baby's childminder. She's very worried about the baby.'

I could hear Shona retreating through the tunnel and into the cave.

'The baby is fine,' she said. 'Don't you think I know how to look after a baby? This should be my baby. I should be holding a baby now. It was my turn. It was my turn.'

'What was your turn?' I asked.

'Kelly,' she said. 'Kelly was carrying my baby. That baby was for me, and it was for Mark to say sorry.'

'Kelly was carrying your baby?' I asked. 'But she was going through the menopause. She can't have been pregnant.'

'Wrong,' the marchioness said.

'Why did no one tell me?' I asked. 'That whole business with the harp. Why did you let her carry it if you knew she was pregnant? You should have known how dangerous that would have been.'

She was silent. She squirmed; I could see her silhouette undulate in the corners of my phone light.

'She could have lost the baby doing that,' I continued. 'And I nearly broke my foot. What were you thinking?'

I had angered her. The air sparked between us. I had to find a way to pacify her.

'This should be my baby,' she said. 'I should be the one carrying the baby, holding the baby. It was my turn.'

'I understand that the last few weeks have been difficult with your husband dying . . .' I began.

'No, they have been difficult because I lost my baby,' she said.

'What do you mean?'

'Kelly lost the baby. She was my surrogate. After what happened with the harp I sent her to a cottage on the estate, thinking she'd be safe there, as long as she rested. That's where I've been. But she had a miscarriage. I was with Kelly when she lost my baby. We had the saddest time. We had so many plans.'

Rain fell, only drizzling, but there was a chance it would become torrential.

'She was the one who called you, you know,' she continued. 'She pretended to be your sister's neighbour. She would do anything for me. It's why she posted that note through your door. She was worried about you. No, not about you – *by you*. She was worried by you. She saw you as a threat.'

'She posted that note? That's insane. Completely insane.'

'Yes, it was,' the marchioness said. 'But she loves me. She just loves me.'

'What was she hoping to achieve?'

'That you would leave, probably. We were to have the baby together and raise it in the castle. Like a kind of commune . . . Maybe she sensed you would endanger it.'

'But she was so helpful,' I said. 'She helped me find Shona.'

'Who?'

'The childminder!' I shouted. 'The baby's childminder!'

'Whatever,' she said dismissively. 'All I know is that she wanted a baby and I wanted a baby. It made sense for us to have a baby and raise it together, because she couldn't find a man and my husband couldn't have children and there is a problem with my womb. They call it inhospitable.'

'You mean hostile.'

'Huh?'

'Hostile. The term is hostile womb. You have a hostile womb,' I said, detecting some mania in my own voice.

'What difference does it make? Hostile, inhospitable . . . it's all the same language. It's all made to make me less of a woman, less of a *human* . . .'

I could hear the rain pattering on the railings, an increase in the frequency of its fall. I worried about how wet the baby was getting, how unwell this might make her.

'I was going to make it all up to Mark,' she continued. 'Because he could have a niece or a nephew to replace the child he'd lost, the child I'd killed. There was a plan. Although my husband should have died much sooner than he did. I had been assured that he would not suffer a long and painful death, but it was. That haunts me every minute of every day.'

I heard a man's voice behind me. The sound of other people in the desolation of this moment filled with me with indescribable relief. The marchioness hadn't heard the voice. The sound of the waterfall must have muffled it.

'You know Mark's my brother,' she said. 'Of course, you know that. You're not stupid.'

I didn't know that. I was stupid.

'It's because of him that I am where I am. I mean not literally, here in this moment, by this beautiful waterfall, in this darkness with you and this baby. It's because of him that I'm a marchioness. He was one of the estate hands long ago and one summer I was at the estate, during the summer holidays, and David saw me and invited me into the castle. He taught me all about the Classics.'

'Heather.'

It was Mark. He was standing behind me. He shone his phone in my face. I flinched. He redirected the light toward the marchioness. 'You told me you'd never come here again,' he said to her. 'You promised me.'

'You shouldn't have come,' she said.

'Everyone's been looking for the baby, Heather,' he said.

'I wanted to show her the falls,' the marchioness said. 'I wanted her to see how beautiful they are.'

'Come on,' he said. 'It's not going to bring her back. Nothing will.'

I wondered what her plan with my baby had been. I knew not to ask, if asking alone would nudge her into executing whatever it was she had been working on.

'You're going to give the baby back to Emma now,' he said.

'Emma? Who's Emma?' she asked, baffled.

'Camilla,' Mark said. 'Emma is Camilla.'

The marchioness stepped towards us, cast only in the light from Mark's torch. I inched forward. She held my baby in her arms and looked at her. She looked so deeply into her as if she were searching for something. But then she moved away, closer to the railings, and she held my baby aloft. She dangled my baby over the gorge.

I screamed. That's all I can remember. My own screaming. The raw leonine pitch of my screams.

'I'm so empty, Mark,' she said. 'I'm so empty. I don't feel anything. It's just nothing all the time.'

She turned around, her arms still extended. My baby dangled like a cub, legs swinging alternately in the air, with no sense of the threat she had been in.

Slowly, Mark approached her and took the baby and then passed her to me and I seized her, clutched her, held her so close that I had to tell myself to loosen my hold for her sake. I retreated into the tunnel, through the cave and out the other side, where I found Shona chugging anxiously on a menthol cigarette for all it was worth.

She dropped it on the wet ground and ran to the baby, feeling her cheek with the back of her hand. 'Wee thing's freezing,' she said. 'Let's get her home.'

Together we made our way back down the hill with Shona steadfastly lighting the path ahead.

Chapter 44

'Let me give you something for your eye,' Mark said, referring to my current ocular flare-up. 'I get the same thing. You need steroid drops. It's when the pinguecula becomes inflamed and it looks like conjunctivitis, but it isn't. I've got some at the cottage. I'll drop it in before you head off.'

'Thank you,' I said and I let him into the house.

He went through to Shona's living room and sat on the sofa. I sat down in the armchair next to him. For a while, he said nothing but looked around the room, studying Shona's belongings and piecing together her personality from what he saw, his eyes lingering on the *Live, Life, Love* sign illuminated by twinkling red and green Christmas lights on her mantelpiece.

'It was her first husband,' he said. 'He was strict and authoritarian and, you know, an oppressive type. I don't think she really recovered from being married to him, and even though she was happier with David, and even though he treated her well – like a goddess – I don't think she ever properly dealt with the first one. It was a long time – ten, twelve years. I think it changed her, the way she was programmed, if you get what I mean.'

On the sofa next to Mark was the duvet under which I had slept the night before, folded and put to one side with a pillow stacked on top. He looked odd sitting next to it. Shona had said we could stay with her after our adventure at the falls. It had been a restless, wakeful sleep, and yet I had been exhausted. I supposed that was to be expected given what had happened and how much worse things could have been.

'Heather had been looking after Agatha, my daughter,' Mark continued. 'She was six at the time. My wife had died a few years after she was born and her death, after the diagnosis, came in a matter of months. I was in denial about it and I wasn't coping. This was around the time that Heather married David and she took Agatha under her wing because she could see that I couldn't deal with it. She loved her like she was her own. It sounds like a cliché but it's true.'

I could see that Mark was struggling with this, because his voice started to quiver and he spaced his sentences far apart so that he could get some purchase on his words. I wasn't sure whether to tell him that it was okay; he didn't need to tell me any of this, but I knew that that was to do with my own discomfort with difficult things and that, if he wanted to tell me what had happened, I should allow him to. I didn't need to make things better for him. Things could be uncomfortable.

'Can I get you some tea?'

He shook his head. 'No, I'm fine, thanks.' He cleared his throat and straightened his back. 'Heather used to take Agatha to the falls whenever they stayed at the loch house. Agatha thought it was the most magical thing, that one minute you could disappear into the darkness of the cave, and the next, come out the other side and see this incredible waterfall. Heather was so good at creating wonder and mystery for her.

These were things I couldn't do. I couldn't see that there was anything but sadness in the world, but Heather showed Agatha the opposite – she showed her the magic. Also, I think that for Heather, spending time with Agatha freed her because she was this beautiful source of light and hope when she had been in the darkness for so long.'

'Heather?'

Mark nodded. 'Her ex-husband wasn't violent or verbally abusive or anything like that but he had this incredible power over. She felt like a prisoner in her own head – do you know what I mean? And she always felt she had no choice because he had told her so, that because she was brought up in poverty, you know, on a council estate, because she had nothing, she was lucky just to have a roof over her head.'

'Kelty?'

'Huh?'

'Was the council estate in a place called Kelty?'

'Aye,' he said. 'Why?'

'I got lost there with her a few weeks ago on our way back to the estate. She told me she wanted to stay and have a look and I couldn't understand why.'

'That's where we grew up,' he said. 'I'm surprised she even got out of the car. She always said it was the last place she'd ever go.'

'But she always seemed so exotic. I could never place her.'

'That was exactly what she wanted people to think.'

'What happened with her husband? Her first husband.'

'She left him. Upped and left.'

'Where were they living?'

'Basingstoke.'

'Basingstoke?'

'Yes, Basingstoke,' he said. 'It's in England. In Hampshire.'

'I know where Basingstoke is,' I said. 'It just surprises me. I can't really picture it. She made it seem as if she'd had this jet-set lifestyle.'

'No. It was a very normal life, from the outside anyway. She worked as a teaching assistant in the local school. That's where she met Kelly. They worked in the same school together,' he said.

'They worked together?'

'When she married David, she asked Kelly to move up to Scotland and work as her housekeeper. She had been her only friend and she didn't want to be without her.'

'I just don't get it,' I said. 'I can't see her working with children. She had that rule about no children on the estate and she was so uncomfortable with the baby.'

'Heather loved working with children,' he said. 'But she was so worried about another tragedy. She didn't want to take any risks. That's why she had a blanket ban. The problem was that her drive to have children was just so strong.'

'Is that why she left her husband?'

'Partly that. He didn't want children, and she felt suffocated. That's what she said. Her husband was controlling, you know. We never saw her. He didn't want her to have a relationship with her family, not that we were much of a family. That was all part of the problem. She had no friends. It was just him and her job and that was it, that was her life. She left with nothing and without telling him because she had tried to leave the proper way, you know, by saying that she wanted to leave him, but he wouldn't let her. She told me that she could feel the stress of it all the time. Even when she wasn't with him, she felt this tension that she knew would kill her if she didn't do something about it. And then one day she had had enough. She left and came to the castle. The marquess remembered her from when she used to work in the stables in the summer holidays and he let her live in the cottage in the walled garden until she found her feet. But over time they grew close. Something in him wanted to protect her. She has this vulnerability that makes people so protective of her . . . it's incredible, really. They want to look after her.'

The normalcy of the cottage in the walled garden made sense to me at that moment. It was a halfway house, where Heather was laid to rest and the marchioness had come to life.

Outside the house there was the sound of beeping, of a large vehicle reversing. I could hear Shona in the corridor shouting something about the bloody bins, rattling and crashing as she ran to the front door. Empty bottles clashed violently inside the cavernous plastic walls of a blue and yellow IKEA bag. The door slammed behind her.

'But it all changed with Agatha.'

Mark stood up and moved toward the window. He parted the net curtains with a finger. I peered outside. Shona was remonstrating with the bin men. He removed his finger from the net. The curtain fell.

'If you come out of the cave, away from the viewing platform and back up the hill, there is another path down to the falls, which, before the accident, used to lead to this little place where you could swim in the pools. Now, there are barriers and bridges, but then, you could swim and play and that's what they loved to do, but, on this day, the weather turned. The rain became torrential, so much so that Heather could hardly see a thing. And she couldn't see that Agatha had been swept away by the current.'

He looked up at the ceiling to stem the flow of tears.

'I'm so sorry,' I said. 'I'm so, so sorry.'

He shrugged and sniffed. I walked over to him and wrapped his hand in mine.

'Thank you,' he said.

I withdrew my hand, and I sat back down.

'Agatha's happiness was the only thing that mattered to me,' he said. 'When the grief and the pain get too much for me, I think, at least she's with her mother. At least she did not have to go through life without her mother.'

'But you've had to go through life without her,' I said.

Chapter 45

Even though it was December in Chiswick – my erstwhile favourite time of year in my erstwhile favourite place – I felt an emptiness. Christmas lights illuminated the High Road and the roasted chestnut vendor had pitched up outside Waterstones, wafting out the nostalgic aroma with the aid of a little battery-operated fan. All the ingredients for a pleasant Christmastime were there, but I could not attain the sense of joy I yearned for.

The flat felt cold and unwelcoming, and I found the din of the trains, the cars, the buses and the planes more intolerable than ever. And there were people all over the place. I couldn't get away from them. I thought I would love being within a stone's throw of my coffee shop where they wore the serious black aprons, but I felt silly paying the money they wanted me to pay for the coffee, having experienced life with a Sage machine and Nespresso pods.

But at least I was closer to Hannah. She had, however, found herself a man I didn't like very much. He was the one she had met on the Tinder date that had wrenched her away from Scotland and from me. There wasn't anything radically bad about him, but I could see that he wasn't right for Hannah because he was dull and had a rodent quality and, most importantly, I knew she was settling and that made me sad.

She invited the baby and me over for Sunday lunch and her boyfriend was there, providing a running commentary on her gravy-making, telling her to add cornflour when she was absolutely refusing to and she was telling him to fuck off. While I found witnessing this exchange painful, it made me so grateful that I was no longer married because, as a bystander, I could see how harmful being in a long-term, committed relationship was to a person.

After we ate, she sent him out to get pudding from M&S, which was a good forty-minute round trip, factoring in driving, finding a parking space, locating the pudding and buying the pudding. It meant that we could talk without his ferrety head swivelling about between us.

'What do you think?' Hannah asked.

I said nothing which, between sisters, was saying everything.

'Come on,' Hannah said. 'You can tell me.'

'I'm going to tell you something the marchioness told me.'

'You're giving me advice from Princess Nut-Nut?'

'She's not mad,' I said. 'She just had a terrible time.'

Hannah smiled.

'What she told me,' I continued, 'was that a husband can be either an anchor or a weight. A jailer or a liberator.'

'But I'm not talking about marriage,' she countered.

'Not yet,' I said. 'But you might, and things have a way of gaining momentum. You have to decide which a man will be – a jailer or a liberator. Once you know, you can act accordingly. You may decide that you would prefer not to be jailed. Or that you require no liberating, because you are already free.'

The baby was sitting on my lap, sucking on a Yorkshire pudding.

'You sound like a podcast,' Hannah said.

I nodded sagely.

'Things aren't as black and white as that, and you know it,' she added. 'Why does a husband have to be a jailer or a liberator at all? Why can't they just be someone you have Sunday lunch with?'

'Because Sunday lunch is the easy part,' I said.

We shared a peaceable silence. The winter sun was low, perching on Hammersmith Bridge.

'Does that mean you're going live like a monk for the rest of your life?' she asked me.

'I think I'd probably love that,' I said.

'But what are you going to do about James? Or not? Do you even need to communicate with him again now that he's an actual criminal.'

'I spoke to him.'

'When? You didn't tell me.'

'Just before I left Scotland.'

'And?'

'His case is coming up for sentencing,' I said. 'He was repentant. He said he had definitely hit rock bottom.'

'No shit.'

'He wants to be able to see the baby. For me to bring the baby on visiting days. I told him I would need to think about it, you know, because he nearly tried to kill us – which he denies.'

'Visiting days?' Hannah said. 'What a joke. Go all the way up to a prison in Scotland to visit him?'

'They'll probably move him south when he's sentenced.'

'Makes no difference,' she said. 'He deserves nothing from

you. He should ask for nothing. And he should get nothing. *Nothing.*' She pounded her fist on the table like a gavel and our cutlery clattered. A fork fell off the table and I bent down to pick it up. 'What about Mark?'

'What about him?'

'Well, there was something there, wasn't there? I can't have been imagining it.'

I shrugged. I pushed the fork prongs into my fingertips. They formed yellow dimples on my skin. 'I think I have to leave all of that in the past now and move on,' I said. 'They've put the estate up for sale. Mark has power of attorney over Heather. She's in a mental health unit somewhere, I think. I'm not sure where.'

'The one her husband was in?'

I nodded.

'Jesus,' Hannah said. 'Unbelievable. Unbelievable that you went there to get out of the madness here, only to find it madder.'

'Yes . . . but it made me feel less mad.'

'It's all relative,' Hannah said.

I could hear footsteps outside the flat. Hannah's new boyfriend opened the door. He stood in the doorway, legs wide apart, holding up a pie, jangling his keys.

Chapter 46

Hilary found me in Gail's on the High Road while I was researching how to be an Uber driver on my laptop. I was dismayed that I'd have to go through the process of getting a Private Hire licence to become one. I thought it would be a lot simpler –I thought I could be an Uber driver while I went back to university, having been inspired by Shona, studying what I wasn't sure. Hospitality, I thought. I had enjoyed running the castle even if it had been for only a fortnight. Or perhaps I could do something sexy like an MBA.

Hilary said she had just been passing, but I wasn't buying it. How could she have possibly just been passing when she lived eight miles away in St John's Wood? She was obviously either stalking me or having me followed, having taken a leaf out of her son's book.

She offered to buy me a coffee and, begrudgingly, I agreed. I told her to get me a cinnamon bun and she recoiled at the prospect of having to procure carbohydrates against her will. She sat down, placing the little steel tray in front of me.

She got straight to the point. 'Where's my granddaughter?'

'She's with my sister,' I said.

She snarled. 'I would have liked to see her.'

'Well, I'm afraid I wasn't expecting you–'

I looked around myself in mock incredulity, and she shuffled in her seat for a bit and fiddled with the rings on her fingers.

'I have some information to impart.' She cleared her scratchy vulture throat.

'Firstly, James has been sentenced to six months in prison, which, according to the solicitor is a good outcome.'

I looked at her indifferently.

She continued: 'And secondly, I'm afraid I will have to sell the flat.'

I looked up sharply from my latte. 'What?' I bellowed. 'You can't!'

Around us, everyone went quiet.

'I'm afraid that I can,' she said. 'You see, money's tight at the moment. All those lawyers' fees. Reducing James's sentence to six months didn't come cheap, you know.'

'Money's tight? You live in a mansion on one of the most expensive streets in London.'

'Yes – and it's very expensive to live on one of the most expensive streets in London.'

'But the flat is in James's name,' I said.

'It isn't, darling,' she said. 'I bought that flat. It's mine.'

'But it's our marital home,' I said.

'Theoretically,' she said.

'Theoretically?' I repeated.

Hilary straightened her back. She took a sip of coffee.

'Where do you expect us to live? You are literally kicking us out.'

'I thought you could come and live with me,' she said. 'You said it yourself: I live in a mansion on one of the most expensive streets in London. Who wouldn't want to live there?'

'Me! I wouldn't! Not in a million years. Not now – not ever!'

Hilary downed the rest of her Americano and placed it meditatively into the saucer. 'Think about it,' she said.

She got up and walked away, clubbing the other customers on the way out with her Prada Saffiano.

•

I walked back to the flat, past the florist, past the little coffee shop. There was an altercation between the cheesemonger and the butcher because the queue for people picking up their turkeys was blocking the entrance to the cheese shop.

I texted Hannah: *On my way back. 5 mins.*

As I was about to press send, a call came through on my phone. I didn't recognise the number. I decided to leave it in case it was James (although his prison-mandated calls usually said *No Caller ID*) or Hilary, having found a way to phone me from another number. I figured that if it was important, whoever was calling would call again and leave a message. The person did call again and did leave a message. I got out of the cold and the rain and stood in the shelter of the Tube station. I struggled to hear because of the clatter of a train pulling into the platform overhead. When it moved off again I heard Vanessa's voice tailing off in the message. She told me to call her back urgently.

She was coming after me to sign the paperwork I had refused to sign; I was sure of it. I had no idea how she had managed to get hold of my new number.

There was a text: *It's not what you think. Call me asap.*

I called back.

'Emma?' she said.

'How did you get my number?' I asked.

'Your sister.'

'Hannah gave you my number?'

'Yes,' Vanessa replied, 'but only after she gave me the Spanish Inquisition.'

'How did you get Hannah's number?'

'It's on her LinkedIn.'

'Oh,' I said.

'Look, it's not important,' she said. I was already irritating her and we had only been on the phone for thirty seconds.

'If you're planning to blackmail me about James so that I sign those papers, you needn't bother. There's nothing you could do that could make his situation worse.'

'No,' she said. 'That's not why I'm calling . . . although I am sorry about that. I regret that I did that. That wasn't cool.'

'Not cool . . .'

I was excited about unleashing the diatribe that had been for so long gestating inside me when she raised her voice and spoke over me.

'Emma, stop talking and listen. You need to listen to what I am about to say.'

I ceased.

Vanessa continued: 'I called because we've had an offer for the business. An Emirati businesswoman has made us an offer.'

'Why?'

'Doesn't matter why, she just does. Because you are a major shareholder, I will need you to agree to the sale.'

'What if I don't?'

'I think you're going to want to,' she said. 'I think you will want to agree to it very, very much.'

Chapter 47

I bought the castle.

The baronial entrance hall was mine. The orangery was mine. The walled garden was mine. All the cottages were mine, even the one that burned down that I had to rebuild was mine.

Some things were no longer mine. Stolen blueberries in a shopping bag. Special chocolate hazes. Wine bottles in the bottom of my closet. Handsome arresting officers. Trauma consultants in lovely footwear.

The hope I had harboured for a particular kind of family life – the one I never had, the one I thought I wanted – after a proposal spelled out in tiles on a Scrabble board one cold December night, a moment of dazzling ingenuity at a desolate time.

And a mother-in-law. Or a certain incarnation of her. A new version of Hilary emerged, one that I could warm to: one that gave her granddaughter unimposing, unconditional love. She established herself as a mediator between James and me, and I was grateful for that. In the end, she decided not to sell the flat on Avenue Mansions, so that James, on his release, could live there and would not have to live with her.

She did not get involved in the bidding war I had with the twins for the purchase of the castle in which I saw them off.

I was sure that she would have tried to sabotage it, but I was wrong. Someone or something had chastened her. Given that Mark had power of attorney over his sister, he chose me as the buyer in the end. It was a Beautiful Day.

I asked Mark to continue in his role as estate manager. I said he could move into the dower house on the estate and, once she was deemed stable enough to leave her facility, Heather could live with him. A few nights a week he invited me over for dinner and I'd walk back to the castle, with the baby in her buggy, on the path through the woods that he had made for us.

I opened the castle all year round. I bought a little coffee truck and parked it by the walled gardens. We built a visitor centre with a café and gift shop, both of which Shona managed. She was an exemplary employee, just as long as I did exactly as she told me. We rented out the cottages as holiday lets. My scary cottage on the hill was the most popular of all – always fully booked. I suppose that people love a thrill, especially if they know they can escape it. I designed castle merchandise, going off to trade fairs all over the world, and Mark came with me. Strictly business of course.

And I kept the house on the loch, in case I ever needed somewhere to run away to.

Acknowledgements

I would like to thank Olivia Davies at United Agents for her brilliance and conviction, and Alison Rae, my excellent editor at Polygon – a true pleasure to work with. It is an honour to be on her list.

Thanks also to Zoe Ross, Esther Walker, Siân Jones, Thea Lewis-Yates, Sarah O'Reilly and Charlotte Nation for their encouragement, advice and friendship.

And, with the deepest gratitude, my family for their love and patience.